DANCE
WITH THE
DEMON

DEALS WITH DEMONS 2

STACIA STARK

DANCE WITH THE DEMON

CHAPTER ONE
DANICA

The sun was out, the birds were chirping, and I could barely control my rage.

"What do you mean you sold it?"

Gary gave me an impatient look. "You missed out. Someone else wanted it more. They outbid you."

I kept my voice low as I leaned against the counter. Deep, beneath my failing shields, my power roiled, dark and deadly.

"You said no one used black monkshood."

"Yeah. It was weird. Someone bought my entire stock. I was chatting to Merrill and he said someone bought his as well."

"That's fucking great."

"It's not personal. It's business."

Gary stood straighter on his stool in front of the counter, squaring his shoulders as I took a deep breath. Adult gnomes were between four and five feet tall, and Gary was too proud to lower the counter to his own height so his customers would have to bend.

Power seethed around my body. For the first time, true fear crossed Gary's face. Then it hardened. "Watch yourself, Danica."

I shuddered, fighting for control. Someone had placed a suppression spell on my power when I was a kid, and now that it was slowly crumbling, my power tended to spark with strong emotion.

A few weeks ago, two of my marks were killed in front of me. Both held information about my mother's killer, and both were killed by arrows which shouldn't have taken down a lesser demon—let alone a high demon. When I'd asked Cara to investigate just what made the arrows so special, she'd told me to purchase black monkshood. Apparently, it could be used in a spell to discover if the arrows contained a poison found in *any* of the realms.

Unfortunately, black monkshood only grew in the middleground– the mysterious, dangerous realm that had long been home to those fleeing other worlds. I'd called Gary the moment I learned what I needed, and a few hours later, someone had beat me to it.

"How much did they pay, Gary? You didn't even give me the opportunity to outbid them."

He sniffed. "You couldn't have outbid them. They had deep pockets."

That made it worse. If someone had bought up all the black monkshood hours before I could, they'd done it because they knew I was onto something. *Or* they wanted me to *think* I was onto something. Whoever had fired those bolts into the demons I was questioning had prevented me from learning who had killed my mother. And now they were covering their tracks.

All because Gary was incapable of keeping his word.

"I trusted you," I hissed.

More magic leaked from me. The store was darkening. Maybe if I pulled the gnome's head from his shoulders, he'd think twice before double-crossing me.

No, Danica, then he won't be able to think at all.

Gary thinned his lips and I snarled. "Who were they?"

"I don't know. I'd offer you security footage, but that camera doesn't work."

My shield cracked. Power began to slide from me as I trembled, blind with fury. He had promised. *Promised* he wouldn't sell it. He had *dared* lie to me.

"Daddy I'm scared!"

Gary had two kids. Young boys who constantly caused havoc. Last time I was here, I'd played hide and seek with them.

Now, Ziprick was clutching his dad's leg, staring at me like I was a monster. His brother scampered close, practically climbing up his dad's leg as he stared at me, white-faced. I glanced around at the thick, dark purple power that had leaked from me, filling the store like smoke.

I *was* a monster.

Gary held Ziprick to him, glowering at me. "Get out."

Words escaped me. My throat ached and my power disappeared back beneath my shield as if it'd never been there.

Oh, how I wished it had never been there. I stumbled to the gutter outside Gary's store and heaved, bile creeping up my throat as tears pricked my eyes.

I'd been *excited* to chip away at the suppression spell when I found out about it. After rejecting the tiny ember of power I'd had my entire life, I'd thought I could finally use my power to keep myself safe.

Instead, it constantly slipped through when it was least convenient. Samael's words ran through my mind on a loop. *"That suppression spell would've crumbled eventually. Likely at the most inconvenient time possible. And you would've been all alone, with no idea what was happening to you, and no way to regain control. Your magic flares with great emotion. Who brings that emotion out in you, hmm?"*

I hated that he was right. And I lived in terror that I'd invertedly use my power on my sister. I needed help. But the world would burn before I'd voluntarily ask Samael for it.

Every time I thought about the demon, I had to restrain the urge to go to him. Some days, it was because I dreamed of stabbing him in the gut and watching him bleed out. Other days, it was because I longed for the feeling of safety I'd briefly had in his arms.

I was losing it. And I needed to head to the Mage Council to file the paperwork for my last bounty. I glanced back at Gary's store and my chest clenched. The look on his face. The terror in his kids' eyes. If this was what my power did, I didn't want it.

Straightening my shoulders, I turned and began walking toward the Mage Council. The Durham Mage Council Facility was two blocks away, in what was once the Durham County Human Services building. The building had been more pleasing to the eye when it was owned by the government. The Mage Council took paranoia to a whole new level, and now it was thick gray stone and small windows with bars on them. The thought of working inside the facility all day made me shudder.

The facility was quiet. A group of mages and bounty hunters had been sent to Raleigh, where someone had decided to wake up a troll. The troll had already done a couple million dollars of damage, and since the unseelie king hadn't sent anyone to kill the troll, it was now the Mage Council's job.

I signed in and made my way to the check-in counter.

My bounty had been a banshee who'd decided to torment her neighbor after they had an argument about the length of her grass. She'd spent the next week screaming and wailing all night, every night. Her screams created blind terror in anyone who heard them, and there had been a spate of car accidents on her street.

I'd shoved ear plugs deep into my ears and given her a look that told her that today was not the day. She'd received a hefty fine from the Mage Council, but from the look of retribution on her face, her neighbor was likely to regret reporting her. I had a feeling I'd be seeing her again.

I waited until the mage finished with the bounty hunter in front of me, and handed over my paperwork, receiving three hundred dollars in return. Then I took the elevator to the fifth floor where I hovered in front of Charles, waiting for my next job.

The mage raised one eyebrow as he skimmed his screen. "Says here you're on leave."

"Excuse me?"

"Yeah. No jobs for you."

"I'm not on leave. I brought a bounty in earlier today." I spoke with the exaggerated patience of a woman who was struggling not to lose her shit.

Charles shrugged and shifted his gaze behind me at where a line was forming. "Take it up with Albert."

"You bet your ass I will."

Albert worked on the ninth floor. I stalked toward his office, noting his receptionist was nowhere to be seen. It was eight pm, and she'd probably gone home. Good. I kept walking, knocked once, and opened the door.

The most powerful mage in North Carolina was standing in front of a large closet, the door open. Inside the closet was what looked like an old trunk. The trunk was open, but all I could see was a grey blanket covering whatever treasures he had hidden away. My curiosity was officially piqued.

Albert ruled his mages with an iron fist, and he occasionally liked to confiscate weapons and spells he didn't approve of. If they were deemed to potentially be dangerous to a human bystander, they ended up in his office.

As a contractor, my weapons had always been safe. But I bet if I could peer inside that trunk, I'd find plenty of goodies from his mages.

Albert slammed the lid down on the trunk, threw a dark cloak over it, and closed the door. Then he turned to me, red slowly creeping up his cheeks. I'd pissed off the man who would decide whether I could pay my rent. Awesome.

"Sorry, Albert," I smiled sunnily. "Your receptionist wasn't around so I figured you'd have a few moments free."

He stared at me, his eyes piercing. "Take a seat."

I did, but my mind was on the trunk. What was in it? Why would Albert be so worried about me seeing inside it?

"Charles just told me he couldn't give me my next

bounty. Apparently, I'm on *leave*."

Albert sat behind his desk, his face still red. "I think we're both well aware of why that is."

"Why don't you spell it out for me?" I'd never liked Albert, but up until now, I'd respected him. I had a feeling that was about to change.

"The recording, Danica."

My hands wanted to fist, but I forced them to lay on my lap. Four weeks ago, Samael had been betrayed by a demon he'd trusted for centuries. A coven of insane witches had planned to kill him. They wouldn't have stood a chance against a high demon, except that they'd been harnessing power from each demon they'd killed. After Samael had been betrayed and taken unaware, they'd clamped him into Naud Chains.

I hadn't forgotten that those chains were only accessible by the Mage Council.

One of the witches had been recording the entire exchange. She'd died when Samael turned the coven to ash, but her phone had continued to capture the video, and Vas had missed it when he'd searched for any tech. That recording had fallen into the hands of the Mage Council. Samael had assured me that Albert would be keeping the recording locked up and hidden from prying eyes.

But obviously I would still be dealing with the consequences.

"I saved Durham– and the world– from a coven of witches who were about to be bloated with demon power. You're welcome."

"You saved the most powerful demon in this country

from certain death."

I gave him squinty eyes. "Samael was approximately three seconds away from saving himself. The power he had gathered was… indescribable."

"Regardless, I found it necessary to take the recording to the other members of the council."

Oh yeah, this was bad.

"And?"

"And saving a demon from humans is not in your job description."

"Those humans would have killed you. You realize that, right? They wouldn't have stopped at the demons."

"Regardless."

"So, what, because I dared save Samael's life, I'm now fired?"

"No. You're on temporary leave while the council conducts a review. You'll be notified of the council's decision once the review is complete."

I stared at him. We both knew I was fired. This was just his way of keeping it clean.

"This is horseshit."

Albert's gaze dropped to my arm, and he stared at the intricate gold design for a long moment. It was too damn hot to wear a long-sleeved shirt today, and half of Durham already knew I was bonded to Samael. But I still had to resist the urge to cover it up.

"You had the opportunity to break that bond. If Samael had died, we would be having a different discussion."

I'd known the consequences when I made my decision. I'd known damn well that I could've broken the bond and continued with my life. Except that if I had, we'd now be dealing with thirty insane witches who suddenly had an infinite well of power. I'd make the same decision again. But the fact that there was still a recording of that decision meant I was screwed.

I wasn't getting anywhere with Albert. It was obvious what would happen next. The review would find that I was a liability to the Mage Council. My days of working here were numbered.

I was surprised they hadn't already taken away my access to the facility itself. I was guessing they would wait until the review was completed. The council liked to do everything by the book.

My power pressed against my shield, and I envisioned a thick steel door, ruthlessly holding it back. I wouldn't let Albert see how much I cared.

"My record speaks for itself," I said. "You've made the wrong choice here."

His expression was carefully neutral. "You're entitled to think that."

I shook my head, got to my feet, and stalked out of his office.

It was as if I was sleepwalking as I made my way back into the elevator and down to the lobby. Working for the Mage Council hadn't been my life's dream, but it had allowed me to interrogate paranormals who might've seen my mom before she died. And, it had allowed me to pay my bills.

Panic climbed up my throat. I had a few weeks of living expenses saved, but that was it. I needed to find a new job.

Fast.

My phone vibrated and I fumbled for it, almost dropping it as I pulled it out of my pocket.

I'm here, at a table near the back.

My sister. Shit. Luckily Meredith's was a four-minute drive from the Mage Council.

On my way.

SAMAEL

"The grimoire is authentic."

I narrowed my eyes. "Are you sure?"

Gloria, the witch I kept on retainer, sniffed in obvious offense. "You have your areas of expertise, demon. And I have my own. This is one of Cyprianus's Black Books."

Satisfaction roared through me. Cyprianus was a demon who enraged Lucifer, challenging him for power several centuries ago. Lucifer had ensured he was captured and forced through the closest portal. He hadn't known where the portal led to, and he hadn't cared. Unfortunately, for the humans in this world, Cyprianus had arrived, incensed, and determined to make Lucifer pay.

Cyprianus wrote nine Books of the Black Arts. When Lucifer learned what he was doing, he sent his best assassins to find him and kill him. They succeeded, but not before Cyprianus distributed the books amongst humans who had the most power, with the hope that they would one day be able to access that power and take down Lucifer himself.

The coven of witches who managed to wake the demigod and open the portals seventy years ago had used one of the Black Books to do it.

The grimoire in my hand would be added to my collection. I had six of them, with just three more to go.

"You allowed yourself to be taken by the witches so you could get your hands on this book," Gloria let out a hoarse laugh.

I gave her a slow smile. "Did I?"

She laughed some more, and I turned, taking the grimoire with me as I stepped onto the balcony. I launched into the air, rising to my penthouse, where I landed and tucked the grimoire away in my personal safe.

My thoughts turned to Danica. While she likely hoped otherwise, I hadn't grown bored and decided to allow her complete freedom.

To deal with the little witch, I had to tamp down all my instincts to dominate. The instincts that made me want to make her *beg* for me. I had to continually remind myself that if she were the type of woman to submit, I wouldn't be half as interested. Her commitment to disobedience and determination to buck any and all authority both frustrated and intrigued me.

Centuries of existence had taught me patience.

That patience wasn't infinite, but I had enough time to allow Danica the illusion of freedom while I aligned all the chess pieces on my board. And then she would be mine.

CHAPTER TWO
DANICA

It had been four weeks since my sister agreed to have that first drink with me. Now, we met at Meredith's once a week, exchanging pleasantries and tiptoeing around the subject of our childhood. We were both trying.

But we had a long way to go.

I found it difficult to move past the fact that my sister had never gotten in touch— even after I visited to tell her mom's death hadn't been an accident.

And Evie? She couldn't forgive me for not fighting harder to stay. For not running away from Austin and coming back to her. For staying away for so long.

"Sorry I'm late." I slipped into a chair and Evie glanced up from her phone. She had a wicked smile on her face, and I raised one eyebrow. "What's that look for?"

"This guy I've been seeing–" she frowned. "What's wrong, Dani?"

At least she was calling me Dani again. That was progress.

"Nothing," I attempted a smile, and my sister simply raised one eyebrow, glancing away. Her gaze landed on a group of werewolves who were taking shots at the bar. One of them tipped his head back and recognition swept through me. Matt. I'd met him when I interviewed his alpha a month ago. He was looking better than he had that day, but I had a feeling Nathaniel wouldn't be pleased to learn that such a recently turned werewolf was drinking.

Meredith's was a squat, brick building with a small outdoor area that was rarely used. Wobbly stools lined the beaten-up bar, the floors were scuffed and chipped, and the lights were dim. It was one of my favorite places in Durham.

I turned back to Evie. Silence stretched between us. I didn't want to admit what was bothering me, but she had a right to know what was going on.

"I terrified a couple of kids today." The words tasted like ash.

Evie's face creased. "What do you mean?"

I took a deep breath. It was time to tell her the truth. "It turns out my father wasn't human. Or mage. Do you remember that dark fae guy who was hanging around mom for a few years before we left?"

Evie's eyes flashed at the reminder, but she put it away, frowning as she took a sip of her rum and coke.

"I don't think so."

"You were probably too young. Anyway, I think he might have been my father. My power is dark. Likely unseelie. Someone put a suppression spell on me when I was a kid."

Evie gaped at me, her eyes wide. I almost laughed. She looked like a Disney princess who had just learned that the birds who helped her get dressed every morning were dead.

My sister took after my mom. Huge, aquamarine eyes, thick, glossy blonde hair, perfect skin, and curves in all the right places. When we'd taken family photos, I'd always felt like the odd one out with my dark hair and petite frame. Now I knew why.

"But suppression spells are only for witches who've been sentenced by the High Coven."

"Yeah. Except they weren't suppressing witch magic." The magic I'd inherited from my mom was a trickle at best. "It was unseelie power."

Evie tilted her head. "So, you're like, uber powerful now?"

She kept her voice light, and I attempted a smile. "I don't know how powerful. Ever since I worked that case for the demons…" both of our gazes dropped to the gold mark on my arm, and I ground my teeth.

"The suppression spell has been wearing away?"

I nodded. "Apparently these types of spells are usually reinforced every few years."

"What has this got to do with the kids?"

Bile crept up my throat at the reminder of Gary's kids. Their little faces, such a pale gray they were almost white.

"When I get… upset, I have a hard time controlling my power."

Evie's gaze turned knowing. I'd scared the shit out of her the first time I lost control of my power, holding a witch in place, and forcing her to answer my questions.

She cleared her throat. "You did that to the kids?"

"God no. But I threatened Gary– their father. In front of them. My power leaked out of me and rattled the roof. They were terrified."

"You didn't hurt anyone?" her voice was very careful.

"No. But I could've. I'm telling you now, so you know. If I ever lose control, run."

"You won't hurt me."

"I may not know what I'm doing," I warned her. I needed her to take this seriously. "This suppression spell... it hid my power from me all these years, and whenever a piece of the spell crumbles, my power overtakes me. It usually happens when I'm enraged, and it boosts my anger into a new stratosphere. It's like my power is a river and I'm caught in the currents without a life jacket. Anyone close to me is at risk."

"You won't hurt me," she said again. I sighed, and she gave the hint of a smile. Evie had always been able to out-stubborn anyone. Even me. "What are you going to do about it?"

I signaled for another round, and across the room, Mere caught my eye with a nod. "I'm going to find someone who can reinforce the suppression spell."

She gaped at me. "What?"

"I don't need this power. I don't want it. It was helpful when I was working with the demons and being targeted by those crazy witches, but that's done now."

"If you have access to that amount of power, it can keep you safe."

"Not at the expense of everyone around me."

"I think you give yourself too little credit. Why don't you find someone who can help you learn to control it?"

Samael's face flashed in front of my eyes, and I closed

them in a bid to make it disappear. It didn't. When I opened my eyes, my sister was smirking at me.

"You were thinking about *him*, weren't you?"

"Samael can't be trusted."

A couple of months ago Samael caught me in his tower, with one of his demons dead on the floor in front of me. He'd bonded me to him, and we'd made a deal. If I could find out who was murdering his demons— and kill them within two weeks– he'd let me free.

During that time, we'd gotten… close. Despite my hatred of Samael and everything he stood for, I hadn't been able to help myself. We were drawn together like magnets, and at one point I'd been moments away from sleeping with him.

Then I saw the true Samael. The Samael who'd refused to release me from my bond over a technicality. After I'd saved his life, I might add.

Evie raised her eyebrow, tucking a stray curl behind her ear. "Have you seen him since…"

"I made the mistake of saving his stupid life? No. He's been suspiciously absent from my life. But you know what hasn't been absent? This stupid mark." I held it up and the gold seemed to sparkle in the light. I ground my teeth. The mark on my arm proclaimed that I belonged to Samael. And each time I dropped my shields even a little, I could feel his masculine presence down the end of that bond.

"Have you thought about asking him for help?"

"He can't help me with this. Besides, he's a demon. What does he know about unseelie power?"

Just the word "unseelie" made me shiver. I didn't *feel*

half unseelie. But I'd also been magically neutered for most of my life.

"Uh-huh." Evie's mouth twitched and I scowled at her.

"He's dangerous. Besides, I have a new plan. I met a witch when I was investigating the demon murders. Her name is Selina. She was the one who was able to tell me my power wasn't all witch. I'm going to see if she'd be willing to help me find someone who can perform a suppression spell. Otherwise, maybe she can train me to keep my control."

In the meantime, I had to accept that I couldn't be trusted around anyone who could piss me off. So basically the entire population of the world.

Evie grabbed my hand and squeezed. "Go to Gary and explain what's happening with your power. Apologize. He'll understand. And in the meantime, if you can't trust yourself to buy things from him, let me know. I can go for you."

I smiled. This was the least awkward conversation we'd had so far. Maybe there was hope for us yet.

"Okay," I said. "But after what I did, there's a pretty good chance he'll just ban me from his store."

"All you can do is try."

"You're right." And now I itched to go talk to him.

Evie's eyes gleamed. "Go apologize. I'll wait here and order us another drink."

Gary's was just a couple minutes away, further down Main Street. "I won't be long." I got to my feet and scanned the bar. The werewolves were busy chatting up a group of light fae women. The goblins in the corner were speaking in hushed voices, and Mere was keeping an eye on the group of human mercenaries near the door. No one here would be likely to mess with my sister.

"I see what you're doing," Evie said mildly. "I can take care of myself."

I grinned at her and strode out of the bar.

DANICA

I squinted at my phone. Ten pm. Adult gnomes didn't need much sleep, and Gary was known for keeping his store open until two am some nights. I turned right as I walked out of Meredith's, heading down Main Street toward Gary's small store.

High above me, I heard the rustling of wings. I surveyed the night sky. The sound had only lasted a split second, but I knew what I'd heard. I'd thought I was going crazy over the past few weeks but I wasn't. Samael still had his people watching me.

I suppressed the urge to call him and give him a piece of my mind. The demon was leaving me alone for now. I had no desire to rouse his interest once more.

I slowed my steps as I approached Gary's store. The lights were out, which was unusual this early.

Maybe I'd emotionally scarred his kids so badly that he'd had to take them home.

I pushed that thought away and pressed my face against the glass, peering into the darkness.

"Oh my god."

I threw open the door and bolted across the small store, dropping down to Gary's side.

Someone had bashed his skull in. His head was caved in on one side, blood leaking onto the floor of his shop. The rest of his body was so broken that it looked like little more than mush.

My hand shook as I pressed it to Gary's neck, searching

frantically for a pulse. I jolted as he opened his eyes. Still alive. I had no idea how, but I was keeping him that way. I pulled my phone from my pocket.

"I'm getting you help," I promised. His eyes were dark with pain, and he opened his mouth in an attempt to say something. "Just rest, you're going to be okay."

I called an ambulance. He'd be taken to the paranormal hospital, where the doctors and healers would work together to save his life.

The operator was calm. "An ambulance is on its way, Miss."

I left the phone line open as instructed. Gary was still attempting to speak. He would open his mouth, strain for a while, and then his eyes would slide shut.

His hand twitched, and I took it in mine.

"Did you hear that? The ambulance is on its way. They'll heal you right up, and I swear I'll kill whoever did this."

"Boys," he managed to get out. "Protect them."

"I will."

"Promise me."

"I promise."

I took a frantic glance around. Where the hell were his kids?

"You guys can come out now." I closed my eyes when there was nothing but silence. I'd terrified them a few hours earlier, and now their dad was dying in front of them.

"I know I scared you today, but I'm here to help. Your dad wants me to look after you."

I returned my attention to Gary. Pride shone in his dull eyes. He'd instructed them to hide, and they were doing exactly as he'd said. He flicked his eyes to my left and I peered between the shelves lying on the floor.

The store was a wreck. Someone had almost killed Gary, and they'd ransacked his store. I turned back to Gary. His face was so broken it was almost impossible to recognize him. But his terror was clear. My instincts roared at me.

I needed to get the kids out.

I grabbed my phone, hung up on the operator, and called my sister.

"Evie. I need you to get to Gary's now. Do you know where it is?"

"Next to that tattoo parlor everyone loves, right?"

"Yeah. I need you to take his kids and keep them safe for me. Can you do that?"

I knew she could. Despite my hatred of the witches, they'd always protect children.

"Of course. I'll be right there."

I hung up, and a tear slid from Gary's eye as he stared silently at me.

"Who did this to you?"

He opened his mouth, and his eyes rolled back in his head as he passed out. Fuck. I turned and crouched next to the shelves in the direction he'd flicked his eyes.

Nothing. For a couple of kids who were like hurricanes every time I entered this store, they were now so quiet it was as if they weren't here.

I cracked my shield and sent out a tiny tendril of power. There. In the corner of the store. I picked my way over the weapons and spells that littered the ground, ducking around the few shelves that were still standing.

Nothing.

I frowned. "Are you boys invisible?"

A tiny squeak, followed by a hushed 'shhh.'

They were *in* the wall somehow. I ran my fingers over it, looking for some kind of trigger. Then I cracked my shields again.

It was warded. Heavily. Gary had paid a pretty penny for such a good ward. I didn't have time to hesitate. I pulled out my Nim Cub, sliced my arm, and lifted my hand.

The ward snapped, disappearing as if it had never been there. As soon as it was gone, I could see the opening mechanism, hidden in the corner of the wall.

I flicked it, and the bottom half of the wall swung open, revealing two little gnomes, who blinked at me with wide eyes.

"You're Cilibim, right? And you're Ziprick?"

Gary had taken a human name when he first came through the portals. He'd said it was to help him integrate with the locals. But he'd given his kids Gnome names.

"I'm Cil, and he's Zip," Cil told me solemnly. "Is our dad going to be okay?"

"I've called for help," I said, unwilling to give them false promises. "Your dad asked me to look after you."

They exchanged a look, clearly wondering why their dad would trust their safety to a woman he'd kicked out of his store just a few hours earlier.

"I won't hurt you. I promise." It *killed* me that they were frightened of me.

The kids looked at each other again, their gray faces wearing identical expressions of distrust. Finally, they stepped out from their hiding place in the wall.

Sirens sounded in the distance.

"I need to check on your dad, okay?"

They nodded, following me back over to Gary, who was now unconscious. I was going to find whoever had done this to him, and when I did, they were going to pay and pay and pay.

I checked his vitals. Gnomes were lesser dark fae, and they were usually pretty fast healers, but Gary didn't look any better. My chest clenched.

"Danica?"

I glanced over my shoulder. Evie's face drained of color as she looked around the store.

"Who did this?"

"I don't know. But I need you to take the kids and keep them safe. I'll come see you after."

Evie nodded, her mouth firming. Then she gracefully picked her way over the rubble lining the floor until she was in front of the kids. She knelt down.

"My name is Evie. What are your names?"

They told her and she grinned. "What cool names. I have some people who want to meet you. Will you come hang out with me?"

Cil shook his head. "We're meant to stay with Danica."

"I'm Danica's sister. She's going to come hang out with us once she's looked after your dad, okay?"

They both looked at me and I nodded. "I'll be there as soon as the healers are looking after your dad."

Zip shook his head. "I want to stay with dad."

"You heard him," I made my voice firm. "He wants me

to keep you safe."

Cil narrowed his eyes at me, suddenly looking older than his years. "You'll find the man who did this to our dad. And you'll kill him."

"Yes."

Evie made wide eyes at me and I shrugged. They had a right to know the truth.

I knelt down next to Gary again. Still unconscious.

The sirens were getting closer. My gut told me to get the kids out. If they'd seen whoever did this, they could be in danger. I met Evie's eyes, and she nodded. A few soft words later, and the kids were pressing gentle kisses to their dad's cheek before filing after her.

I went still. Gary wasn't breathing.

I leaned down and started CPR.

CHAPTER THREE
DANICA

Rose arrived as Gary was being loaded into the ambulance. I stood in the store and watched, my hands fisted.

Rose cleared her throat. The bounty hunter had never liked me, and she hated demons even more.

"What do you want?"

She smiled. "Danica Amana, you're under arrest–"

That was enough to make me rip my gaze from the ambulance. "What the fuck are you talking about?"

Satisfaction gleamed in her eyes. Rose's father had been killed in a demon summoning gone wrong. He was an idiot for attempting to set a demon on his business partner, and he'd gotten what he deserved. And I'd told Rose exactly that when she'd pissed me off during my last investigation.

She obviously carried a grudge.

"Witnesses heard you screaming at this gnome earlier today. Apparently, you choked him with power."

"Since when does the Mage Council care about lesser fae?"

If anything, I was expecting the

dark fae to begin an investigation into what had happened to one of their people.

Rose ignored me. "And just a few hours later, he ended up dead, with his store nothing but rubble. And you were conveniently here to find him. Did you have a moment of regret, Danica? Is that why you called an ambulance?"

"You guys think *I* did this?" My hands fisted. Rose noted it and smiled.

"It's ironic, really. Soon, there will be a bounty on *your* head. Traitor." She sneered at me, her gaze dropping to my arm.

That's what this was about. The Mage Council was still punishing me for not breaking the bond with Samael.

"Fine, I'll come in," I said. I wanted to talk to Keigan anyway, and maybe I could get Mella to do some research for me. I needed to know if there were any similar cases in the area.

"Oh you'll come with me, will you?" Rose simpered. "Thank you for doing me that favor, Danica Amana." Her eyes hardened. "Hold out your fucking hands."

For the first time, true fear hit me.

The witches who had tried to kill Samael had used these chains on him. With enough time, the sheer force of his power would have snapped them, but while I *had* power, Samael *was* power. I'd had a glimpse of it when he'd killed close to thirty witches with little more than a glance. And yet, those chains had blocked his ability to access that power. If they'd made *Samael* unable to access his power, I'd be completely helpless.

If Rose put those chains on me, I was screwed.

Betrayal stabbed through me like broken glass. Four and a half years I'd been a contractor for the council. Not only had they fired me, but now, they wanted to put fucking Naud chains on me?

I bared my teeth at Rose. "If the mages want me to answer some questions, I will. But if you think I'm wearing those chains, you're dreaming."

Not only were the chains guaranteed to render me powerless, but they were meant to humiliate me. The Mage Council did the same to Mella, the selkie who was chained in the facility's library. Since they'd hidden her skin from her, she was already completely powerless, but they'd put her in chains anyway. Because they wanted to prove a point.

Look what happens to the people who betray us.

Rose planted her feet. "Don't make this more difficult than it needs to be."

"I've had a very bad day. I'll come in, but I'm not wearing the chains. Don't push me on this."

"I can have backup here in two minutes."

I laughed, and it echoed through the room. It didn't sound anything like me. "Bring your backup," I dared her. Then I dropped my shields.

Power greeted me like a long-lost lover, caressing every inch of my skin. It urged me to make an example of the bounty hunter who'd dared to try to chain me.

Rose went white. She was very still. *Prey.* That's what she looked like.

"What about now? Would you like to chain me now, Rosie?"

Wow, unseelie power made me into kind of a dick.

But Rose wasn't holding out the chains anymore. She handed them to another bounty hunter. The *backup*. He'd arrived while I'd been attempting to control the power that urged me to kill everyone in sight. I bared my teeth at him.

Then I packed my power away, shoving it down beneath my shields. It hurt.

"Let's go."

I followed them out of the store. Out the corner of my eye I saw movement. Vas.

His expression was hard as his gaze took in the bounty hunters behind me. I gave him a nod. I was fine.

He tilted his head disbelievingly and I nodded again. Last week, I'd taken Vas to the shooting range. It had been hilarious trying to teach a demon who was a walking weapon how to fire a gun. He was the only demon I still talked to, and the only good thing to come out of my deal with Samael.

I'd always been low on friends, and Vas was quickly becoming more like a brother.

A flap of invisible wings, and he was gone. I got in the back of Rose's car and sat quietly. Rose got in the front, and I was small enough to enjoy the goosebumps that rose on the back of her neck.

Oh, she wouldn't have had a problem with me behind her if she'd clamped Naud chains around my wrists and removed my ability to access my power. I refrained from telling her I didn't need my power to kick her ass.

The Mage Council Facility was a few minutes' walk away, and if Rose had been thinking clearly, she would've taken the opportunity to march me down Main Street and humiliate me further.

The short drive didn't give me much time to consider my options, but I ran through them anyway. Option one: tell the mages about the kids. Cil and Zip would be questioned about whatever they saw. Unfortunately, I highly doubted the mages actually gave a shit about Gary. They were bringing me in to put me in my place. The kids would be further traumatized.

Option two: leave the kids out of it. Evie would keep them safe, and I could visit them when I was done being grilled by the mages. They'd be comfortable, surrounded by the witches who— while I couldn't stand most of them— would probably be delighted to have kids in the house again.

Rose parked the car and I stepped out. I didn't know the bounty hunter who'd been sending wary glances over his shoulder at me from the passenger's seat. He must be new. He circled the car and approached me from behind. I snarled at him.

"If you think I'm going to allow you to walk that close to me, you're wrong."

If I gave these assholes an inch, they'd stab me in the back and have me in those chains before I could blink.

The bounty hunter gave me the side eye. He had six inches on me and his fist was the size of my face. He stood poised on the front of his feet as if ready to lunge at me. I'd pull him off balance and bury my knife in his gut before he got the chance.

Time slowed down as we both stared at each other. I softened my knees and he squared his shoulders.

Anytime, buddy.

Rose jerked her head at him and moved away from me, allowing me to follow them both in. Mages and bounty hunters were gathered in the lobby, mostly silent, all eyes on me. Someone had tipped them off that I was being brought in. Ben, the power-hungry coward and pain in my ass, leaned against the wall near the elevators and gave me a wide smile as we approached.

Rose pressed the button for the paranormal elevator. The elevator we used when bringing in dangerous bounties. What a nice touch.

Ben winked at me. "Danica Amana brought in for questioning. I never thought I'd see the day," he drawled.

"I'm not surprised by your mental inadequacies. As always, your train of thought is stalled at the station."

The male bounty hunter snorted, and Ben glowered at me, stepping close. His hand twitched as if he'd like to smash his fist into my face. I ignored him, sauntering into the elevator as soon as the doors opened.

Rose pressed the down button. They were taking me to the interrogation rooms. Just a few weeks ago, I'd stood in one of those rooms with her and questioned a witch who'd been suspected of killing demons. Now, I was going to be the one interrogated.

Life was funny.

The elevator doors opened and my eyes met Keigan's. He was pale, his mouth turned down. He narrowed his eyes at Rose, and the look on his face clearly communicated his disappointment. She shifted on her feet and looked away.

"Danica," he murmured. "I'm sure this has just been a big misunderstanding. We'll get this cleared up."

"I don't think so. They tried to put me in Naud chains, Keigan."

He blanched and Rose flushed. "Naud chains? What were you thinking?"

"Albert's orders," Rose said.

Keigan ignored her. "I'll speak to him," he said to me. "We'll figure it out."

I had a feeling we wouldn't figure anything out, but I nodded and followed Rose to interrogation room three. Yes, she remembered the last time we were here too. She'd been so terrified of Vas she'd nearly pissed her pants, and now she was attempting to prove that she was in charge.

I sat down on one of the metal chairs and both bounty hunters leaned against the wall. The room was silent as we waited. Rose had her head bowed and was silently studying the ground. If she hadn't been such an asshole from the moment I met her, I'd probably feel sorry for her. She'd imagined she would bring me in here in Naud chains, humiliating me in front of everyone. Instead, I'd walked freely behind her, while Keigan— a mage she looked up to— had made it clear he was disgusted by all of it.

The door swung open, and my eyes met Albert's. He was dressed in a gray suit, his eyes hard, a deep pillow crease on his cheek. Clearly, he hadn't lost any sleep after firing me.

"Danica," he said. I nodded at him. He jerked his head at the bounty hunters, and they left the room.

The door opened once more. Keigan. "You're entitled to a representative," he said. "Would you like me to stay?"

I smiled at him. "Sure." It was more for him than me. He

was clearly miserable, his face pale and his brow furrowed. If I said no, he'd likely just stand outside the door, wringing his hands. I didn't know *why* Keigan had taken me under his wing when I first began contracting for the Mage Council, but he was the only person here who truly gave a shit about me.

Keigan took a seat next to me. Albert didn't seem pleased, but he didn't object, sliding into the chair on the opposite side of the table.

"Do you know why we brought you in?"

Oh, is that what they'd done? I gave him a look that said he knew damn well I'd brought myself in. He sat back in his chair, tenting his hands on the table in front of him.

"Rose said the Mage Council got wind of my argument with Gary."

"Yes. A few hours later, the gnome ended up almost dead. He may still die."

My stomach twisted. "I have no motive to hurt Gary."

"Then why were you seen screaming in his store? Why did a bounty hunter nearby report a wave of dark power? If you went back tonight and lost control, it will go better for you if you admit it now."

"I went back to apologize. I found Gary crumpled on the floor. His shop looked like someone had tried to ruin everything he owned."

Or, like someone had been looking for something. Had his goods been broken because someone wanted to hurt him, or were they broken by someone who was looking for something?

I hadn't paid enough attention. I'd been too focused

on getting the kids out and keeping Gary alive. I'd kept up the CPR until the ambulance arrived and the fae healer had managed to get his heart beating again.

I needed to get back to his store and take another look.

"Amana?"

"I'm sorry, what was that?"

Albert gave me a hard stare. "Take me through it step by step."

I complied, telling him exactly what had happened from the moment I arrived, but leaving out all mention of the kids. Albert let me run through it, nodding along, and then studied his notes.

"It says here that the gnome has two children."

"His name is Gary."

He surveyed me, his eyes hard. "Where are the children?"

"I don't know. I haven't seen them. I'm unsure why this is Mage Council business, to be honest. As you're *well* aware, Gary isn't human."

"You don't need to be sure. All you need to know is that when a bounty hunter connected to the Mage Council but bonded to a *demon* is seen threatening a resident of this city, the Council takes notice."

I heroically restrained myself from rolling my eyes. Albert smiled at me. It wasn't a nice smile. "Why do I get the feeling you're not being entirely truthful, Amana?"

I shrugged. Keigan cleared his throat. "It's late," he said. "Danica has told you her version of events. With the gnome–" he glanced at me and his eyes softened "with *Gary* still unconscious, you have no reason to hold her here."

Albert ignored the other mage. My power licked at my shields, itching to teach him a lesson he'd never forget.

"It doesn't take a demon to know that Amana is lying," he said. Then he turned to me, his expression stony. "Either you tell us exactly what happened now, or you leave me no choice but to administer a truth spell."

My mouth hung open. Next to me, Keigan got to his feet. "This is outrageous!"

The door slammed open, leaving a dent as it hit the wall. All of the oxygen in the room was immediately sucked out as the high demon stepped inside, his eyes on mine.

Power, thick and deadly crept up the walls and along the floor. It radiated from him, silent yet dripping an obvious threat. His silver gaze ignored everyone else in the room and methodically scanned my body as if searching for bruises.

He looked like a fallen angel, with his lush mouth, sharp cheekbones and a jaw that looked hard enough to break your hand– if somehow you defied all odds and managed to punch him in the face.

I hadn't seen him for weeks. He'd been allowing me to skip Monday dinners, which were mandatory for everyone bonded to him. I'd hoped his choice not to make attend his stupid dinners also meant he'd chosen to leave me alone.

I should've known better.

"Little witch," Samael purred, "just what trouble have you gotten yourself into now, hmmm?"

I would kill him. I'd kill him so dead that I'd make what the witches had wanted to do to him look like a day at the spa.

"I'm fine," I told him. "Butt out."

Albert went sheet white, and Keigan began to tremble. Samael just laughed.

"I don't think so." He turned to Albert. "I must have misheard you. You didn't just threaten *my* witchling with a truth spell, did you?"

His tone was one hundred percent possessive male. His eyes dared Albert to misstep, and the corner of his mouth tipped up in sardonic amusement.

"No," Albert ground out. His gaze flicked to me, and my shoulders wanted to hunch. The disgust was clear on his face.

Samael smiled. "In that case, we'll be leaving. Come, bounty hunter."

I'd had dreams of him ordering me to do just that. I shoved the vision away and ground my teeth as I got to my feet.

"Thanks, Keigan," I murmured.

"Be careful, Danica."

"You know it."

I walked out the door. Rose was hunched against the wall as if she was attempting to blend into it. The male bounty hunter was nowhere to be seen.

Samael followed me out, turning sideways through the narrow doorway. His wings couldn't fit, even tucked in tight. I'd had dirty, dirty dreams about him and his wings.

Albert and Keigan followed us out, and Samael turned his head, glancing over his shoulder.

"Attempt to put Naud chains on Danica again, and I'll burn this place to the ground."

His gaze lingered on Rose, and surprisingly, she didn't

piss her pants. She did turn white, her mouth a thin line as she nodded.

"Oh, and Albert… don't think I've forgotten that the witches who attempted to kill me were using those filthy chains. When I find out exactly how they got their hands on them, your name better not come up."

Albert said nothing, simply watched as Samael turned toward the elevator.

I ground my teeth but kept walking. The elevator certainly wasn't made for Samael's wingspan. He pulled me into him and turned, arranging his invisible wings. The elevator doors slid closed, and my eyes met Albert's. I knew what it looked like. He couldn't see the fact that there was nowhere else for me to stand, feather's brushing every inch of my body and likely pressed against all three of the elevator walls.

No, it just looked like I was Samael's toy.

"I can't believe you just did that."

"Believe it, witchling."

My hands fisted. "You made things a hundred times worse. I was handling it, Samael, and now you made them think I'm one of your subjects."

"You *are* one of my subjects."

I snarled at that, managing to turn within his arms and his gaze dropped to my lips. "There's that mouth I can't stop thinking about." His voice was low, intimate, and my breath caught in my throat.

"Don't play with me, Samael."

"Oh, little witch. I would like nothing more than to play with you. Unfortunately, you insist on running from me."

"And I always will," I vowed. He merely smiled.

The elevator doors opened to the lobby. Thankfully, at this time of the night, it was almost empty. I was so furious I was shaking. "You undermined me."

Samael's gaze turned cold, but he didn't say a word until we were out of the lobby and on the sidewalk.

"I helped you. You may thank me now."

"The underworld will freeze over before I thank you for messing with my life."

"It's not as hot there as most people think," he said. "I felt the wards on your apartment. You've been practicing."

"Don't change the subject. Wait, when were you at my apartment?" I wouldn't thank him for making me attend those ward lessons. I would not.

The gleam in his eyes told me he knew I was appreciative despite my annoyance at him. I gave him squinty eyes.

Samael raised one eyebrow. "You have much more to learn. Your power is unique but potent. If you truly want to be able to defend yourself, you need to train."

I swallowed. While I was grateful for the help he'd given me, our 'sessions' had been torture. Not only was Samael a strict, merciless teacher, but I'd been forced to sit with him for hours.

Wards weren't the only things I'd learned during those hours. I'd learned that the tiny crease that appeared between his brows when he was concentrating… it made my stomach flutter.

I learned that the pride in his eyes when I succeeded made me feel like I could take on anything and walk away.

I learned that the scent of him— cedar and citrus and

male– made my heart thump harder in my chest.

I learned that despite my every instinct warning me away from the demon, my body didn't care.

He stepped closer, and I backed up, until I was leaning against one of the concrete slabs that protected the building from anyone who thought they could ram it with a car or truck.

"I missed you," he breathed, leaning down until his head was almost buried in my neck. "Did you miss me?"

I didn't miss him. I *craved* him.

"Absolutely not."

"Ahh Danica, you wound me."

"Blah blah. Get out of the way, Samael, I have places to be."

"You're going to talk to the gnome children."

"Yes."

"Would you like some help?"

I smiled sweetly. "When I need someone to be so scared they piss their pants, I may give you a call. When I want to talk to two traumatized kids, you can stay far away."

Something I couldn't catch flashed over his face.

"Very well. I'll see you soon, Danica."

"I don't think so."

He merely shook his head at me. The expression on his face said I was the most adorable thing he'd ever seen. I barely resisted the urge to punch him in the nose.

With a snap of invisible wings, he was gone.

Chapter Four

DANICA

vie lived in Trinity Park— deep in witch territory. Most of the houses were old, huge, and steeped in history— all things witches were delighted by.

I was so tired I could barely see straight, but I managed a sloppy parallel park and made my way up the steps leading to the coven's wide porch.

I'd once played on this porch with Evie. We'd swung on that porch swing and climbed the huge tree in the front yard.

The coven's house was painted a cheerful buttercup yellow with white trim, it was large enough to house a solid third of the coven, with extra guest rooms for nights when they got together for meetings or to work on their spells.

Evie opened the door before I could knock.

"You're okay."

"Yeah."

"What did the Mage Council do?"

"Threatened me with a truth spell."

Her face turned white, and then she flushed. "Let them fucking try."

Magic sparked around her and I stared. Evie kept her magic hidden away, but since I'd been in Austin, she'd turned into a powerhouse. There was something about it—

"Danica."

I surveyed the witch standing behind my sister. "Gemma."

Last time I'd been here, I'd lost control of my power, holding the coven leader in place and ruthlessly questioning her. The look on her face told me she would never forget it.

"The boys are in the living room."

She gestured for me to follow her. I gaped at Evie and she clamped her mouth shut, her eyes dancing with humor.

I'd forgotten how Gemma felt about most kids. I'd never been fortunate enough to benefit from the way she loved on anyone younger than sixteen, but I'd seen it happen.

Cil and Zip were sitting on a stuffed gray sofa, a bowl of popcorn between them. On the TV, the news played, and for one long moment, it felt like I'd never left this house. Gail–one of the more senior witches– had always been obsessed with the paranormal news, and insisted on keeping the TV on day and night.

The boys were silent, obviously exhausted, their gray faces drawn and pale, with dark circles beneath their blue eyes. Zip clutched a small canvas bag in one hand and held his brother's hand in the other.

They needed to go to bed. But I needed to find out what they'd seen before they forgot anything important. I crouched in front of them. "Hi guys."

Both of them focused on me. "Hi, Danica," they chorused, and I smiled.

"What's that you've got, Zip?"

He clutched the canvas bag tighter. "It's our treasures."

"What kind of treasures do you have?"

"They're secret."

I glanced at Evie. She grinned at me. "You always looked after our treasures when we were kids."

"You couldn't be trusted not to lose them."

I turned back to the kids. "Okay, I need you guys to tell me everything you remember about tonight. Can you do that?"

They both nodded. Distantly, I was aware of Gemma, Gail, and a few of the other witches filing in.

"Okay," I took a deep breath. "What did you guys have for dinner tonight?"

"Chicken nuggets and mashed potatoes with green beans," Cil said. "I ate all my green beans, but Zip only ate half.

"Dad said I could," Zip stuck his lower lip out.

"I hate green beans," I admitted, and he grinned at me, revealing sharp, pointed teeth. He was still missing a couple of adult teeth.

"I hate them too."

"So after dinner, what happened next?"

"We went back to the store. Dad said he wanted to stay open for a few more hours and we needed to do our homework quietly."

"Okay. So what happened after that?"

Zip reached for his brother's hand once more. "A bad man came."

"How did you know he was a bad man?"

"He was wearing a cloak. Bad men wear cloaks."

My mouth twitched. He wasn't wrong. Anyone who wanted to look suitably villainous had a tendency to buy a black cloak. And that cloak tripped them up and gave their enemies loose clothing to grab them in a fight. Cloaks were for low-level thugs and rookies.

"So the bad man came, and then what happened?"

Cil's eyes filled with tears. "Dad told us to hide."

"Was the bad man in the store?"

"No. He was on the street."

"Okay, so your dad saw the bad man through the store windows. And then you hid in your secret hiding spot? The one I found you in?"

"Yes. Dad used his *I'm serious* voice. If you don't listen to that voice, you get no TV for a week."

"Did you hear anything when you were hiding?"

Zip began to tremble, and Cil threw his arm around his brother's shoulders. "We don't want to talk anymore."

I studied them. I wasn't going to get anything out of them until they felt safer. "That's okay. Gemma and the other witches here are going to look after you." I leaned close. "If you're lucky, maybe Charlene will make you her famous chocolate chip cookies."

"Dad said you had to keep us safe."

I nodded. "I am. This is the best place for you. These witches are the most powerful in Durham, and they'll kick the butts of anyone who messes with you. I'm going to come back tomorrow, okay? Maybe we can talk some more then."

"You're going to find out who hurt our dad," Zip said.

"Yes."

"And then you're going to kill them," Cil stared into

my eyes.

"That's right."

"Danica," Gemma hissed, and I shook my head at her. "They're big enough to hide and keep quiet when their dad tells them to. They're big enough to know the truth."

I turned back to Cil, and he smiled at me. Then he took the canvas bag from Zip and reached inside, pulling out a glittery gold marble. "You can have this."

I grinned at him and ruffled his hair. "I can't take one of your treasures."

"You can borrow it. For good luck, until you find whoever hurt my dad."

"Thanks." I slipped it into my utility belt.

"Holy crap, turn that up."

I didn't recognize the voice, but I recognized the urgency in it. I spun as one of the witches grabbed the remote, turning the news up.

"Sources say the woman was a bounty hunter for the Mage Council before the incident," the news anchor said. "When we reached out to the Council, they refused to comment, saying that Ms. Amana was a short-term contractor who is no longer employed by the council."

I froze. On the TV, the shot cut away from the news anchor, and my face came into view.

I was trapped in a circle of witches, my face ashen. Samael was chained, and the witch recording the show zoomed in on my ankle. White bone poked through the ruin of my skin and the camera zoomed in on the compound fracture. One of the witches in the living room gagged.

My ankle still twinged occasionally. Unless I went back

to a fae healer, it probably always would.

On the screen, I pulled out one of my throwing knives and nailed Veronica in the throat. She went down, choking on her own blood.

"Gnarly," one of the kids said. They shouldn't be watching this. But I couldn't seem to look away.

Samael was staring at me, his silver eyes burning.

"Where the hell did they find Naud chains?" Evie asked.

I rubbed at the back of my neck. "There's only one place they could've gotten them. Shockingly, it's home to the same people who just leaked this."

Albert hadn't taken kindly to Samael's threats. And while he knew Samael would likely consider killing him for leaking this video, he also knew that Samael would then be faced with a power struggle within the Durham Mage Council, which the demon would have to sort out.

On the TV, Mary stepped over Veronica's body and picked up the grimoire. It was impossible to tell how much power Samael was gathering on the video, but even now I could feel the memory of it, hot and potent in the air.

Witches began to flee. I memorized their faces, wondering if Samael had found them yet. These were the witches who'd escaped, and like cockroaches, they were likely to keep coming back for more. Someone needed to spray them with hairspray and light them on fire.

I winced at the direction my thoughts had taken. Turns out, I was still pissed about the entire experience.

The recording continued to play. I was getting to my knees, and I stared at my determined expression, my stomach swimming at the memory. Agony had roared through every cell of my body and I'd been fighting to stay conscious. I'd known that if I passed out, the witches would succeed.

Mary raised her hands. On the screen, I made it up to one foot.

Mary let her power loose, aiming it at Samael. A few feet from me, Gail cursed. I glanced at her, but her gaze was on the TV as the power streamed from Mary, dark and deadly.

I leapt in front of Samael, and he clutched me in his arms. My ward surrounded us, my power glowing like an iridescent, violet and gold wall. A wall that Mary's power was beginning to eat through.

On the screen, Samael clutched me to his chest, and then brushed my lips with his. In the living room, the witches gasped, turning to glance at me.

I couldn't hear him over the chanting of the coven, but I still remembered the languid tone of his voice. *"You're okay,"* he'd murmured. *"My turn."*

On the screen, Samael placed me on the ground and stood in front of me. Mary's power had almost made it through my ward. Samael was talking to me, telling me to drop my ward. His eyes were indulgent. He'd looked at me like–

"You look half-dead, Danica." Horror saturated Evie's voice.

I attempted a grin. "Spoiler alert, I made it out okay."

She simply shook her head at me, and I turned back to the TV. I did look half dead. I'd had a vicious head wound, a broken ankle, and I'd been drained of power.

Onscreen, I dropped my ward, and in the blink of an eye,

Samael turned the witches to ash. He took a step toward me, and I froze. There were no longer any witches alive to make any noise, and the camera caught his next words.

"Danica," he purred. "Are you frightened of me?"

"Of course she is," Gemma muttered. "I didn't raise an idiot."

I glowered at her. "You didn't raise me at all."

Someone hushed me and I scowled. On the screen, Samael was picking me up. Vas appeared, offering to take me, and Samael clutched me to him, the movement clearly possessive. Shit.

He kissed my forehead, and there were several gasps. "A forehead kiss!" one of the younger witches said. "You know what that means!"

"What does it mean?" Zip asked.

"It means the king of the demons has a big fat crush–"

"Shhhhh!" several voices cut the witch off.

The video ended and the news anchor stared into the camera. "Our sources say members of the coven were direct descendants of the McCormick coven. The McCormick coven was responsible for the opening of the portals seventy-two years ago."

A tiny hand touched my shoulder and I jolted. On the sofa behind me, Cil beamed at me.

"You're friends with *Samael*?"

"Uh…"

"More than friends," someone muttered, and I lifted a hand, keeping it behind me and hidden from the kids as I flipped them off.

"Will he help you find who hurt my dad?"

I gave him a look. "Um, excuse me. I don't need his help. I'm an asskicker."

Both boys laughed, and Gemma stepped forward. "Right. To bed, both of you."

I watched as they negotiated, finally agreeing to go to bed in exchange for chocolate chip cookies in the morning. Witches filed out of the living room, shooting me wide-eyed looks, and a vicious headache took up residence in my left temple.

"Dani?"

"Yeah."

Evie slumped on the sofa the gnomes had just vacated. "You almost died."

"I told you that when I visited a few weeks ago."

"Hearing it is different from seeing it. What are you going to do now?"

"I'm going to protect the kids, find out who hurt Gary, kill them, discover who leaked this video, kill them too, and find a new job."

Evie blinked at me. Then she laughed. "At least you have a plan. Can I help?"

"Keep the kids safe. Listen to them when they think the adults aren't listening. If they remember anything about whoever attacked Gary, call me. No matter what time it is. Even if it's something small like the sound of his voice or the way he said a particular word."

Evie nodded. "Want to stay here?"

I perused the living room. It was empty now, but a few minutes ago, it'd been full of witches who'd just seen me help a demon slaughter another coven. If I stayed here, someone was likely to wait until I fell asleep and then try to smother me with my own pillow.

"Maybe another time. I need to feed my cat."

Awkward silence stretched between us. She cleared her throat and leaned against an overstuffed armchair. "I know you hate the coven, Dani. But they were my only family."

Fury burned through me. "I was your family!"

"You were gone. I was a kid." She sighed and ran her hand through her long hair. "Gemma was there when I got my first period. Noelle bought me chocolate when my first boyfriend broke my heart. Ainsley taught me how to ward."

"Because you didn't want anything to do with me."

She shook her head, and it was my turn to sigh. We weren't going to get anywhere tonight. Both of us were too tired. Too resentful.

"Let's talk about this another time," I said.

"Yeah. Another time."

CHAPTER FIVE
DANICA

I couldn't sleep. Every time I closed my eyes, I could see that expression on Samael's face. He had no right to look at me that way– his killing-spree expression tempered with a kind of reluctant tenderness.

I hadn't seen it at the time– I'd been too busy staying alive. But watching him on that screen tonight had made my head ache with confusion.

Lia let out a displeased meow as I flipped onto my side again. I'd rescued the kitten from a flooding gutter, and now I spent my few moments of free time fretting over how I was a bad cat mom.

Parenthood, yo.

"Sorry," I told her. "Don't blame me. Blame that big, dumb demon."

I scowled. Ultimately, it didn't matter *how* Samael looked at me. He'd refused to remove the bond, and even if he'd left me to my own devices for the past month, the fact remained that if he wanted, he could make me do anything he pleased. That thought hung over my head like a guillotine, ensuring I woke up in a panicked sweat at least a few times each week.

I shouldn't be *thankful* that he'd left me alone. His little stunt at the Mage Council tonight had proven that he could change his mind at any time. I felt Samael down the other end of our bond continually. My shields blocked me from most of it, but every minute of every day, I knew he was there, waiting me out.

If he wanted, Samael could order me to do anything he wanted. And like anyone bonded to a demon, I would be forced to obey.

Lia shoved her face against mine. I was hyperventilating, I realized. Panic ripped through my chest and my throat tightened. I sat up in bed and pulled Lia into my arms, stroking her tiny head.

For the past four weeks, I'd researched everything I could about how to kill high demons. I'd found nothing. The demon was playing with me right now. He may be interested in me as a woman, but he'd been alive for longer than I could comprehend. Sooner or later, he would become bored, and the orders would begin. I'd lose all free will and be nothing more than a puppet. I had to find a way to protect myself before that happened.

You don't want to kill him.

I let out a shaky breath. I didn't. I could admit that to myself now. But I needed *something*. I needed a way to protect myself, so Samael would know if he ever truly wielded that bond against me, he was dead.

When I was investigating the demon murders for Samael, the witches had placed a compulsion spell on a high demon, forcing him to attack me. I'd broken his arm and his neck, and he'd still been trying to kill me.

Samael had exploded his head with a wave of his hand.

How did I even go up against someone that powerful? Compared to the tornado of his power, mine was a gentle breeze on a summer's day.

I forced my mind away from Samael. I had more than enough to focus on— problems I could actually solve.

I needed to check out Gary's store. I lifted my phone closer to my face. Four am. Awesome. I wasn't going to get any sleep tonight anyway, so I may as well get back to work.

I gently placed Lia on the bed next to me and sat fully up. I'd head to Gary's and see if I could find anything helpful. Then, maybe I'd be able to sleep.

Ten minutes later, I was walking out to my car. I caught movement out of the corner of my eye and froze.

"You can come out," I muttered sourly. "I know Samael has someone watching me."

Earlier, it was Vas. But he wasn't usually stuck to me like glue. I think he'd happened to be in the area more than anything, and he'd promptly run back to Samael to tell him I was being taken in by the Mage Council.

A demon dropped down next to me. He was fast, and my heart thumped at his sudden movement.

"Who are you?"

"Inferus, ma'am."

I stared at him. "Don't call me ma'am."

"Yes ma'am."

I heaved a sigh. "How long have you been watching me?"

"Since the moment you left Samael's tower four weeks ago, ma'am."

"Call me Danica."

The look on his face told me he would *not* be calling me such a thing. I growled. I missed Vas. If Samael had decided to temporarily stick someone with me, I would rather deal with the demon I knew and liked.

"Where's Vas?"

"Away, ma'am."

"Call me ma'am again," I gave him a wide grin, complete with crazy eyes. "I dare you."

Inferus took a single step back. I turned and strode to my car. The demon lifted into the sky, where he'd follow me. I didn't bother calling Samael to complain. The demon would find it amusing, murmur something filthy which would make me picture him naked, and Inferus would still end up following me around until Samael decided to call him off.

The drive to Gary's only took a few minutes. I parked around the corner and moseyed down Main Street. At this time of the morning, only a few cars were coming and going, and the few people walking down the street kept their heads down, minding their own business.

Gary's block was intersected by Mangum Street to the west and Corcoran Street to the east. The guy in the cloak could've come from any direction. But some of the traffic lights at the intersections around here would have cameras. I needed to talk to Steve.

One day he'd call in all the favors I owed him, but hopefully that day wouldn't be any time soon.

The stores either side of Gary's– a tattoo parlor and a bakery– both kept human business hours. But there was a bar on the corner that might prove helpful. At the very least, maybe some of these stores had cameras positioned on their doors or windows. Even a reflection of the guy in the cloak could help.

The Mage Council had left Gary's store unlocked. Assholes. This store was his livelihood, and the damage done to his business was monumental. Maybe I could set up some kind of GoFundMe for when he got out of the hospital.

I flipped on a light and scanned the wreckage in front of me. My heart hurt. At the time, the devastation to the store had been peripheral as I focused on Gary and the kids. Now, it was a stark reminder of how they'd nearly lost their lives. I had no doubt that if the man responsible for the brutal attack on Gary knew his kids had seen him, he would've killed them without a thought.

Oh, I was going to enjoy hurting him.

I scanned the space. Nothing out of the ordinary. I methodically worked my way from behind the counter across the store to where I'd found the kids, and back toward the door.

Nothing.

Frustration welled, but I forced it down. I'd question potential witnesses, talk to the kids again, and hopefully, Gary would regain consciousness soon and tell me what he knew.

If his brain was still working correctly of course. I rubbed my eyes with the heels of my hands. "Fuck."

My phone buzzed and I gratefully took the distraction, glancing at the screen. Cara.

Get to the Mage Council. I have something to show you.

I typed a quick reply. *I'm fired, remember? I highly doubt I have access.*

I strode back toward Gary's counter and rifled through one of the drawers until I found a spare key. Then I locked the door behind me as I left.

I can get you in. Just get here. Now.

My curiosity was officially piqued. I drove to the Mage Council's facility just in case I needed to make a quick getaway. If I was caught in the building, they'd likely kill me quick, hiding my body somewhere it would never be found.

Cara was waiting downstairs for me with a tech mage she introduced as Ethan. He pushed his glasses up on his nose and gave me a wide-eyed look.

I scowled at him. "Yep, I'm her. Vicious demon protector extraordinaire."

Cara rolled her eyes. "Charming as ever, Danica."

Ethan walked toward the spelled bowl of water, and I felt him collect his power. If he could truly get around the sign-in spell, then he was a friend I needed to have.

I squinted at Cara. "How'd you know I'd be awake?"

She laughed. "I saw the paranormal news. Your little video has gone viral on the human channels too. I don't know many people who could sleep after that."

She wasn't wrong. Ethan muttered to himself, and the bowl turned green. I peered at it, barely breathing. The spell was designed to carefully monitor anyone who stepped through the lobby doors. The bowl shouldn't have turned green until each of us had held our hand above it and waited for our palms to be magically read.

Ethan had a slight sheen of sweat on his forehead. If the council found out what he could do, he was dead.

"Thank you," I told him.

"Don't mention it. He shot a desperate look at Cara. "Can I go now?"

"You sure can," she purred, winking at him, and he blushed. Then he glanced at me and practically ran out of the lobby.

"How'd you make that happen?"

"He owed me a favor. Plus, he wants to get into my pants."

We stepped into the elevator and I studied her. "Why are you helping me? Don't you know I'm a dirty traitor?"

She eyed me. "You forget I was working these same streets for years before I was promoted. I know exactly what kind of hard decisions you have to make sometimes. If those witches had managed to steal Samael's power, they would've made the Decade of Despair look like a good time."

The Decade of Despair was the first ten years after the portals had opened. Close to a billion humans had died, and the power struggles while paranormals carved out their alliances and territories…

I shivered. Yeah. The witches would have been worse. Still… "You saw me save Samael's life, right?"

She grinned. "Girl, the way he looks at you? I would've saved him too."

I chewed on that while the elevator doors opened to the 6th floor. The Mage Council's library stretched out in front of us. Nothing but silence.

We stepped inside. I half expected an alarm to start blaring, but Cara was already grabbing my elbow and pulling me toward the restricted section.

Tall, walnut bookshelves stood in rows– the books they held painstakingly organized by subject and author. I breathed in the comforting scent of leather and old paper.

"What are you guys doing?"

I jumped and let out a distinctly un-badass yelp. Cara smirked at me. We both turned.

Mella was standing on the other side of the library in her window. I stared at her. "Do you *sleep* here?"

She gave me a pissy look. "What, did you think Albert unlocked my chains each night and sent me home for eight straight?"

"I guess not." I shrugged. "We're up to no good."

"Excellent." She waved her hand. "Continue."

I grinned. The selkie had been stuck in this library for several decades after doing something to betray the Mage Council. No one knew what it was, and they'd hidden her skin, shoved her in Naud chains, and spelled her into silence.

I chewed on my lip. "Question."

"Answer."

"When Samael was in the Naud chains, he couldn't use his power, but he could still gather it to him."

"Yes?"

"Can you do the same?"

She smiled. "That would mean I'd been gathering power for decades, waiting for my chance to burn this place to the ground, wouldn't it?"

I shivered, and her smile widened. Next to me, Cara

cursed.

I stared at Mella. She stared back at me. All she needed was her skin and she would be uncontainable. Selkies were lesser fae, but if she'd had decades of gathering power... and the rage to fuel it...

Cara jerked her head and I followed her toward the restricted section. Here, the bookshelves here were shorter and wider, and they surrounded a collection of round tables since they weren't able to be checked out from the library. Anyone using them had to sit at one of these tables under the watchful eyes of the librarians.

"You've got to be kidding me."

She grinned. "Trust me. I've got this."

"Are you sure?"

"I've been working here for a while. You'd be surprised how many people can get into this area."

If Ben hadn't snuck into this very section of the library, I wouldn't currently have the Mistilteinn Dagger on my hip. If that idiot could do it without getting caught, Cara could too.

She held her hand up to the ward and I shivered as it licked at us.

"How are you getting through?" I whispered.

"I copied one of the librarian's magical signatures."

My mouth dropped open. Not only was that an elegant solution, but it took serious power.

The ward glowed briefly and then parted, allowing us entry.

"Over here," Cara said, striding toward a squat bookcase near the window.

I wished I had a few hours to poke around in this section. The books seemed to call to me, as if urging me to rifle through them.

Cara crouched and ran her fingers over several books, finally pulling out what looked like a small, unassuming, leather-bound journal. She placed it on the table between us and opened it, rifling through the pages until she found what she wanted.

"Check this out."

I sat and read.

Rowan– mountain ash– witchwood – sorb apple.

The rowan tree has long been known as the portal tree. Before the portals opened, Neo-Druids would place the tree at their gates, demonstrating that visitors were crossing the threshold.

The Norse god Thor was saved from a fast-flowing river by a low-hanging branch of mountain ash.

According to Greek myth, the goddess Hebe protected a chalice of ambrosia, only for it to be stolen by demons. When the gods sent an eagle to retrieve it, the eagle was wounded in the battle. The drops of blood that fell from its wounds sprung up as mountain ash.

European rowan trees have long provided protection against malevolent beings such as demons and are used in charms against black witches and lesser fae. Most importantly, they remain one of the few ways to kill a high demon.

I froze, lifting my head. Cara smiled and pulled something from her pocket, holding it up.

She'd cut the arrow until just the point and a small

amount of shaft remained. I got to my feet and held out my hand, staring down at it. "You mentioned that the wood was strange when you first saw this arrow."

"Yeah. It made no sense, and it made the bolt heavier than it needed to be. I ran a hundred different tests for poison, and I couldn't find anything, which is why I wanted the black monkshood. Then I got to thinking— what if it was the wood that was important?"

I raised one eyebrow. "You're a bit of an obsessive, aren't you?"

"I sure am. Anyway, there's your answer. It's not the arrows themselves that kill high demons. It's wood. From the rowan tree."

My head spun. This tiny arrow would kill Samael. All I'd have to do was slip it between his ribs when he least expected it and just like Vercan, he'd turn to ash.

My stomach twisted. Cara gave me a sympathetic look.

"Now you know you can kill the guy who looks at you like you're the only thing he's ever wanted to look at. What are you going to do about it?"

I slipped the bolt into my pocket. "I have no idea."

SAMAEL

Pure, unrelenting rage unfurled its wings inside my chest as I watched the recording on the TV in front of me. The video had been leaked.

On the screen, Danica threw herself in front of me. The brave little witch had thought she was sacrificing her life to protect everyone in this world.

And yet she would be targeted and ridiculed for it.

"I want them dead."

Sitri untangled himself from the corner of the couch where he'd curled up to watch the recording. Across the room, Lilith raised one eyebrow.

"The power vacuum–"

A knock at the door. Bael poked his head in, his expression somber.

"We have a problem."

"What is it?"

"The Mage Council have officially named Danica Amana as the lead suspect in the murder of Merrill the goblin and the attempted murder of Gary the Gnome."

Lilith sighed. "You have made your obsession with the woman too obvious, Samael. You know what happens to those we consider ours if we do not solidify our claim."

"This is Albert's doing," I said, ignoring her. "And yet, if I strike now…"

"Our plans will be derailed," Lilith said. "Give your little witch the freedom to make her own choices and she will reward you for it."

I almost smiled at that. Lilith clearly didn't know Danica at all. But in this, she was right. For now. Killing Albert would have repercussions which would threaten plans that had been centuries in the making.

"I want an investigation. I want to know every mage who had a hand in these decisions. I may not have the liberty of striking now, but when the time is right, they will learn why they shouldn't have crossed me."

Bael kept his face expressionless. "Very well, I will order it done."

CHAPTER SIX
DANICA

The sun was rising by the time I left the Mage Council. I got in my car and shoved the arrowhead into my glovebox. Then I headed straight to the paranormal hospital in Lakewood Park.

"I'm here to see Gary…"

The receptionist took pity on me. "The gnome?"

"Yeah."

"Room 548."

That was far too easy. I squinted at her, but she was already turning away to answer the phone.

I frowned. She hadn't even asked me for ID. If this was the piss-poor security I could expect from this hospital, heads were going to roll.

I took the elevator to the fifth floor and strode down the linoleum floors, attempting not to breathe in the piercing scents. Every hospital I'd ever been in had smelled like antiseptic and death, and the Lakewood Park Paranormal Hospital was no different.

Two demons I didn't recognize were stationed outside Gary's hospital room. My stomach fluttered.

Samael knew. He knew Gary was important to me, and he'd made sure he was safe. I hadn't been asked for my ID because Samael had already cleared the way for me. I didn't know what to do with that.

The demons watched me approach and I nodded at them. "Is he conscious?"

"No. One of the healers is in there with him now."

I took a deep breath and slowly pushed the door open. The healer was a light fae woman, with a wealth of long hair so light it was almost white. She looked up from the notepad she was writing on as I walked in.

"Ms. Amana?"

"Yes."

"You were the one who found him."

"Yeah."

"You saved his life. His heart had given out under the stress of his body's attempts to heal his injuries. By keeping it beating, you gave him a solid chance."

"How solid?"

"Excuse me?"

"What are his chances of surviving this? Of waking up and recognizing his sons?"

Her light green eyes turned shrewd. "Right now, we're keeping him under. I just healed some of the swelling in his brain, but the damage is severe. Attempting to heal too much at once can lead to a long-term coma that he may not wake up from."

I swallowed. Healing came with side effects. When Samael's healer had healed me, he'd fixed a bad head injury and a compound fracture. I hadn't been close to as hurt as Gary, and it had still taken days before I could leave

Samael's bed. The healer had told me he'd used a light touch so I wouldn't be unconscious for too long. He'd instructed me to return for another healing.

"What are his injuries?"

"Fractured skull, nose, collarbone, ribs, and wrist. His arm was torn almost out of its socket, but it's the internal injuries and bleeding we were most concerned with. So far, we've got that under control, but the swelling on his brain requires a gentle touch."

I couldn't speak. I still hadn't been able to bring myself to look at the figure in the bed. A lump formed in my throat as I stared wordlessly at the healer. Her eyes glinted with sympathy. "I'll give you a few minutes."

My hands shook. How was it that after being worked on by the healers, Gary looked worse? I approached his bed and stared down at him. Maybe it was because they'd cleaned him up, and without all the blood, I could now see exactly how broken he was.

Gary was tough. Gnomes weren't exactly helpless, and I'd seen him throw pushy customers out on the streets when they pissed him off.

He'd get through this. I had to believe that.

"I've got the kids," I told him. "They'll probably wake my sister up at the crack of dawn, and I bet she'll take them for pancakes at her favorite place. She's always been convinced that pancakes are the best comfort food."

He didn't say anything. The tube pushing air into his lungs continued to wheeze.

"I'm going to kill whoever did this to you. All you have to do is recover. By the time you're back on your feet, this will all be fixed. I promise."

My lower lip trembled and I bit down on it hard. The last time I'd seen Gary before he was attacked, I'd lost control of my power and terrified his kids. But that power was exactly why he'd told me to keep them safe. "I've got this, Gary. No one will hurt them."

Gary's room had a stimulating view of the hospital parking lot. Outside, the sun had risen, and it was a new day. I needed to sleep, but I doubted I'd be able to. May as well get straight to work. I called Steve as I walked out of Gary's room.

"I'm at work," he murmured when he answered. Steve worked at Samael's tower. I didn't know exactly what he did, but it was something to do with tech and security systems.

"I need a solid."

"What's wrong?"

I filled him in and he cursed. "I'm sorry to hear that."

"Yeah. I'm going to go threaten some of the people who own stores around Gary's until they hand over their security footage. Can I send it to you?" Steve was great at cleaning up bad video.

"Sure."

"I'll owe you another one."

"This one is on the house."

My eyes burned and I rubbed them. "I appreciate it." I glanced at my phone screen as it beeped. "My sister's calling, I'll talk to you later."

I switched calls. "Evie?"

"Dani, you need to get here. Now." She sounded frantic.

In the background, someone snarled.

"Where are you?"

"I took the boys out for breakfast. Someone set up some kind of magical bomb on our route and the car flipped."

"Jesus. Are you okay? Are the kids okay?" I was already running down the corridor toward the elevator. I pressed the button, cursed, and headed for the stairs.

"We're all fine. Gemma had the car spelled just in case anything like this happened. They couldn't break through the ward."

"Are you still in the car?"

"Yeah. It's upside down. I can hear an ambulance though."

"Is anyone hurt?"

"We're all okay."

"Don't trust anyone except your coven and Samael's demons. Promise me."

"I promise."

I hung up and called Samael. It would take me ten minutes to get to my sister, but she was just a couple of streets from his tower.

"Danica."

"My sister–"

"I know. I'm on the way."

My heart thumped. "Thanks."

I hung up, sprinted down the last few stairs and hauled ass to my car. It didn't escape me that I'd just called the very demon I'd been contemplating killing earlier. And I hadn't even hesitated. The moment I'd known my sister was in danger, I'd reached out to him.

I'd wrestle with that later.

By the time I arrived, paranormals were surrounding the empty car.

"Evie?"

"Over here," she called. I turned. She was sitting in the back of an ambulance, one of the kids on either side of her. Samael stood a few feet away, talking to Vas and Bael.

"I'm sorry, Danica. I didn't see it coming."

"Of course you didn't." She was clutching her arm and I stared at her. "You said you were okay."

"It's just a break," a seelie EMT said. "We'll get it sorted in a moment." He stepped back from Cil. "You're fine, young man."

Cil grinned at him, and then turned the grin on me. "We flew," he said. "You should've seen it."

I closed my eyes. A tiny hand slipped into mine. Zip. He'd hopped out of the ambulance. I glanced at the EMT and he nodded. "Also fine."

I crouched down. "I'm sorry this happened to you," I murmured. Zip nodded solemnly. "Our treasures are still in the car."

I blinked at him. "The marbles?"

"We have other treasures too." His steady gaze told me quite clearly that he expected me to reunite him with those treasures. Despite the situation, my mouth curved.

"I'll get right on it."

Vas made his way over to me, his expression hard. I stood back up and walked a few steps away from the kids.

"What do we know?"

"Your sister saw people in dark cloaks. That was it.

After the car flipped, they surrounded it and ordered her to get out. Said if she cooperated, they might let the kids live."

I would make them hurt before I killed them.

"They weren't expecting the ward."

"Nope. Evie said the head witch of her coven created it. She did good. There are some very upset, cloaked assholes walking around Durham."

They were going to be much, much more upset when I got my hands on them.

"Do you have our treasures?" Zip stared up at the demon, who planted his hands on his hips.

Vas's mouth dropped open. "Wait. You have treasure? What kind of treasure?"

Zip gave him a distrustful look. "It's *our* treasure. It's still in the car."

"If I find it, will you share it with me?" A smile trembled around Vas's mouth as Zip lowered his chin, gazing up at him stubbornly.

"No."

Vas laughed. "I thought not. I'm on it."

I met his eyes. "Thanks."

The kids had been traumatized and their dad wasn't around to comfort them. If they needed their favorite things to make them feel more secure, so be it.

And as soon as they were feeling better, I needed to talk to them again. They were being targeted because they'd seen something that could help them identify the guy in the cloak. He wouldn't bother going after them otherwise.

I could feel eyes on me, and I lifted my gaze, meeting molten silver. Samael seemed deep in thought and I strode over to him. I was about to do something I was guaranteed to regret. Unfortunately, my regret didn't matter. Evie and the kids could've *died*. My sister was powerful, but I wasn't going to paint a target onto her back.

"I need a favor."

Samael watched me, his silver eyes steady on my face as the wind rustled his hair. A few strands caressed one of his sharp cheekbones and I clamped down on the urge to push it off his face. His hair had grown a few inches in the last few weeks.

"Hello, bounty hunter, I'm well, thank you. And how are you?"

"Yeah, yeah, can you help me or not?"

He narrowed his eyes at me, and then his lips curved. I scowled. I *hated* when he smiled. It did something exceedingly uncomfortable to my chest.

"As always, I'm here to cater to your whims."

The words held a bitter aftertaste. I stepped away. "Forget it."

"No." He caught my wrist. "You will tell me what you need."

"I hate the way you order me around, you know that, right?"

He simply raised one eyebrow. I wrestled with the urge to kick him in the shin.

A headache was blooming in my right temple and I rubbed at it. "The safest place for the kids is your tower. I think they saw something last night, and someone wants to shut them up."

Samael raised his eyebrows. When he spoke, his tone

was haughty. "When I need someone to be so scared they piss their pants, I may give you a call. When I want to talk to two traumatized kids, you can stay far away," he mocked me.

Well I deserved that. "On consideration, I may have been hasty. Look, I can't risk my sister, or the kids," I blew out a frustrated breath and he simply angled his head.

"I will help you in this."

"Thank you."

He held up one hand. "But we will make a deal."

It always came down to deals with him, and I somehow never saw them coming, even though he was a demon.

"What kind of deal?"

"On Friday night, I am signing a treaty with the unseelie king. There will be a ball. You will attend as my date."

Today was Wednesday. I ground my teeth. "It's always some kind of bargain with you."

"Yes. Because it's the only way you'll spend time with me. Why must you be so stubborn?"

I pointedly looked down at the intricate gold design on my arm. "Why do you think?"

Silence. I chewed on my lower lip. Samael let me think about it.

I didn't want to go to his stupid ball. But the fact remained that the demon was doing me a solid. I was still pissed at him, but if the kids were safe, I'd be able to focus on hunting down the deadbeats who'd tried to hurt them. Not to mention, if I was going to a ball filled with dark fae, there was a chance I could get a lead which could tell me who my father was.

"Fine."

"Gracious as always," Samael glanced at the kids, who were listening intently to something Evie was saying. She was probably telling them a story. "We will go now."

With that decree, Samael turned to Bael, murmured a few words, and placed his hand on my lower back as he led me toward Evie and the kids. I peered up at the demon. He *really* needed to stop with the possessive body language.

Vas wandered over to me and slipped the kids' bag into my hands. I peeked inside and smiled. A cheap, beaded necklace, a collection of shiny marbles, a broken watch, an old, tarnished amulet, three brightly-colored plastic rings– obviously from a gumball machine– and a handful of coins from various realms. Evie and I had kept a similar collection as a kid, only ours had included various components for spells at Evie's insistence.

Everyone fell silent as I approached. "Hey guys, so we have a new plan."

I handed the bag of treasures to Zip and his eyes lit up as his hand darted out and grabbed it. My gaze got stuck on Evie, who was cursing as the healer jostled her arm. But within a few moments, the strain around her eyes had disappeared as the bone knit back together. Her face tightened once more when I told her where I was taking the kids.

"You don't trust me anymore."

I stepped closer. "I trust you more than anyone," I admitted. "You did everything right. But I won't have you targeted by these people. I couldn't handle it if this shit got you hurt, or worse."

She studied my face for a long moment and then finally nodded. "I'll help you get them settled in."

I smiled down at the kids, who were squabbling over something. "How would you guys like to see the tower?"

"*Samael's* tower?" They gave me big eyes, their little gray faces lit up in awe. It was exceedingly cute.

"Yup."

"With *Samael?*" Zip asked.

My lips trembled and I jerked my head toward the demon standing a few feet away, his mouth tight as he read something on his phone. "That's him, right there."

I'd blown their minds. They stared at Samael as if they expected him to burst into flames. He looked up from his phone, finding all eyes on him. He raised one dark eyebrow and slipped his phone into his pocket. "Are you ready to go?"

The boys jumped up, running at him. "Are you really Samael?" "Do you know Lucifer?" "How tall is your tower?" "Can you set things on fire?"

Evie nudged me with her elbow and grinned. "Turns out he's good with kids."

I blinked at that, but she was right. Samael was answering each question with serious intent, his focus entirely on the boys. His palm lit up with a ball of demon fire as we watched, and the gnomes danced excitedly on their feet at the sight. I didn't know what to make of that, so I shrugged.

"Let's go."

We bundled the kids into the car Bael had ordered for us. The demons thought of everything. Once we arrived at the tower, the kids were obviously in awe, their eyes huge as they stared at everything.

"They will stay on the floor below mine," Samael said. "I have a nanny on staff."

I blinked at that. "You have a nanny? Do you have kids?" The thought did something to my gut, made it twist in a way I didn't enjoy.

"No. Some of my staff do, and I like to be prepared."

I was learning more and more about this guy. I nodded, and we all stepped into the elevator. Evie had insisted on staying to help get the kids settled in, and her eyes were almost as wide as the gnomes' as the elevator opened to the kids' floor.

Cil let out a gasp. "Wow, cool!"

We exited the elevator to a room that was clearly designed for kids. A huge TV offered some kind of video console that the boys crowed over, and the bookcase next to it was full of games. One corner of the room held a mini-library, complete with beanbags and shelves bursting with books. Another corner was clearly created for younger children, with a huge box filled with toys, a motorized car big enough for a toddler to sit on, and a rocking horse.

Four pinball machines took up most of the far wall, and a small boy was standing in front of one of them, slamming his hand into the buttons. He turned as we walked in, and the three boys eyed each other.

"Zip, Cil, this is Brokk," Samael said. The boys weren't shy. They immediately headed toward the pinball machines, talking a mile a minute.

"Who's the kid?" I murmured.

"One of my employees had to investigate a murder in South Carolina. I told him he could leave his family here to ensure their safety while he was gone."

"He's a demon." Talk about stating the obvious.

Samael gave me a look. "Yes."

For some reason, I tended to forget that demons had children. That they had families like everyone else.

"Why can't his mom protect them?" I'd seen just how powerful high demons were.

"She's light fae. A healer. She has few combat abilities."

So, the kid was half demon, half light fae. What a combination.

"I want to stay with them," Evie said. I glanced at her. She was sticking her chin out the way she did when she'd already come to a decision and had no intention of changing her mind.

Samael shrugged one shoulder as Sitri stepped off the elevator, a human woman with him.

"This is Martha," Sitri said. "She works as the nanny here whenever we need her."

"I'm still staying," Evie said.

Martha smiled at her. "Sitri filled me in on what happened today. I think it would be great for you to stay."

I hesitated. Did I want to leave Evie with the most dangerous demon around? Samael smiled at me, likely well aware of where my thoughts had gone, and I sighed. He wouldn't hurt Evie. I trusted him that much.

"Sounds good," I said. "I need to get back to work, but I'll be in touch."

I gave my sister a hug, and waved to the boys, who were

already competing with each other in one of the games. It made loud, siren-like noises that made my head ache.

Samael was silent in the elevator next to me. I skimmed my gaze up his huge body until I found his face.

"Tell me you didn't release that recording." I didn't think he had, but it was best to cross off all the suspects on my list.

Surprise flashed across his face. It was there for less than a moment, but I caught it.

"Why would I do that, bounty hunter?"

He only called me 'bounty hunter' when I was pissing him off. Good. Why should I be the only one wrestling with my anger?

"To isolate me so I'll have nowhere to turn and you can swoop in?"

It sounded ridiculous, and a slow smile crept across Samael's face.

"We both know I have no need to isolate you. It's only a matter of time before you wake up in my bed each morning. Where you belong."

"Keep dreaming."

"Oh, I will." He studied my face, and his eyes darkened. I'd seen that look on his face a few times now, and it never boded well for me. "You haven't slept."

"It was a crazy night." It was almost noon now, but I needed to get moving. Some cameras were programmed to record over their video every twenty-four to forty-eight hours.

"Humans who are low on sleep have poor reflexes."

I sent him a look. "Please, demon-splain my life as a

human to me some more. This is real fun."

The elevator doors opened and I cursed myself for not paying attention to the button he pressed. I stayed on the elevator and he merely took my elbow and hauled me into his penthouse.

"Why can't anything with you ever be easy?"

He raised one eyebrow. "You stole the words from my mouth."

"I don't have time for this, Samael."

He lowered his head, tucking his chin and narrowing his silver eyes at me. I knew that expression. That expression was 100% pure, male stubbornness, and it told me he wasn't backing down.

"You will sleep or I will make you."

"I'm sorry, I must have misheard you. I know you didn't just threaten to send me to sleep like a child."

"Not like a child. Like an exasperating woman who risks her life as if it means nothing."

I took a deep breath. He was a demon. He had no concept of bodily autonomy for anyone but himself. Until I got this stupid bond removed, it was my job to teach him. The world would be better for it.

"Listen. I'm an adult woman who can choose when she takes a nap."

"I don't think so."

I ground my teeth and my power roared, slamming against my shields. Samael gave me an amused look.

"Does your power itch to hurt me, witchling?" He took a step closer. I yawned. My eyelids were so heavy. The mark on my arm seemed to radiate relaxation and comfort.

I forced my eyes open. When had I closed them? Panic made my heart race.

"What are you doing?"

"You're mine, bounty hunter." His expression was cut in grim resolve. "That makes it my job to take care of you when you choose not to look after yourself."

I stepped back and almost stumbled. Samael was there, lifting me into his arms.

"Let me go."

"No."

"I'll kill you for this."

A chuckle that made my hands fist.

"Sleep, little witch. You may attempt to kill me once you have rested."

He always did this. He'd do something that made my heart stutter, like putting guards on Gary's door, and then he'd immediately follow it up with something that made me long to rip his heart out, like this shit right here.

"You're only making me hate you more." My eyes had closed again. I forced them open, only to find him staring down at me, something like regret in his eyes. It disappeared in an instant.

"If you want to hate me for taking care of you, so be it."

I opened my mouth to tell him to stop twisting things. He wasn't taking care of me. He was taking away my control.

But my eyes had already slid closed.

CHAPTER SEVEN
DANICA

I woke up angry. This wasn't *uncommon* for me– I typically harnessed a healthy amount of rage just to get through my day. But the fury that swept through me warned me that I wasn't going to be happy when I opened my eyes.

The heady scent of cedar and citrus was my second clue. I opened my eyes and sat up. Once again, my knives were on the table next to Samael's bed.

I stared at him. One second to reach across and grab a throwing knife, another to aim… I could have it buried in Samael's throat in less than three seconds.

"So what, you put me in your bed and then watch me sleep like a creepy creeper?"

His lips twitched. He was sitting a few feet from the bed, his legs stretched out in front of him as his eyes scanned the book in his lap.

"Tell me that isn't the McCormick coven's grimoire."

He looked up and gave me a wicked smile. "I'm not in the habit of lying to you."

I wrestled with that. I hadn't wanted the grimoire to fall into the wrong hands, but that didn't mean that Samael's hands were the right ones.

"What are you going to do with that?"

He was silent and I cursed. I knew what he'd do with it. Anything he damn pleased.

"You snore."

"Do not."

I sure did. My nose was broken a few years ago, the cartilage turned to mush. I hadn't been able to afford an experienced healer, and he'd described the cartilage in the tip of my nose as a 'mosaic'. While he'd managed to straighten it on the outside, he'd warned me that things were 'a little fucked up,' on the inside.

And now I snored.

"What time is it?" I was so mad I couldn't even look at him.

"Three pm. Your body wanted to sleep for longer, however I knew you would want to get to work so I lifted my compulsion."

"That's real fucking good of you."

I threw his blankets off me. If I wasn't so furious, I'd be fighting the urge to roll over and go back to sleep.

"Vassago located the cameras close to your gnome friend's store. Steve is working on them now."

I almost stumbled. "Thank you."

He was silent while I pulled on my jeans. I didn't even care that I was standing in my underwear and a t-shirt. When he spoke again, his voice was very quiet.

"I don't like it when you're displeased with me."

He said it in a tone that suggested I get over my

displeasure real quick. I scowled over my shoulder at him. "Displeased? Try fucking furious."

His nostrils flared. "I'm not used to taking others' emotions into account. I see a problem and I fix it."

I had a feeling that was the closest Samael ever came to an apology. In his mind, the problem was me. I was tired. So he fixed it. I could see the twisted demon logic even if I couldn't get past the missing piece of autonomy.

I shook my head. If Samael had his way, this would be my life. Always falling in line with whatever he decided was the correct choice for me.

I slid my Mark II into my spine sheath and strapped it on. "Every time you do something like this, it makes me *loathe* you. You realize that, right?"

A hand clamped down on my shoulder, turning me in place. Samael's expression was hard, and a muscle twitched in his cheek.

"I have lost *everyone* who ever mattered to me," he hissed. "I won't lose you too."

I opened my mouth, but his power was already slamming into me, crushing my shield as if it was made of paper. The world around me disappeared. The only thing I could feel was his hand on me.

I stared up at my father who had turned a sickly white. "Your grandfather is dead," he said. "Our enemies have conspired all these years, chipping away at his power and turning those closest to him."

I didn't understand. How could grandfather be dead? He ruled the underworld.

I twitched, raising my hands to Samael's chest. His

hand clamped down harder on my shoulder.

Outside, the sound of screams assaulted our ears. My father pulled me toward a window. "Look," he ordered. "Look at what he has done."

Our palace was surrounded. Someone was using their power to keep my grandfather's body high in the air, a gruesome display for all to see. His throat was cut, his eyes missing. He was old enough and strong enough that, given a chance, he could heal such injuries, but the crowd would behead him long before that happened.

Who could be powerful enough to kill him? I began to shake.

"They will do the same to me, Samael."

"But why, father?"

"Because our enemies wish to have no challenge when they take your grandfather's throne." He suddenly grabbed me. "Look away."

It was too late. My mother's body had been raised next to my grandfather's. My gentle mother, who tickled me, told me stories, and whispered that she loved me more than life itself.

"Take your sister." My father pressed her into my arms. Alette was only one. She didn't know what was happening, but even she knew it was bad. She began to cry, and my father sent her to sleep.

"You will run, Samael. You will run, and you will grow up, and when you return, you will kill your enemies and take your grandfather's place on his throne."

"But—"

"Look after your sister. You know where to go."

I did. Recently, my father had begun running drills, timing me as I ran through the hidden passages within our home.

"Get to the River Styx. The ferryman will take you to Hades. He knows where to hide you."

"Come with us."

My father was already drawing away, his face hard. He had loved my mother more than life itself, and I knew these would be some of the last words he ever spoke. He pushed my bed to the side and opened the hidden latch, revealing the passageway. He took Alette from my arms, watched me climb down the short ladder, and then pressed a kiss to her sleeping face.

He handed her to me and began to gather his power.

"Go, Samael. And remember, you will lay waste to our enemies."

I stared at him. "I will," I promised. "Goodbye, father."

"Goodbye, son."

I ran and ran, holding my sister tightly in my arms. Alette was small but heavy, and I panted, sobbing for my mother. Long minutes later, I forced myself to wipe my tears as I cracked open the door to the dungeon, tiptoeing through the silent cell and outside.

"What did I say? I told you he'd be here."

Hands grabbed me, ripping Alette from my arms.

"Your father truly thought you could escape? His arrogance knows no bounds." Niyax, my grandfather's second. He'd betrayed him.

Niyax smiled at me, pulling me toward the crowd. Soldiers surround me on all sides, hundreds, thousands of them.

I screamed, reaching for my sister. He waved a hand and one of his men dropped her on the cold ground. He lifted his sword, impaling Alette's tiny body.

I roared, drowning in agony. My sister loved me. I told her stories, cuddled her when she was sad, promised to teach her everything I knew about the secret passageways in our home.

She was supposed to grow up. We were meant to be siblings for the rest of our lives.

Alette was the baby. Loved and doted on by all who knew her.

I was supposed to protect her.

The demon in front of me lifted his own sword. "Goodbye, Samael."

My power engulfed me. It tore through my body like wildfire. Too soon. I wasn't supposed to come into my power yet. I was too young. It would rip me apart.

But it would also rip these demons apart. I would be with my family. But first, I would make these men suffer.

Demon fire streamed from me, and the men around me began to scream. My body shook with the overload of power, but it spread, destroying everything in its path.

Moments later, I was alone. The men who had killed my family were nothing but ash, floating on the breeze. The taste of it filled my mouth, got stuck in my nostrils and I choked on it as I gasped, falling to my knees.

I crawled to my sister, blood pouring from my mouth and nose. I took her tiny body in my arms and lay down, waiting to die.

Long moments later, a face appeared above me.

"Time to go, Samael."

The ferryman.

"No. Let me die."

He laughed, the sound hoarse, and reached into my pocket, withdrawing a coin. "I made a deal with your father. Besides, you're not going to die. You're much too powerful for that." He gently took my sister from my arms, ignoring my attempts to hold her.

I tried not to glance back, but I couldn't help myself. My father's body had joined my mother and grandfather, his mouth still frozen in a snarl.

"We'll bury them somewhere pretty," he promised. "Now let's go."

The memory faded. I stared at Samael, my chest so tight I could barely get the words out. "Your family."

"I apologize," he said, his face turning blank as he stepped away.

"No. It's okay." I raised my hand toward his face, let it hang awkwardly in the air, and then dropped it. "I'm sorry. How old were you?"

"Eight of your years."

"What happened to the people who did it?"

"I killed most of them. But not enough. One of them took my grandfather's throne, and he sits on it still."

"Your grandfather was the ruler of the underworld?"

A sharp nod. I studied his face. At eight, the amount of power he'd used had been unimaginable. If I hadn't seen it through his eyes, I wouldn't have believed it. I'd thought him powerful when I watched him destroy the witches, but compared to turning an army to ash as a child, killing the coven was likely as mundane to him as washing his hands.

Samael had been tasked with protecting his sister, and he'd failed. Bile crept up my throat at the memory of her tiny, fragile body. It had happened centuries ago, but Samael's memory was crystal clear.

I wanted to discuss this more. To ask who had raised him. I was suddenly desperate to know what else had shaped him into the man he was today.

"You wish to get back to work," he said. "Go."

"Samael."

He turned away, but I didn't miss the tiny hint of vulnerability in his eyes. The stiffness of his shoulders. He was sad. And I was about to do something stupid.

I followed him, and he turned back to me, any hint of feeling gone from his blank face.

I slid my hand up his chest and marveled at the ridges of his muscles. My hand seemed to have a mind of its own, sliding up to his neck. Both of us barely breathed. Finally, he stiffened, his eyes burning.

"Don't pity me, bounty hunter."

"I don't."

He glowered at me, and I shook my head. "It's not pity. It's sympathy."

I rose onto my tiptoes and pressed a kiss against his chin. And another against the corner of his mouth. He lowered his head, and I brushed my lips against his. To date, our kisses had been full of lust and frustration. This was… gentle. Samael went exceedingly still… as if I was a wild animal he didn't want to startle. His lips softened against mine, and his hands fisted by his sides, as if he was barely restraining himself.

I stepped back. "I'd better get back to work."

He gazed at me, and I was pretty sure the demon saw more than I wanted him to see.

"Steve's office is located on the third floor."

"Thanks."

My mind whirled as I stepped into the elevator. My last sight of Samael was him standing in front of the window, his legs spread as he stared down at his territory. Alone.

Steve raised his gaze from his work as I walked into his office. "You look… rested."

"Shut it. What have you got for me?"

"We have three shots of the suspect in the cloak. They're not great. Gary's cameras seem to have mostly been for decoration.

Goddamn it, Gary.

"Any of them give you anything good?"

"The tattoo parlor had a functioning camera."

Steve pressed a few buttons, and I leaned closer as the video began to play. "He's got his hood up."

"Yeah. Smart guy. See how he's hunching his shoulder and turning his face away here? He knows exactly where the cameras are."

I watched the video, but it didn't tell me anything I hadn't known. The asshole who'd hurt Gary came from the west. He walked quickly but not overly suspiciously. Steve pulled up the three still shots from the video and I studied them. The cloak shifted slightly as the guy turned toward Gary's store and I squinted. "There's something about him that seems familiar."

Steve raised one eyebrow. "Yeah?"

"Yeah." I shook my head. I couldn't place it. "Can you print these out for me?"

"Already have."

"Thanks."

Steve gave me a sympathetic look. "Good luck."

I left Steve attempting to clean up the pictures and drove to Selina's, my mind replaying the memories Samael had shown me.

He'd been so young to witness such horror. To lose his entire family. And then he'd come into such a terrible power, right when he'd had vengeance on his mind. What did that do to a kid?

When I was sent the pictures of my mom's body, sprawled on the street as if she was trash... my world had stopped turning. I suddenly had no goals, no plans, nothing except the need to find whoever had killed her and make them pay.

Something told me Samael was the same.

Selina lived on the outskirts of Trinity Park, close to West Club Boulevard, which separated Trinity Park from Walltown. She'd added several squat pots of flowers on either side of the steps to her porch, and bright pink flowers spilled out of them— the pots already struggling to contain them. Her lawn was still as green and lush as ever. I had a feeling that Selina's lawn stayed perfect year-round.

She opened the door as I got out of my car, beaming at me.

"Danica. I was just thinking about you."

I couldn't help but smile. There was something disarming about Selina's friendliness. I relaxed fully in her presence, which was something I didn't do around most people.

"How do you look so good all the time?" I asked. She was wearing a turquoise dress with purple flowers dotted across it, dangly earrings which almost brushed her shoulders, and her hair was in a simple messy bun. Her dark skin glowed, and her feet were bare— toenails painted a bright coral.

She reached out to hug me as I made it to her front door. "I'll take the compliment. Come in."

Selina turned and gestured for me to follow her inside. She bypassed the stairs and instead chose the kitchen. I took a seat at the counter and frowned. Selina hadn't just been thinking of me, she'd obviously known I was coming.

She poured me a glass of sweet tea and offered me a plate. "Help yourself."

"You didn't need to do this."

"Something told me you hadn't eaten lunch." She took her own plate and we both loaded up on fried chicken, mashed potatoes, and green beans.

"You need my help."

I gave her a hard stare. "You know it's really annoying when you do that."

She burst out laughing. "Give a witch some credit. You look exhausted, and you're attacking that food like you've never eaten before. You have a grim look about you, Danica. What happened?"

I filled her in, starting with the way I'd threatened Gary.

She waved her hand. "He obviously forgave you if he asked you to take care of his boys."

I shook my head, reaching for my tea. "He had no choice."

"He could've asked you to take them somewhere else. The very power that scared him also gave him the certainty that you'd keep his children safe."

"Mmmm."

Selina shook her head at me, her long earrings dancing. "You're having control issues."

"Yeah. When I first realized I had this power, I didn't want it. As soon as I find whoever killed my mom, I'm out of here, and this amount of power is wasted on me, you know? And then I realized I could use it to help me search, and to protect me along the way, and I started thinking 'hey, maybe it's not that bad after all.'" I used my finger to draw a star on the condensation forming on my glass. "But I don't want to be this person."

"You don't want to be feared for your power."

I nodded.

"When I was a kid, no one knew I had any power," she said.

I angled my head. "I can believe that." Even now, Selina kept her power tucked away so tightly that I couldn't sense if she was a gray witch, or wholly white. I occasionally got a glimpse of a deep well of power, but only if I was paying attention.

"My power manifested young, but it wasn't celebrated. My mother had fallen in love with my father at a young age. She was black, he was white. She was a witch, he was a human. Their differences were stark, but they had a deep love for each other. Unfortunately, while I still have a deep respect for my father, I can recognize that his ignorance around power did no one any good.

"He'd insisted that my mother break from her coven. We weren't living with them, but he didn't approve of her visiting, even weekly. Once she left, he made it clear that he was completely disgusted by magic. Any urge she had to use her power was met with disdain and revulsion."

"I can't imagine how hard that must have been."

Selina nodded. "My mother was a powerful witch. To her, using that power was as natural as breathing. When I was born, she couldn't feel any spark of power within me. For a while she mourned, wondering if her insistence on never using magic while she was pregnant had magically crippled me. After a few years, she had decided it was a gift. She had moved far from her coven, and we lived in a human neighborhood, close to where my father worked. Everything was great. For a while."

Selina swallowed, briefly closing her eyes. "My mother was a smart woman, but she was young. Her parents had been abusive— her father an alcoholic, and when she met my father, she'd fallen so deeply in love that she'd lost all reason. When he decided I would be sent to a human school, she didn't object. After all, it seemed likely that I had no power."

My lips went numb. "But you did."

"Yes. I was small, shy, and one of the few mixed kids in my neighborhood. I was confused, torn between different worlds— my father was a human, my mother was a witch.

My father was white, my mother was black. Every question I had about magic went unanswered. Every concern I had was swept under the rug. By the time I went to school, I felt like I didn't belong anywhere."

"Let me guess, the little psychopaths made it worse."

She laughed. "Kids can be cruel. I was bullied. One girl liked to put paint in my hair, and she would whisper in my ear that her mother had told her *my* mother was a witch, and I was going to hell. It didn't take long before I was going home crying each day, begging my parents to let me homeschool. Unfortunately, they both agreed that I needed to learn to solve my problems and not run from them. One day, this little girl decided to get physical. She pushed me off the swing and called me a filthy word. I snapped."

Selina sighed, pushing her plate away.

I leaned one elbow on the counter. "Did you kill her?"

"No. But almost. My power was uncontrollable. My mother was called, and she arrived to find that I'd wrapped the swing around the little girl and was hoisting it higher and higher in the air as it tightened. I had created a ward, and none of the human teachers could get through to stop me. By the time my mother managed to pull me from my frenzy, I'd broken several of the girl's bones."

"I'm sorry."

"So am I. That was the end of human school for me, for which I was grateful. But my mother realized I needed to be trained. By then, she was so used to suppressing her own magic that she needed her coven's help. My father threatened to leave. She took me anyway. They divorced a few months later."

"She should've taught you how to use your power."

"Yes. And you need to be taught the same. I was a child with witch power. You are something *more*. But without training, the result is the same. You can't expect to be able to control something that has been suppressed all these years. The only differences between you and the seven-year-old me are your age and the amount of power you wield."

I picked at my cuticle while I thought it through. Attempting to ignore my power hadn't worked. "You think you can teach me how to avoid scaring the crap out of people unintentionally?"

"I can teach you what I was taught. Your power is different, but the underlying rules should be the same."

I took a sip of my iced tea and squared my shoulders. "Okay. Let's do it."

Chapter Eight
DANICA

I was so tired I was almost shaking when I left Selina's an hour later. We'd started simple, and she'd had me raise and lower my shields over and over again. When I'd asked why we were doing something she'd specifically warned me not to do, she'd told me she was hoping I would learn exactly how exhausting it was to do something so unnatural.

"Your shields should rarely be lowered. You need to learn how to make them almost translucent. Your power should be able to flow through your shields when necessary."

I'd shrugged and complied, raising and lowering my shields what felt like a thousand times. Finally, Selina had made me reach for my power while raising and lowering my shields. By the end of our lesson, I'd felt the tiniest spark of power while my shield was still up.

My phone vibrated in my back pocket, and I pulled it out as I got into my car. I kept the door open and turned the key in the hope that the air conditioning would get to work. A trickle of sweat ran down my back, beneath my t-shirt.

"Danica Amana," a voice said.

I frowned. The voice was familiar. "Who is this?"

"Mariam. We met a few weeks ago when you were looking into the demon murders."

Mariam. The light fae representative. "How can I help you?"

"You may be able to help us," her tone was wry. "I saw the video."

I was so tired that it took me a moment to understand what video she meant. When I did, I clenched my teeth. "You and the rest of the world."

She laughed. It sounded like tinkling bells. Tinkling bells I wanted to punch.

"It seems that you are currently unemployed."

There was no point lying. "Yup." I popped the p and she chuckled. Glad my current circumstances were so amusing to her.

"We may have an opportunity for you."

"An opportunity?"

"Yes. Can you meet with me to discuss it?"

"When?"

"Does now work?"

Typical fae. There was only one schedule, and it was their own.

I chewed on my lower lip. It was getting close to dinner time. I needed to question anyone who'd been around when Gary was attacked before their stores closed. But I also needed to earn enough to pay my rent.

"Give me an hour."

I drove back to Gary's store and went from door to door along the street, displaying the useless picture of the man in the cloak and generally making a nuisance of myself. No one could give me anything even remotely helpful. The bar on the corner had been hosting a private party, which had gotten loud. Any sounds Gary may have made, or any smashing of his store, had been lost to the bad pop music that night.

Pissed off, I scowled down at my phone. My mood turned darker. Instead of heading to the fae representative's office, which was close to Samael's tower in the center of Durham, Mariam had instructed me to go to Hope Valley, where many of the high fae lived.

It had added ten minutes to my trip each way, but I was more concerned with the neighborhood itself.

Before the portals opened, Hope Valley had already been one of the most prestigious areas in Durham. And many of the residents had been just fine while the world turned to shit, retreating behind their huge gates and into their panic rooms. I'd seen an interview of a human who lived in the area after the portals fell, and he'd been most befuddled by the fact that people had attempted to break down his door while fleeing from the werewolves who'd rampaged through the city.

When the fae arrived, many of the high fae decided they enjoyed the neighborhood. Something about the sprawling homes had obviously reminded them of their world. The light fae, in particular, tended toward the gaudier mansions, and they offered humans deals they couldn't refuse when they wanted their homes.

Within a decade, almost all the humans had left the neighborhood. The holdouts had soon discovered that living in a fae neighborhood meant dealing with pixies stealing their food, goblins terrorizing their children, and the occasional banshee screaming bloody murder.

I didn't mind the lesser fae. It was the high fae– and their deep sense of entitlement– that rubbed me the wrong way.

Dover Road backed on to what had once been a country club but was now a small forest. I slowed my car and crawled along the road, fascinated despite myself. Then I double-checked the address. Yup, I'd gotten it right.

My car couldn't have looked more out of place in this neighborhood, and a light fae couple who were out for a walk sneered at me as I pulled into the drive and pressed the intercom.

"Name?"

"Danica Amana."

The gate slid open, and I drove up the long drive, my mouth falling open. It looked like a hotel. The sand-colored house sprawled over what had to be twenty-five thousand square feet. Multiple columns supported the four-storied monstrosity, and a group of light fae guards waited for me outside the front door.

I parked and stepped out of my car, finally closing my mouth.

One of the guards stepped forward, his pale blue eyes intent as he took in my weapons.

"This way, Ms. Amana."

The fae's pointed ears told me he was high-fae, but he registered as low on the power scale. I followed him into the cool of the house and up one of the two staircases leading to the second floor.

We stopped outside the first door on the left, and he rapped his knuckles on the door.

"Come in."

Mariam was sitting behind a commanding wooden desk. My gaze skipped the rest of the room and got stuck on the desk. The grain of the wood swirled in a way that made it almost look like marble.

The polished wooden floors gleamed, while the walls were done in crimson. The furniture was solid, clearly expensive, and mostly wood. For all their love of the ornate, the fae preferred to surround themselves with natural textures like stone and wood whenever possible.

Mariam smiled at me and gestured for me to take a seat. I wasn't sure what kind of powers she had, but she'd always smelled of salt water to me. Her blonde hair had been pulled back in a simple braid, highlighting her impeccable face and sharp cheekbones. Her eyes were so blue they appeared almost violet.

"Nice place you've got here."

If she heard the sarcasm in my voice, she didn't respond to it.

"The seelie king occasionally uses this home when he visits. Thank you for meeting me here. I appreciate it. The subject we are about to discuss is… delicate."

Delicate and clearly confidential. I was officially interested.

The fae male left, closing the door behind him. Mariam took a moment to examine me, and then finally let out a long breath.

"Over the past few weeks, we have had some incidents."

"What kind of incidents?"

Mariam hesitated and it was clear that she wasn't thrilled about disclosing these incidents.

"I can't help you unless you tell me what happened."

"First, I need your word that you are no longer associated with the Mage Council."

I raised my eyebrow. "I thought you said you saw the video."

She stared at me silently and I heaved a sigh. "I am no longer associated with the Mage Council. I'm officially fired."

Mariam's gaze dropped to my hip. The Mistilteinn Dagger was in my belt sheath, and I hadn't bothered pulling my t-shirt over it. Mariam had just used my own lie-detector against me.

Sneaky. I could respect that. My opinion of her increased a notch.

"Okay," she nodded. "Several light fae artifacts have gone missing recently."

"What kind of artifacts?"

She went silent again. I waited her out. This was like pulling teeth.

"The kind of artifacts that should have been kept in the fae realms," she said finally. "However, some of their owners are both overconfident and stubborn."

"Lay it out for me."

"Three weeks ago, the first artifact was stolen. It's called the Belt of Thor."

"What does it do?"

Mariam's lips twitched like she was holding back a sneer. She clearly thought I should know all about the fae and their most valuable artifacts.

In my mind, I got to my feet, told her to go fuck herself, and walked out the door. Then I woke up in a week or two to find my electricity was shut off.

I kept my ass in the chair and gave Mariam squinty eyes.

She sighed. "The name of this artifact means 'strength belt' or 'power belt' in Old Norse. Some know it as the Girdle of Might."

"So, what, it makes people exceptionally strong?"

"It was said that the Megingjörð Belt doubled the strength of Thor himself."

"Yikes." If it doubled the strength of a god, what would it do in the hands of a paranormal with a grudge? My mind presented me with the thought of someone like Veronica with the belt and I shuddered. The witch had been crazy and powerful enough.

I took out my phone and opened the notes app. "Where was it stolen from?"

"My office."

I gaped at her. No wonder she was barely giving me any of the information I needed. Mariam had fucked up.

"My king had asked for it to be kept safe in this world, as he is currently having some… issues with his enemies." She waved her hand in the air. "There have long been rumors that the belt can also increase the owner's natural power along with strength. Those rumors are false, but symbols have their own power, and the seelie king found it more convenient to remove the symbol completely."

"You tried it, didn't you?" I gave her a wink and she merely sniffed and said nothing. The fae couldn't lie, and she simply shrugged, leaning back in her chair.

"Ogma's Amulet went missing next."

"Ogma?"

Mariam's expression said she found my knowledge of the gods wanting. I waited her out.

"Ogma is the Dagda's brother. He's also Lugh's half-brother."

I raised my eyebrows. Even I had heard of Lugh and the Dagda. Like the two main families in any soap opera, they cultivated infidelity, revenge, and plenty of drama. Only this soap opera involved incredible power.

Mariam nodded at whatever she saw on my face. "Ogma invented Ogham, which was used to create the old Irish alphabet."

"Okay, so what does the amulet do?"

"It provides the owner with great knowledge. Knowledge that is confidential and priceless. However, only those with fae or demon blood may use it."

I frowned at that. "Demon blood?" She clamped her lips shut and I almost rolled my eyes. "So it's knowledge about the fae, huh?"

She stared at me. I heroically held back a smirk. "How did the amulet go missing?"

"The amulet's power works in a unique way. While not quite sentient, it has often gone missing over the centuries, always finding its way to the one who needs its knowledge the most."

"But it hasn't shown up?"

"No. We would know if the amulet had been activated and used, as it then would have made its way back to us. Instead, it is still missing. We would not have worried, except that the other artifacts are missing as well."

I entered the amulet into my phone.

"Anything else?"

"Hrunting is also missing."

I gaped at her in stunned silence. When I could talk again, I stuttered out my words. "The sword that Unferth gave Beowulf? How much power are we talking here?"

She gave me a thin-lipped smile. "That sword was created by mortals. Hence why it proved ineffective. However, that sword *will* lead those with enough power to another much more important sword."

"An important sword like the one Beowulf found in the cave? That sword was melted when he killed Grendel's mother."

"Was it?"

Wow. Okay. "Who was the sword stolen from?"

"A light fae named Aubrey. He's somewhat of a weapon collector. The sword was stolen from his house."

"So whoever has been stealing these artifacts already has a belt that can make them exceptionally strong, an amulet that can give them incredible knowledge, and a sword that can lead them to another sword known for killing monsters. Do I have that about right?"

Mariam raised one eyebrow. "Indeed."

"Suspects?"

"There are few who know what these artifacts can do. But we have become… overconfident."

I raised one eyebrow, and Mariam sighed again. "The artifacts were created several millennia ago. Some of them by the gods themselves. They were lost in various worlds, found, and lost again. They do not require power to wield them. They are their own power."

So literally anyone could pick them up and use them in any way they chose– whether they were human, werewolf, fae, or demon.

"Okay. I need a list of anyone who knew about the artifacts and anyone who could've had access to them."

Mariam nodded and reached for a piece of paper, handing it over. I scanned down the list of names and barely suppressed a sigh.

"Let's start with the belt. Any video footage?"

Mariam looked offended at the suggestion. "It was in my personal office."

"Anything else I need to know? Anyone who you came into contact with who made the hair on the back of your neck stand up?"

She shook her head and I put my phone down. "I require a five thousand dollar deposit which will pay for any incidentals, bribes, and travel necessary during the investigation."

Mariam frowned at me. "I don't think you realize just how important these artifacts are. In the hands of humans, werewolves, or other paranormals, they could wreak destruction across this world. Seelie artifacts can do everything from suppressing demon magic, to taking power from the world around them for the user to wield. If you can return them to us before they are used, I will pay you a hundred thousand dollars."

Somehow, I managed to stop my mouth from dropping open. "Okay. I still need the deposit. And I need to talk to your receptionist."

"She is waiting outside. You may interview her in here."

Mariam got up and opened the door. I took the opportunity to take the seat behind her desk. When interviewing witnesses and suspects, always take the position of power.

Mariam disappeared and her assistant walked in, raising her eyebrow when she saw me behind the desk.

"Adelina?"

"Yes." Her face was blank but her eyes radiated dislike. I'd met her once before with Vas. She'd attempted to block me from seeing Mariam, and I'd pulled out the big guns, threatening her with the demons. I wouldn't like me either.

"Take me back to the day the belt went missing," I said. "Did you notice anything out of the ordinary?"

She sat down, stretching her legs out in front of her. She wore a pale pink suit and a set of pearls. Her eyelashes were so long they gave me the willies.

Adelina cooperated, taking me through every minute of her day. Occasionally, she flipped through her daily planner or took out her phone to check a detail.

No, she hadn't noticed anything out of the ordinary, and all the people who'd had a meeting with her boss that day had been trusted to the fae.

I let her go and leaned back in Mariam's chair. With the way the fae were determined to keep their business to themselves, this was likely to be a long, complicated investigation. An investigation without the few resources I'd had with the Mage Council.

My hands fisted. Fuck those guys. I was going to solve this, get my money, and be set for at least the next few years if I lived frugally.

Mariam opened her door, her eyes narrowing as she took in my position in her seat. She walked toward me, handed me a check and hovered, clearly waiting for me to get out of her chair.

I stood. "I need to take a look around your office tomorrow. Is that going to be a problem?"

"No. I will tell everyone to cooperate."

"Okay. I also need Aubrey's information, along with anything you can tell me about where the amulet was last seen before it disappeared."

"I will email the information through to you."

"Thank you."

I got in my car and drove home, where I had a nightmare that Odin was trying to kill me.

CHAPTER NINE

DANICA

I messaged my sister as soon as I opened my eyes the next morning. Evie said Cil and Zip were doing okay. They were quiet, but their new friend and the toys and games at Samael's had them sufficiently distracted.

I called the hospital. Still no change in Gary's condition. I hung up, fed Lia, showered, and drove to Mariam's office.

The fae representative's building had been decorated in gold and whites, with the kind of thick, lush carpet that screamed wealth. Adelina and I ignored each other as I strode through the small waiting area and past her marble counter, heading toward Mariam's office.

A group of pixies flitted by, their voices so high pitched I held back a wince as they gossiped amongst themselves.

Mariam was waiting in her office for me, and she nodded as I stepped inside.

"Good morning."

"Hi. Where did you keep the amulet?"

She gave me a look, but I didn't exactly have time to be polite. Today, I needed to go talk to the kids, follow up with Steve, and go to the stupid ball with Samael. I also needed to go through Gary's schedule in the weeks leading up to his attack.

Mariam got to her feet. She wore a white dress that I would've spilled something on within five minutes, and her feet were clad in gold stilettos that perfectly matched the gold accents in the wallpaper.

She crossed the office, opening a cupboard next to the wall with the floor-to-ceiling windows. In the cupboard was a safe.

I cracked my shields down and stared at the fae.

"Where's the ward?"

A muscle twitched next to her eye before she could hide it. She must be *very* upset if she'd let her glamor slip. "This safe wasn't warded."

"I'm sorry, I must've misheard you. You can't have told me that you had no ward on the ancient fae artifact which was created by a *god*."

She glowered at me and turned away. After a few moments of pacing back and forth, she threw up her hands. "I should've warded it," she admitted. "But this is one of the most secure buildings in Durham. No one knew the amulet was here. And this office is monitored at all times."

All signs were pointing towards her assistant being involved. The only problem? Fae couldn't lie, and I'd made sure to ask her yes or no questions. Adelina hadn't expected the amulet to go missing.

I turned to the safe. I could crack it in about fifteen minutes, and my safe-breaking skills were rusty as hell. If someone knew the amulet was here, they could've snuck in at any time.

Half an hour later, I stalked out of Mariam's office. Then I paused, my gaze going to the pixies who were sitting on one of the tables in the seating area, their tiny legs hanging over the edge.

I crouched in front of them. "Hi."

The pixie closest to me flapped incandescent wings, her magenta eyes taking me in. "You're investigating the missing amulet."

"I am. Can you guys tell me anything?"

They all shook their heads. A sudden thought occurred to me and I smiled at them. "Do you work here?"

They nodded. "I am the pixie queen's assistant," the first pixie said. "She has me bring her requests and petitions to Mariam, who takes them to our king."

"So, you must be here a lot, right?"

She nodded and her friend let out a laugh that sounded like tiny bells ringing. "Most days. Our queen has many petitions for the king."

"Have you noticed anyone going into Mariam's office over the past few weeks?"

"Just Mariam and her guests. And the humans who use their tools."

I went still. "The cleaners?"

"Yes."

I ground my teeth and scanned the list of names Mariam had given me. They were divided into groups, and there were no humans amongst them.

"Are there many cleaners in this building?"

One of the other pixies, a tiny male dressed in green pants and a white shirt nodded, his wings fluttering as he rose into the air. "There are many humans here. They don't like us."

His dark frown said he didn't like them either.

My curiosity was piqued. "How do you know they don't like you?"

"They call us rude names. And one of them attempts to use their sucking machine to make us disappear."

Sudden fury ripped through me. "The vacuum?"

He nodded. "We were nice to the humans when they first started working here. But they weren't nice back."

"I'm sorry they weren't nice to you. Don't judge us all based on those assholes. Thanks for talking to me. If I have any questions later, can I talk to you guys again?"

They all nodded, and I got to my feet. I stalked back into Mariam's office, throwing open her door.

She jerked her head up and I scowled at her. "Cleaners, Mariam?"

"I'm sorry?"

"Human cleaners. Why would you need cleaners in a fae building anyway?"

"This facility— and my position— was designed to be a bridge between the fae and every other race in this world."

I was sure that somewhere, that logic worked for the fae. Personally, I had no fucking idea how. They'd invited humans in here. Humans who would get an up-close look at the wealth and power the light fae held after coming through those portals. How exactly would that help create a relationship of respect?

"So you thought hiring human cleaners would… what? Make you more approachable?"

Mariam flushed. "I didn't make that decision."

"Okay. This time I need a list of *everyone* who had access to this office. Including the humans."

She picked up the phone, murmured a few words to someone and hung up.

"Adelina will have it for you."

"Thank you."

I turned, walked out, took the list from Adelina's outstretched hand, and scanned it.

The fae had hired Crystal Clear Cleaning. I Googled the company as I stepped into the escalator and headed back down to the lobby. How like the fae to completely forget that they had a team of humans accessing their buildings.

I got back into my car and headed to Samael's tower.

Zip and Cil were snuggled up next to Evie on the sofa when I arrived. Evie was reading them a story and she glanced up at me, but I waved my hand, indicating that she should keep going.

"And they lived happily ever after," she said a few minutes later. The kids looked up.

"How's our dad?" Zip demanded.

I stepped further into the room. "He's doing okay. He hasn't woken up yet, though. I need to ask you guys a few questions."

They nodded and I sat next to Zip on the couch. "Okay you guys, I need you to think back to everything that you and your dad did over the past week. Let's start with the weekend. What do you do?"

They blinked at me and Evie jumped in. "You guys go to a lesser fae school, right?"

"Yes. I'm in the *advanced* math class," Cil said. "Zip's in the math class for *babies*."

Zip's mouth twisted and I leaned close. "I wasn't any good at math either."

He looked up at me. "You weren't?"

"Nah. I liked to read."

He grinned. "I like to read too."

"Awesome. Okay so when you finished school on Friday, what did you do next?"

"Dad took us to the park. And then he had to work, so we went to Merrill's."

Merrill was a goblin who ran a store similar to Gary's, only he specialized in locating weapons, herbs, and spells from other realms. The two store owners had a begrudging respect for each other, even though they were competitors, and had struck up an unlikely friendship.

Cil gave Zip wide eyes and I squinted at them.

"What?"

"We're not meant to hang out at Merrill's without dad," he admitted. "We told dad we were visiting our friend Kir."

Lying to their dad. They'd started young. "Why doesn't your dad like you visiting Merrill alone?"

"He says he has dangerous stuff in his store. But Merrill makes sure we don't play with anything that could hurt us."

"Okay, so you guys went to Merrill's. Then what happened?"

The boys shared a look. "Dad had to work most of the weekend," Zip said.

"He's always working," Cil frowned. "But he took us to the park again on… Saturday? And then he had a business meeting on Sunday, so he said we had to go and entertain ourselves."

I narrowed my eyes at them. "You went back to Merrill's, didn't you?"

They both nodded solemnly. "Merrill is fun," Zip said. "He lets us play in his stock room. It's huge."

The boys took me through the rest of their week, but nothing stuck out to me. "Does your dad have a calendar or a notebook where he writes down his meetings?" I hadn't seen one when I poked through his store.

"Yeah," Zip said. "It's usually in his pocket."

In that case, I needed to get back to the hospital and see if it was found on Gary when he was taken in. Then I'd go home, throw on a dress, and get back in time for Samael's ball.

The door to the balcony opened and the demon himself strode into the room. Samael looked distracted, clearly lost in thought until his eyes narrowed on me, taking in my ripped jeans, utility belt, and t-shirt.

"You don't look ready for the ball."

"Cinderella has been busy. What time does it start?"

"Seven."

"Surely a hedonist like you wasn't intending to be on time?"

He gave me a slow smile. "I have a dress for you."

"Uh-uh. I have my own clothes."

"You agreed to go as my date. My dates wear what I choose for them."

"Do they?" I crossed my arms. "Do they really?"

Evie let out a choked laugh and I gave her a look. The

boys were staring at us wide-eyed, clearly entertained. I ground my teeth. "I'll see you guys later. Samael, we'll talk about this elsewhere."

"As you wish." He held his arm out for me and I ignored that, stalking past him and into the elevator. I pressed the button for the lobby. He stepped inside and glanced at the buttons. The light behind the G disappeared and reappeared around the button for his penthouse. I scowled at him.

"Grant me this favor," he crooned, and I shook my head as the doors opened and I was once again in his territory.

Of course, this entire fucking city was his territory.

"I don't think so." A thought occurred to me. "How about we make a bargain."

His eyes turned feral. The demon did so enjoy his bargains. "What kind of bargain?"

"I wear your dress, and I only have to stay for two hours."

He stepped closer, and every nerve in my body seemed to come to attention. "You wear my dress and accessories, and allow my team to help you get ready. You stay four hours."

"Three hours and I'll wear the dress and let them help me with my hair. If you have shoes, I'll take them too. But that's it."

He raised his hand, and I barely breathed as he tucked a lock of my hair behind my ear. Satisfaction radiated from him, and I had a feeling I'd agreed to much more than he'd expected. Sneaky demon.

"Very well." Two women walked through the doorway in the direction of his bedroom, and I shamelessly stepped behind Samael. He'd had this planned, and now I was stuck.

"Wait, wait, wait. It's only five pm. I have things to do! I'll get back here in an hour and you guys can pretty me up then."

Samael seemed entirely too amused by my cowardice. "I don't think so. As my *date*, you will need to look the part."

The women were already approaching, both of them impeccably put together. The woman on the right was clearly unseelie fae, her pointed ears and dark hair displayed to her best advantage. She took one look at me and clapped her hands.

"In the shower please." She shared a look with her partner. "We have work to do."

SAMAEL

I closed my file on the little witch and lifted my head, gazing out the window of my office and to the city below me. The more information that my people found about Danica, the more my suspicions proved correct.

If she was who and what I suspected, she could lead me to everything I'd ever wanted. But only if I managed her carefully. Without enough oversight, I risked losing everything.

Including the witchling herself.

I ground my teeth. For the past weeks, I'd allowed her absence at Monday dinners. After her fury when she realized I wouldn't be removing my bond, I'd given her some time to cool off. However, my patience was drawing to an end.

A knock sounded at my door.

"Enter."

Bael stepped in, a thick file in his hands. "Ag believes one of the grimoires may have surfaced in Myanmar. He's leaving after you sign the pact with Finvarra."

My every sense sharpened. I itched to go hunt for the grimoires myself, but my enemies watched me too closely.

Nine black books. The search had taken centuries, as had the forming of alliances across the realms. With the grimoires in my possession, and an army of paranormals at my disposal, I would finally be able to strike.

My vengeance was so close I could almost taste it.

Unfortunately, there was still one unknown. One tactical consideration that had to be accounted for with every step.

Thanks to my suspicions about who and what Danica was, the playing field had changed.

Finding the grimoires and striking at my enemies quickly had just become more important than ever.

"How is Danica's training?"

Bael studied my expression, keeping his own neutral. "She is learning from the witch. Selina."

I nodded. "She's powerful. That is acceptable. For now."

"We need to talk about the traitors," Bael smoothly changed the subject.

Two demons had betrayed me to the McCormick coven, and where there were two, there were more. Just a few years ago, I wouldn't have thought it possible, but my enemies had a long reach, even from the underworld.

I waved my hand. "What do you know?"

"Sitri has examined Malgron and Botis' electronics."

I leaned back. Sitri had a unique ability to use his power to create backdoors into sophisticated systems and dissolve encryptions. Never had the power been seen in a demon before, but it had proven incredibly useful over the years, as human technology began to catch up to where it had been before the portals opened.

"And?"

"They were careful. They knew we would inspect their electronics if they were caught. We are now comparing timestamps when they were off shift. Any of our people who were supposed to be working, or who were rostered off during the same periods will be questioned."

I gave a short nod. Questioning my people left a bad

taste in my mouth. It was also terrible for morale. But I couldn't risk my plans being disrupted.

Not now, when I was so close to taking back my throne.

CHAPTER TEN
DANICA

"**S**urely we're done now. This is getting ridiculous."

And my voice was perilously close to a whine. The woman who'd ordered me into the shower shook her head at me, clamping her fingers around my chin so she could hold my face still.

If she squeezed any tighter, I was liable to snap my teeth at those fingers like a rabid dog.

Her name was Dorielle, and she'd introduced her partner as Linetta. The other woman was a human– and apparently one of the most well-known hairdressers in the country.

She'd tutted over my split ends, given me a trim, and curled my hair in soft waves before piling it on my head in a complicated arrangement that left a few tendrils falling down to frame my face. I didn't know exactly what she'd done to make it so glossy, but even I had to admit that it looked better than it had in years.

Meanwhile, Dorielle had taken over my makeup. I'd sternly told her that makeup wasn't covered under my agreement with Samael, but she'd almost had a stroke when I began slapping on foundation.

She'd convinced me that the process would be much faster if I allowed her to take over.

I was a sucker. That's what I was.

My nose itched and I raised my hand. Dorielle hissed at me and I scowled. I was damn glad Samael couldn't see this.

Dorielle's fingers tightened. I shifted in place. "Are we done yet?"

Dorielle let out a growl that sounded otherworldly. "I would already be finished if you knew how to stay still."

I refrained from telling her that staying still and quiet was one of my best things when I was hunting my bounties.

Finally, she used a tiny brush to swipe lipstick over my mouth. Maybe no one had told her that you could lift the tube up and paint it on in a much shorter time frame.

She stepped back, and I rolled my shoulders, getting to my feet.

Linetta handed me the dress and I stepped into it, allowing her to zip me up. I curled my lip as she held out the torture devices she considered shoes.

I could walk in heels. In my late teens, I went through a stage where I was determined to be like normal women. I knew how to kill a man in a hundred different ways, but I'd wanted one piece of normality in my life.

I'd practiced walking in them until I was able to master the small steps and slow roll of my hips. When my trainer— Edward Sutton— had caught me wearing them, he'd given me a slow smile that I knew meant I was in deep shit.

The next day, he'd made me train in heels. And the next. He'd explained that if I was going to do something as foolish as wear ankle-breaking devices, then I was going to learn to swing a sword, throw a knife, and most importantly— engage in hand-to-hand while wearing them.

He'd taken something I'd been convinced would make me like other women and ruined it. I'd barely worn heels since.

I slid them on and Linetta held out a velvet box. I shook my head. "That's a nope. The makeup wasn't included in my deal with the demon and I let you guys paint my face. There's no way I'm wearing his sparkly stones."

Both women stared at me. I ignored them and turned to the full-length mirror in Samael's bedroom. Even I could admit I looked good.

"Okay," I said. "Let's get this over with."

A deep voice made me jolt. "Now that's the attitude."

I didn't know where Samael had gotten ready, since we were currently standing in his bedroom, but I almost swallowed my tongue as I looked at him.

A tux should soften a man up a little. It should hide his rough edges and fool the eye into believing the man is tamed, if not harmless.

The tux wasn't doing its job. Samael oozed danger. His silver eyes scanned me, and while his expression didn't change, I practically choked on the satisfaction wafting from him.

My dress was a purple so dark it was almost black. It shimmered in the light, falling over my skin like water. While the dress fit like a glove, Samael had obviously memorized where I liked to keep my weapons. The fabric draped over my right thigh, allowing me easy access to my

Mark II, which I'd switched from my spine sheath.

My Nim Club was tucked into the sheath around my neck– connected to a leather lanyard covered in sparkly gems. It looked cheap next to the dress, but would hopefully appear to be a necklace with the end tucked into the low neckline and the sheath beneath my breasts.

"You rip the breath from my lungs."

I flushed as Samael stepped closer. Distantly, I was aware of Linetta and Dorielle hightailing it out of Samael's bedroom. I cleared my throat.

"You clean up nicely yourself."

His bowtie was the same deep, dark purple as my dress. We were going to be matchy-matchy. Cute.

"There's something you need to know," Samael said. His eyes were burning with what looked like retribution and I stiffened.

"What?"

"The Mage Council have publicly named you as the lead suspect in the attack on Gary the gnome.

I reached out a hand to steady myself on the vanity. "Excuse me?"

"I'll kill them," he said it casually as if stating that he'd order them a drink. "But in the meantime, you need to keep a lookout for any bounty hunters with a point to prove."

I had a pretty good feeling Rose would've told everyone and anyone about my little reaction to the Naud Chains. And the demon who'd appeared and scared the crap out of the mages.

I sighed. "You can't kill them, Samael. You need them. You know that as well as I do."

Samael had a symbiotic relationship with the mages, and unless he wanted to end up taking responsibility for the safety of every human in the triangle, he needed them alive.

No paranormal wanted to return to the Decade of Despair. Even humans could cause damage to paranormals if they had both the numbers and the sheer desperation.

"I don't need all of them," he said silkily.

I shook my head. "It wouldn't matter if you killed them now anyway. Word will have already spread. They're doing this to distance themselves further from me after leaking the video. It's diabolical, really."

"I am sorry."

If I thought about it for too long, it made my chest ache. "Me too." Time for a change of subject.

"I got a new case today." I didn't know why I was telling him, but he looked pleased that I was.

"What kind of case?"

I filled him in. "So far, they've lost a sword, an amulet, and a belt. But there will be more. Someone is targeting the seelie."

"They have long collected artifacts of power. It surprises me that they would risk losing them."

"Yeah, well, I think it surprised the hell out of them too." I angled my head. "Question."

"Potential answer."

"Mariam told me that some of the light fae artifacts can suppress demon magic. Is this something that the light fae themselves can do?"

"Yes. They would have to be extremely powerful, or the demon would have to be young and unshielded. They would also usually require the demon's cooperation." He studied my face.

"What is it?"

"Nothing. Just thinking."

He looked displeased and I changed the subject. "Do you have somewhere I can put Misty?"

"Misty?"

I held up the Mistilteinn Dagger and Samael's lips twitched. "It needed a nickname," I explained.

Actually, while I had the dagger in my hand…

"Why were you seen near my mom's body?"

Surprise flashed over his face. "You want to talk about this now?"

"The last time we were supposed to have this conversation, it was derailed by a demon under a compulsion spell. Every other time we've been interrupted."

He took a step closer. "And now you have your dagger in your hand." He smiled, but not like it was funny. "You don't think I killed her."

"No." I'd already used Misty to question him when I found out he was close enough to the body to leave a magical imprint behind. Only the most powerful creatures left an imprint that could be picked up by magical investigators. Power leaked from them constantly.

"Tell me you didn't have anything to do with her death, Samael." My throat tightened and I stared at him. "You lost everything as a kid. Can you imagine wondering if I was responsible? I need to know, without a doubt, that you didn't get my mom killed."

His face softened, and he raised one hand, cupping my

cheek. "I had nothing to do with her death," he vowed. "I was in the area because my enemies had begun targeting those I cared for." The dagger didn't glow. He cleared his throat and if I didn't know him better, I would've thought he looked... awkward. "I had been seeing a witch. When I learned that a body had been found…"

"You thought it was your lover."

He nodded. Something uncomfortable twisted in my chest. "Did you love her?"

I clamped a hand over my mouth and took a step back. What was wrong with me? Next, I'd probably ask Samael if she was prettier than me.

Surprise flashed across his face, followed by a feral delight. I closed my eyes, cheeks burning. "Don't say a fucking word."

"I don't need to, witchling," he purred. "Your reaction tells me everything I need to know."

I took a deep breath, opened my eyes, and attempted to ignore the satisfaction glittering in his silver eyes. "Can you... tell me anything about my mom?"

His expression softened. He knew what it was to lose a mother.

"I forwarded everything I found on to the investigators. However... she was a witch, so the humans were uninterested in solving her murder. The covens were at war with one another, and there were too few resources to cover the surge of murders."

A tear slipped from my eye and Samael looked like I'd stabbed him. "There is something else we can try."

"What is it?"

"My bond with you… it allows me to share images, memories."

Like he had with the memory of losing his whole family. I opened my mouth to demand he do it right now, and he shook his head.

"I will not show you the memory now, Danica. We will choose an appropriate time."

I let out a slow breath but finally nodded. I had no doubt that after seeing my mom's body, I wouldn't exactly be in the good state to accompany him to his ball.

I held Misty out to him and he took the dagger from me, disappearing within his apartment where he tucked it away— likely in a hidden safe. Surprisingly, I didn't demand to see where he'd put it. I trusted Samael to give it back to me. I frowned.

I reached for the tiny, useless sparkly purse I'd been given, tucking my phone inside. The purse could fit two throwing knives, and I slipped them in as well. I didn't expect shit to go down at Samael's fancy party, but it was best to be prepared.

The demon returned, reaching for the velvet box. I gave him a look and shook my head. I wasn't wearing his jewels. He merely smiled at me and opened the box, revealing a… knife sheath. A knife sheath on a lanyard. Only his was somehow… classy.

I stared. The leather was black, polished to a gleam, with cubic zirconia set in regular intervals along the strap. While I'd bought my lanyard with the understanding that it would look like a cheap necklace, Samael's looked anything but cheap.

My hands itched for it. I met Samael's gaze. His expression was carefully neutral, but his eyes told me how much he wanted me to take it. I fisted my hands, and he waited me out.

"Your current lanyard and sheath will stand out amongst those in attendance," he said finally. "They will wonder what it is and come to the conclusion that you are armed. I know you don't enjoy drawing attention to either yourself or your weapons."

Andddd he was chipping away at my determination not to take anything else from him.

"You had this made for me?"

A muscle ticked in his jaw and he nodded. He rightly assumed that knowing he'd had someone create this for me made it less likely that I'd take it. But he didn't lie to me.

I wanted it. I knew at a glance that it would fit my Nim Cub perfectly— and Samael should know, I'd been unconscious and armed in his presence often enough.

"Thank you," I said. Samael tensed, obviously still expecting me to refuse. Joke was on him. If he'd attempted to get me to borrow a gaudy diamond necklace, he would've been waiting until the end of time. This… this was different.

I reached for it, and he let out a slow breath, some of the tension draining from his body. Pleasure sparked in his eyes as I pulled off my other sheath, slipped my Nim Cub out, and replaced it with his gift.

He took a step closer. Then he leaned down and brushed my lips with his. I allowed it. He held out his arm and I took it, allowing him to lead me to the elevator.

"I thought you'd want to fly down."

Samael shook his head. "Not tonight."

The elevator opened to the ballroom on the 70th floor. I'd been here once before, on the night that I stole a strand of Samael's hair, broke his ward, and stole his dagger. I'd been so pumped with adrenaline that night that my vision had tunneled, my focus entirely on the demon at my side.

I surveyed the room, studying the high ceilings. Balconies jutted out at regular intervals, a few of them with their dark curtains pulled.

"What's wrong?"

"If I wanted to kill someone here, I'd sit up in one of those balconies with a gun or a crossbow."

Samael gave me an indulgent look. "My security would never allow such a thing."

I rolled my eyes. Arrogance, thy name is Samael. I let my eyes scan the rest of the ballroom. An orchestra was set up in the corner furthest from the door, and couples were already swaying on the dance floor, while demons and dark fae gathered in small groups.

Like the light fae representative's headquarters, the ballroom had been done in gold and white. But while their building leaned toward ostentatious, Samael's ballroom was muted elegance.

Agaliarept approached, eyeing me as he murmured a few words to Samael. It was the first time I'd seen him since he fell into a coma, and he was looking healthy. He'd definitely dropped a few pounds though. I nodded at him and he gave me the barest acknowledgement before walking away.

Agaliarept didn't like me. To be fair, he hadn't liked

me before I saved his life. Keeping him from hitting the big slide was the final nail in the coffin that held our potential friendship. Maybe he was embarrassed that his ass had needed rescuing.

Steve walked past, then did an exaggerated double take. I gave him the stink eye and he moved closer.

"You guys look good together," he murmured while Samael said a few words to Bael. I glowered at him.

"Don't make me throat-punch you."

Steve chuckled and I nudged him with my elbow. "Any more luck with the video?"

His brow furrowed and he lifted his hand, nudging his glasses further up his nose. "No. You know, my grandfather was a tech guy before the portals opened. He managed to stay alive through the Decade of Despair by hiding out in my family's cabin in the woods for most of the decade. And when he talks about the technology before they opened…" he shook his head. "Seventy years since the world turned to shit and technology is only just catching up to where it was when my grandfather was working."

"The world stopped. There couldn't be any technological advancement when people were busy trying to stay alive."

He nodded. "I know. But it's a damn shame. Because if the portals had never opened, humanity would likely be far, far ahead of where we are now." Steve flushed, looking past me, and I realized Samael was no longer talking to Bael. Instead, he was giving Steve a considering look.

I linked my arm through his, and he shifted his gaze to me, surprise evident in his eyes. Steve made a quick escape and Samael allowed me to steer him closer to the bar.

Waiters were doing the rounds with champagne, but I had a feeling I was going to need something stronger tonight.

I tensed as voices raised behind us, and my hand slid toward my thigh. Samael caught it in his, lifting my hand to his lips as he glanced over his shoulder.

"The unseelie king is here," he said, and my heart thumped harder in my chest.

"Why did your pulse rate just increase?" Samael's eyes flashed dangerously, and I merely raised one eyebrow at him.

"I want to talk to him."

"I don't think so." His smile wasn't quite a baring of teeth, but it was close. "I once vowed that you'd never meet him."

I rolled my eyes. I'd mentioned the rumors of the unseelie king's beauty when I was trying to distract Samael after one of his people had been murdered.

"I don't care how pretty he is, Samael. I want to talk to him."

"And why is it so important for you to speak to him?"

I gave him my best 'duh' look. "Because I'm dark fae. There's a tiny chance he could know who my father is. And if he doesn't, he might be able to point me toward someone who does."

Samael's hand had left mine, something like shock dancing across his face. *That's right, demon. I put the pieces together all by myself.*

An important-looking guy approached him, and I used his moment of inattention to slip away, heading toward the corner of the ballroom where a crowd had gathered around the unseelie king.

He *was* beautiful. His dark hair curled slightly on his head, and his eyes were the gold of ancient coins. They seemed to glow as he stood surrounded by fae guards and curious guests. He was tall, and something about the way he stood, with his wide shoulders slightly angled, made me picture him swinging a sword. Power swirled around him, and I was sure a woman lucky enough to see beneath his tux would find nothing but hard, sculpted muscle.

There was something slightly feral about his expression. His eyes said that he was endlessly amused with the bowing and scraping, but beneath the amusement, I caught a glimpse of dull rage. I forced myself to step closer.

His eyes found mine.

"Ah, the woman escorted by Samael himself," he murmured, his voice low, but it still seemed to carry over the crowd. Heads turned my way and I ground my teeth, fighting back a flush. Few things annoyed me like public attention.

The king smiled, his eyes still on me. "Leave us," he said. I took a step back, but it was everyone else who was melting away, other than a few guards who took a couple of steps back. One of them shot me a warning look and I resisted the urge to flip him off.

"Hi," I said stupidly. The unseelie king smiled indulgently.

"Hello. Your name?"

"Danica. And you?"

Surprise flashed over his face and he laughed. The ballroom seemed to go silent at the sound. There was something musical and yet deeply sexual about his laugh. I swallowed.

"You're enchanting. My name is Finvarra. My closest friends call me Fin." He winked at me, and I raised one eyebrow as his gaze left me, lingering somewhere behind me.

He was flirting with me in an effort to get under Samael's skin. Oh, I had his number. I merely smiled and took a step closer, lowering my voice.

"I was hoping you could help me with something."

"Of course."

"My father was unseelie. He left my mother and she never told me who he was. I'd like to know if you have heard of any unseelie who were with a witch a few decades ago, or if you can direct me toward anyone with this information."

Surprise crossed his face for less than a second, but I caught it. He leaned closer and seemed to breathe me in. His power swept along my form, and I could feel it nudging at my shield. I fought to keep my hands away from my knives. His power was endless— like Samael's. Both men could rip my shields down and stab into my deepest well of power with little more than a thought.

"You're not one of mine," the king's voice dripped amusement. His gaze languidly scanned my body from head to toe. "More's the pity."

I wrestled with that for a long moment. It made sense for me to be half dark fae. I knew it had made sense. And if I wasn't dark fae I was–

Samael was suddenly next to me, and I was impressed that he'd held himself back for so long. "Don't force me to break our alliance already, Finvarra."

Finvarra merely laughed again, and I almost shivered. Samael's hand wrapped around my upper arm and a ball of fury settled beneath my ribs, burning through my chest as it grew larger by the second.

These men were two of the most powerful beings on this planet. And yet all they cared about was their pissing contest.

"I have another question," I purred. Fivarra's eyes narrowed on my face and he nodded.

"Why is it that you only care about the high fae? Where is the same interest for the rest of your people?"

"Excuse me?"

I merely smiled. "You heard me."

Finvarra's eyes turned cold, and dark power radiated from him. I stood my ground, but the temperature in the room plummeted. My breath began to fog.

"Would you care to repeat that, human?"

CHAPTER ELEVEN

DANICA

I ignored the unspoken threat in the unseelie king's voice. He wouldn't dare kill me now. It'd be bad optics.

"One of your people was attacked and almost killed a few days ago. So far, there has been no dark fae interest in this attack. His store was a crime scene and left unlocked by the Mage Council. Truthfully, I don't blame them. They've made it clear they don't give a shit about anyone but mages and humans. But I thought your job was to protect all of your people— even lesser fae?"

A muscle twitched in his cheek. His beautiful face was hard as stone, and he was no longer amused.

"You're correct. That is my *job*. I was not notified of this attack, nor were any of the high unseelie responsible for protecting lesser fae."

"Excuses are like assholes," I began. A hand clamped over my mouth and I jolted. "Everyone has one," I mumbled against Samael's hand.

"That's quite enough, I think," he growled. The fae king stared at me. Then at Samael.

"You have a hellion on your hands," he said, and my eyes shot daggers at him.

Samael pulled me away, removing his hand from my mouth and curling it around my arm once more.

"What was that, hmmm?" He steered me toward a balcony and I followed, distantly aware that every person on that balcony immediately vacated it, giving Samael privacy.

"I'm *glad* I'm not dark fae," I muttered, kicking out at the stone wall with my stupid stiletto. "Although *you're* just as bad. All of you paranormals who call yourselves 'high whatever' while naming those less powerful as 'lesser.'"

Samael stiffened. "Be careful, bounty hunter."

I was done being careful. "The dark fae king is a jackass, but you're just as bad. When those demons were being killed, you had me investigating the high demons. You didn't even *tell* me about the murders of the lesser demons until multiple days had passed. They were an afterthought to you."

Samael laughed coldly. "And I suppose you're the champion of lesser demons are you? Tell me, how many of my people did you drag into the Mage Council? How many did you interrogate with *my* dagger?"

"It's mine now," I snapped. "You gave it to me. And that's beside the point. The demons I brought in were all guilty of crimes. Most of them had escaped their summoners and slaughtered innocent humans."

"If you believe that, then you really were the Mage Council's tool."

I stared at him and he shook his head. "Enough."

"You're damn right it's enough." I turned to leave and he caught my arm.

"Don't think to walk away from me."

I swung at him. I was off-balance, so it was sloppy. He caught my arm and gave me a hard stare. "I thought you wanted to know what you were?"

I laughed bitterly. "Process of elimination, Samael. If I'm not fae, I'm demon."

He studied my face and his brow lowered. "And this displeases you."

I didn't say anything. Damn right it displeased me.

"Your friend will be okay," he murmured, changing the subject.

I felt tears prick my eyes and attempted to turn away. Samael wasn't tolerating that. He pulled me back toward him and an embarrassing hiccup left my throat.

"Gary's a *person,* Samael. His life matters."

He drew me into his arms, and despite myself, I nestled into his chest, drawing his cedar and citrus scent into my lungs.

"It does matter. Paranormal rulers are centuries old, little witch. Some of us have been alive for a millennia. It makes us… forget what it means to care for others."

I got it. When you were at the top of the food chain, you got used to everyone bowing and scraping. You probably started to believe that you were inherently more worthy than the people doing the bowing and scraping.

I sniffed and he heaved a sigh. "It doesn't mean we don't care. It simply means that sometimes we need to be reminded to care. You've done that for me, Danica."

We were in awkward territory now, and I attempted to push my way out of his arms.

"Uh-uh."

I scowled, but I was trapped against his chest. The demon would release me when he damn well pleased and not a moment sooner.

"Why does everything have to be a power struggle between us, Samael?"

He laughed, the sound raising goosebumps on my arms as he pressed my head to his chest. I'd always thought him heartless, but there was his heart, thumping away.

"I don't know, Danica, but I wouldn't have it any other way. You will amuse, delight, and entrance me for centuries to come."

"I think you mean decades."

He was silent and I pushed against his chest.

"Let me go. *Now,* Samael, I mean it."

He released me, angling his head as if confused. Fucker.

"Centuries?"

A languid shrug. "You're half demon, Danica. You'll likely cease aging in the next few years."

The world had just hit me in the face. I was going to vomit. Everyone I knew would crumble into dust, and I would remain. My sister...

My lips were numb. My knees turned weak. Samael reached for my arm again and I retreated, slamming into the outside wall of his tower.

"If you break down here, there will be talk. Come with me, and your precious reputation will be spared."

My eyes found his. I nodded, ignoring the hand he held out. Instead, I turned, stepping back into the ball. Samael was instantly at my side, catching my elbow with his large hand. He steered me toward the door, replying to the occasional greeting thrown our way.

I was vaguely aware of him leading me out of the ballroom and through another door.

"What happened?" Vas asked.

Samael ignored the question. "Take her upstairs and stay with her until I come to you."

He gave me a lingering look, then turned and strode away.

"You look good in a tux," I muttered to Vas. He merely stepped back, gesturing for me to walk up the stairs. I turned toward the door, and he shook his head.

"Samael's orders. Don't make me the bad guy here, Danica."

I sneered at him and picked up the skirt of my dress, stalking up the stairs. The curtains were open, and I made sure to sit in the shadows, staring down at the ballroom below me. The music slowly stopped, and the crowd turned to where a dark fae male was standing on a raised platform. He waited until the room was silent, and then he spoke, the microphone charm in his hand allowing his voice to carry over the crowd.

"Tonight, you bear witness to a historical event like none other. Tonight, the unseelie fae and the high demons join forces in an alliance that paves the way for further cooperation and peace between our races for centuries to come."

He nodded at someone who carried a table and chair up to the platform. The dark fae king sat and signed the alliance while cameras clicked. The room was so silent you could've heard a mouse fart.

Samael took his place, glancing up until his eyes met mine for the barest moment. Finvarra followed his gaze, then shifted his attention back to Samael as he signed the papers in front of him. Both males stood for a few moments, murmuring to each other as the cameras clicked, and then it was all over.

I glanced at Vas. "This seems like a big deal."

He nodded. "It is. You want to tell me why you're so upset?"

"I'm half demon." I swallowed around the lump in my throat, glancing at Vas. "That means I'll have a half-demon's lifespan."

"Ah."

"Ah?"

He shrugged. "I'm not surprised that you're not all witch. I've seen enough of your power. In fact, I'd bet money that as soon as your suppression spell is completely gone, most people would know you're a demon simply by looking at you. I like having you around, Danica. You're fun. I'm not going to pretend to be sad that you're not going to die on me like most humans."

His face twisted and I stared at him. Something told me that Vas, the kid who'd played with humans at the park when he was a small child, was starting to see what immortality truly meant. Those kids would be in their eighties and nineties now. Many of them were likely already dead.

"It's not the lifespan that's the issue. One day, I'm sure I'll be... happy to be given so much time to play with. But I don't want to see everyone I know die, Vas."

"Everyone like your sister."

I rubbed the back of my neck, attempting to ease some of the tension. "Yeah." Let's face it, it's not like I was surrounded by family and friends at all times. "How do I tell Evie that she's going to grow old and die, and I'm still going to stay young and live for at least a few more centuries?"

Vas laughed. "You're assuming something won't take you out before she grows old. You jump into danger with two feet, you never back down from a chance to fight, and you do crazy things like insult the unseelie fae king within moments of meeting him. If I had to put money on who'd live longer, it wouldn't be you."

Vas was humoring me. But I liked it. "Yeah," I said, slightly mollified. "You're right."

"Little witch," Samael's voice was low and I scowled over my shoulder at him. He ignored Vas and I almost rolled my eyes. Samael often wrestled with jealousy, especially if he thought I was opening up to someone who wasn't him. "It's time for us to go."

It wasn't. I'd already checked my phone. Thankfully, the demon wasn't holding me to our deal. I followed him downstairs, watching how the crowd gathered in the ballroom parted for him.

"Danica Amana?"

I peered down at the goblin. "Hi."

Her green face was tight. "I thought you might be here. I was hoping to talk to you."

"Sure."

Samael watched me through darkened eyes as I stepped away from him and closer to the wall, leaning down so I could better hear her.

"My name is Yexa. My father was murdered a few nights ago," she said, her huge eyes filled with tears. She sniffed, shaking her head, and her long pointed ears flapped against her head. "I live out of state, and I just got back. My father's name is Merrill."

That made two lesser fae store owners, one dead, one fighting for life.

"I'm so sorry."

"Thank you. I know you're investigating what happened to Gary, and I was hoping you could help with my father as well."

"How was your father killed?"

"His store was turned upside down." She gave a wet sniff. "Someone beat him to death."

"I'm so sorry for your loss." There was nothing I could say to help her. All I could do was try to find out who'd killed her father. "I'll go check out his store tomorrow," I promised.

"That won't be necessary." We both turned at the low, dangerous voice. The unseelie king stood a few feet away, his guards nowhere to be seen. Dark power poured off him, and everyone was giving him a wide berth.

"Excuse me?"

He glanced at me briefly. "You're excused." Then he turned back to Yexa. "I will send one of my teams to investigate this murder."

The color faded from Yexa's green face. But she lifted her chin. "Wi-with all due respect your majesty, I would prefer for Danica to help me."

The king went very still. "And why is that?"

"Because she knew my father. And she *cares.*"

I gaped at that, but Yexa wasn't apologizing. She hunched her shoulders, staring down at the ground. I fought the urge to step in front of her. To hide her from Finvarra. But the king merely nodded.

"As you wish." His eyes met mine. "You will let me know if you need assistance."

"She won't," Samael purred.

I glanced between both of the men. Their power was radiating from them in dangerous waves as they stared at each other. Next, they'd be whipping their dicks out to see who was bigger once and for all.

"I'm sorry again for your loss," I murmured to Yexa. "I'll be in touch."

I turned and walked toward the elevator. Samael caught up to me within a few strides, and the elevator doors opened as soon as we were within a few feet. The tip of one of his wings brushed my face and my mind presented me with the memory of his wings out, dripping sparks as he killed the demon who tried to murder me a few weeks ago.

Samael looked at the elevator buttons and the floor to his penthouse lit up. I scowled at him. "I'm going home."

"Without your dagger?"

"No." He had me. I wouldn't leave without Misty. Suggesting that he bring it to me would just make the demon laugh at me.

I followed him out of the elevator, heading toward my pile of clothes, which I bundled beneath my arm. I'd bring the dress back in the morning. For now, I just wanted to be alone.

"Stay with me."

"I don't think so." I turned, taking the dagger Samael held out, still in its sheath. His hand caught mine.

"Why did you think you were unseelie?"

I tugged my arm, snarling when his hand tightened around mine. "My power doesn't feel anything like yours. I remembered an unseelie guy who was one of my mom's closest friends when I was a kid. And Selina told me my power was either dark fae or demon. It was a process of elimination."

"I can see how you came to that conclusion." He let my hand go and I stared him down.

"When did you know I was half demon?"

Silence. I laid Misty on the table next to us, just in case I was tempted to do something I'd regret. Of course, the dagger wasn't made with rowan wood, so the demon would simply yank it out, and his wound would heal faster than I could heal a papercut.

"When you created the ward against the witches in that cemetery. Your witch magic was drained, and all that was left was the power of my people."

"Why didn't you tell me?"

"At first, I believed you knew and thought to keep it from me. Then… I decided it would be better for you to learn of your heritage yourself."

"Oh, you did, did you?" I cursed and turned away.

"You're terrified of your power," he growled. "You want nothing to do with me, or my people."

"That's not true." I was friends with Vas.

Samael's voice turned cold. "You truly want me to believe you wouldn't have spiraled during that case if you found out what you were?"

I shook my head. "You have no idea what it's like. I've hunted demons for years, Samael."

He went still. "I'm aware, bounty hunter."

"Everything I thought I knew about myself is a lie."

He laughed. "Ah, but the woman I know will always prefer the ugly truth to a pretty lie."

"You just didn't want to be the one to tell me."

"You hate me enough already. Why would I give you further reason to think poorly of me?"

He was wrong. What I felt for him was… complicated. Sure, there was a healthy dose of hatred in there. I loathed the way he insisted on keeping me in the dark. The way he made decisions about my life without even consulting me. The way he refused to remove the bond between us.

But there were other feelings there too. Feelings that made my heart stutter in my chest every time he dropped the mask he wore for the rest of the world and looked at me with vulnerability. Feelings that made me *need* to keep distance between us, because my instinct was to do the opposite.

I stared at him silently, and he took a step closer, the scent of him calling to me. He leaned down slowly, giving me more than enough time to slam my hand into his chest, to jerk away from him.

I didn't.

He took my mouth like he owned it, like it had always belonged to him, and he was simply reclaiming his territory. I let out a tiny moan and the sound seemed to break some part of his self-control, because he let out a low growl and ripped his mouth away from mine.

I blinked up at him. His eyes glowed, his expression pure, possessive male as he looked at me.

"I am so old that I feel ancient most days. For centuries, little has moved me. Not beauty, not grief. Only vengeance. But when I look at you, I see things I haven't seen before."

"What kind of things?" I whispered.

"Things I want to guard. To keep only for myself. For the rest of time."

CHAPTER TWELVE

DANICA

I scowled at Samael's words, and he grinned at me. The expression was so foreign on his face that my breath caught in my throat. My hand rose, seemingly of its own accord, and I stroked my finger along his lower lip.

His eyes glittered and he leaned down once more. I thought he'd kiss me again, but instead, he gently took the lobe of my ear between his teeth. His hot breath tickled the shell of my air and my stomach clenched.

Samael let out a low laugh and skimmed his lips down the side of my throat.

And then I was in his arms, and he was stalking through his living room and toward his bedroom. His hands were full, so I took advantage of the situation, pressing my own lips to his neck. Then I bit. Hard.

He let out another rough growl and I shivered at the sound. He was gentle as he placed me on his bed, and I stared up at him. Was I really going to do this?

I had a laundry list of reasons why I shouldn't. Why I should climb off this bed, collect my weapons, and get the hell out of here.

I had no reason to roll around naked with the deadliest demon on Earth. Except one.

I wanted him more than I'd ever wanted anyone before. And I had a sneaky suspicion that I'd never want anyone this badly again. Despite everything he'd done, and continued to do, I ached for him.

It pissed me off. But it was the cold, hard truth.

I'd been trying to fight this for what felt like a lifetime, even though it had been less than two months. My willpower was strong, but not strong enough to be able to stare up at the wild, lethal man above me and not want him with everything I was.

"You look good in my bed, witchling. You always have."

I scanned my surroundings. Samael's bed was huge. It had to be, to comfortably fit his wings. At the thought of him lying naked, his wings spread around him, I shivered.

"Show me."

He knew what I was asking. He dropped the shields keeping his wings invisible and I gawked unashamedly.

When they weren't dripping sparks, they weren't as scary. They were tucked in close to his body, and as I watched, he spread them for me. His expression was arrogant, and I got the feeling he was… preening.

I was… speechless at the sight of him. At some point, he'd ripped off his shirt, and the dim light lovingly highlighted the peaks and valleys of his sculpted muscle. His sharp cheekbones stood out like two blades as his face tightened, his hungry gaze exploring me in turn.

His wings should have stolen the show. There

were no words for their color. Jet-black seemed like an understatement. Obsidian barely scratched the surface. They sucked up all the light in the room and reflected it back, making it difficult to pull my gaze away.

But his wicked, mesmerizing face drew my attention, and I couldn't help but focus on his cruel mouth. I wanted that mouth on me.

I slowly brushed one finger along the edge of the closest feather as he silently watched me.

"You're beautiful," I admitted.

He nodded. "I know."

I burst out laughing, and he took the opportunity to climb onto the bed with me and capture my mouth with his. His wings blocked out the light, and it was as if the world had disappeared, and we were the only two people who existed.

I'd seen his claws briefly before, but I wasn't prepared for the way he ran a hand down my dress, slicing it open. I blinked up at him, stunned at the casual destruction of something so beautiful, but he was too busy staring at my breasts to pay any attention to my expression.

Typical male.

He let out a rough groan and my toes curled. It seemed ludicrous that *I* had made the demon make such a sound. The demon who'd been alive for so long that my puny half-human mind couldn't even comprehend such a lifespan.

His hand skimmed along my collarbone; his touch achingly gentle. I shivered, and his gaze was transfixed as my nipples peaked even further. They were so hard they ached, and I gasped as he slowly circled one with his index finger. Just that touch and I was aching for him. It wasn't like me to lie submissive during sex, but every ounce of my attention was focused on the man above me.

He lowered his head, brushed his lips over my skin, and then took my nipple in his mouth. I writhed, and he let out a low laugh, lifting away long enough to give me a look full of sensual promise.

"So responsive," he purred. "I knew you'd be like this."

His claw slid out once more, and he slashed through the rest of my dress like it was tissue paper. My thong disappeared next, and he stared at me for so long that my cheeks heated.

"Uh, Samael?"

His face tightened, and he met my gaze. "I have lived for a millennia, been with women of all races, from every world."

I glowered at him. That wasn't the way to get into my pants. I opened my mouth to tell him exactly that, but his eyes were suddenly blazing as he glowered down at me.

"Never have I seen such beauty."

I gaped at him. He let out an oath and took my mouth once more, his tongue tangling with mine. He tasted like sin, and his body felt like heaven against mine, hard and strong and— for tonight at least— mine. My hands rose to his hair, and the memory of the first time we met flashed through my mind.

I'd stolen a piece of that hair while both of us were wearing masks. I'd been trembling almost the entire time. Who could've known that choice would have led to this?

No one could have known it because you're throwing

your freedom away.

I attempted to push that little voice out of my head, but it was the truth. Demons were possessive, territorial creatures, and none more so than Samael. If I wanted him to release me and leave me alone, I was going the wrong way about it.

"You're thinking too much," Samael murmured against my lips. "I better change that."

I opened my mouth, but he was already kissing his way down my body. His mouth was hot and skilled, and his hands stroked over my skin as if he was memorizing every inch of me.

And then his mouth was pressed against the damp heat of me. I let out a sound that seemed to please him because he chuckled against me, and the feeling made me lift my hips, desperate for more.

His skilled tongue moved over all my most sensitive spots, never staying in one place for long enough.

"Samael…"

He replaced his tongue with one finger, and I saw stars as he slowly pushed it inside me.

"I've been thinking about how I'd make you beg for me, little witch. You won't rush me through this."

I let out a strangled sound and he sent me a wicked grin, then lowered his head once more. He licked, nuzzled, sucked, and he instinctively knew exactly when I was on the edge, about to explode, because that's when he would shift his attention elsewhere.

He teased me for what felt like hours, and I writhed desperately, sweat pouring from me.

"Samael…"

"Beg me, Danica."

The son of a bitch. Even this was a power struggle. But I was so close…

He danced across a spot that made my every muscle tense, and I groaned in frustration as he stopped.

"Fine," I scowled, throwing my arm over my eyes. "Please, Samael."

"Look at me."

I glowered at him, but I was pretty sure it didn't have any heat in it, just pure, unrelenting need. His mouth found me again and he thrust his fingers inside me as his warm lips expertly danced and teased. I made garbled noises that must have been threats, because he laughed once more, and stroked over my clit. Once. Twice.

My breath caught, my vision darkened, and my climax ripped through me, pleasure lighting up my every nerve ending. Samael groaned and kept licking, kept teasing, even as I turned limp. I jolted as he swiped his tongue over my sensitive clit, and my hands found his head to push him away.

"I don't think so."

He caught my hands in his and frowned at me as if I'd attempted to take away his favorite toy. I opened my mouth to snarl at him, but a moan escaped as he applied the lightest pressure to my sensitive core.

I let out a whine, clenching around his fingers, and he growled, his other hand tightening around my own.

A moment later, my mouth fell open in shock as pleasure tore through me again. I shuddered and moaned, my muscles turning completely limp.

I cracked my eyes open as Samael disappeared. He stood a few feet away, undoing his tuxedo pants, and my avid gaze got stuck on his naked body as he dropped them to the ground and stepped out of them.

The man was perfect. It killed me. Because after this night, no one else was ever going to compare.

I could hate him for that. God knows I hated him for enough other things.

My tongue wanted to dance across the muscles that formed the V pointing to his cock. It jutted out, thick, long, and perfectly formed. His wings flared as I stared, allowing my gaze to drift from the arrogant smile on his beautiful face, to the eight pack I itched to explore, to his huge, muscled thighs. Even his fucking feet were sexy.

His wings framed him like a dark curtain, and I wanted hours of time to stroke them.

Then I lifted my hand and imperiously twirled it. Samael raised one eyebrow but a smirk danced around his mouth as he lifted his hands to his hips. He obviously decided to humor me, because he snapped his wings closed and slowly turned.

I almost swallowed my tongue.

His ass was made to be admired by women across all of the worlds. I wanted to sink my teeth into it.

He glanced over his shoulder and *winked* at me, and I couldn't help the laugh that bubbled in my throat. He looked like a fallen angel, but he was already turning back to prowl toward me, the spark in his eyes all demon.

"Do I meet with your approval, witchling?"

I gave him a sour look. As if he had to ask. He smiled.

Then his smile disappeared and his expression was carved in lust as he ran his gaze down my body.

I was still lying spread on his bed, my body clenching with occasional aftershocks from the two incredible climaxes he'd given me. He climbed over me, and his mouth found mine, his tongue stroking deep. He pushed my hair off my face as he lined himself up, and the tenderness in his eyes sent warning bells ringing in my ears.

We both sighed as he breached my entrance, the thick head of his cock stretching me. He allowed me a moment to adjust, and then drove deep. My head fell back as he thrust, slowly working his way deeper until he was pressed entirely against me. I wrapped my legs around his waist and the new angle made us both groan. His cock seemed to have been designed to hit my G-spot, and I was already on the edge again.

He pulled back and thrust once more, and my eyes slid shut.

"Look at me," he demanded, and I managed to crack my eyes open. He cupped my cheek and drove deeper, his eyes drinking in every expression I made.

I had a bad feeling that my face told him more than I wanted him to know, because a deep satisfaction flared in his silver eyes.

Sometimes, the worst mistakes were the ones you made when you knew they were mistakes, but you couldn't seem to help yourself.

"Stop thinking," he growled. He began to piston into me, and my mind turned blank, every ounce of my focus on the feeling of him deep within me.

For the first time in a long time, my senses were fully engaged. I was *alive*. Furiously alive.

And pleasure was roaring through me. Pleasure so deep and so unending that there was no way my body could contain it.

My hands slid beneath Samael's wings, and I scratched at his back, my nails digging into his skin as I arched, urging him on. He let out a rough curse and slammed his mouth down on mine. My tongue tangled with his and I gasped as he pulled almost all the way out before driving back into me.

"Samael…"

My voice was high-pitched, almost begging, and he repeated the movement again. And again. His hand slid down to my clit, and I went still. My breath caught in my throat.

And then my climax ripped through me, carrying me through a wave of bliss, picking me up and then gently dropping me back down to earth.

Samael buried his head in the hollow of my neck and emptied himself inside me.

We both lay still, panting, recovering. I dreamily ran my nails gently up and down his back, the feathers of his wings tickling the back of my hand. He shuddered and lifted his head, giving me a dark look.

"That's not the way to ensure you get any rest tonight, little witch."

He'd hardened inside me already and I gaped at him. With an amused look, he rolled onto his back and hauled me into his arms.

I was cuddling the demon. After having sex with the demon. And right now, I didn't have it in me to regret a damn thing.

Smug, male satisfaction radiated from the man beside me. I could feel it in the low grumble he gave as he pulled me even closer and buried his hand in my hair so he could lift my head and take my mouth once more.

But I could also feel it at the end of the bond, and I frowned as I attempted to bolster my shield once more.

So we'd had sex. So what? I simply needed to remember not to humanize the high demon. No matter how tender he could be with me, I had to remember that Samael was not, and would never be even remotely close to human. He would never understand what it was like to not have people bowing and scraping to perform his every whim. To not be able to bond people against their will. To not *own* sentient beings. He would never comprehend what it was like to not be at the top of the food chain.

And that reminded me.

"How often do you need to feed?"

He went silent, stroking his hand up and down my back. "Why do you ask, little witch?"

Because if he wasn't feeding from me, I wanted to know who he was feeding from.

The jolt of possessiveness shook me enough that I stiffened, and his hand paused.

He nuzzled at my neck, and I shivered. "Is this… jealousy, Danica?" his voice was delighted.

I used his moment of distraction and rolled out of his arms, making my way off the ridiculously large bed.

"I don't think so," he said, catching my wrist. With one yank, I was on top of him once more, his body spread out below me.

I gave him the scowl that little move deserved, and he grinned up at me. I forced myself to look away. That grin made him look younger, boyish, almost… approachable.

"I like you this way," he purred.

"What way?"

"Possessive, jealous, avaricious for your male."

"What did you tell me once? You don't like your tools broken while you're still using them? Well, I don't like to share my toys until I'm finished playing with them."

He threw his head back and laughed, and my gaze dropped to the strong muscle of his throat. I wanted to kiss him there. To mark him. To demonstrate my claim to everyone and anyone he came into contact with.

Yeah, and any hickeys I created would heal instantly. Meanwhile, I was stuck with his stupid gold mark on my arm.

"While your jealousy pleases me immensely, I'm not feeding from anyone right now."

I barely refrained from hissing that I *wasn't* jealous. Anything I said now would just make the demon more amused.

"Then why aren't you starving?"

"I am able to take sustenance from the demons bonded to me. There are enough that they barely notice the slight drain. However, I will need to feed within the next few weeks."

He didn't tell me that if I didn't feed him, he'd be forced

to go elsewhere. But the subtext was there.

He was playing with my hair, stroking his hand through it and occasionally brushing the shell of my ear, the sensitive skin at the base of my neck. It was incredibly distracting.

"My family would have liked you, little witch," he murmured, and I went still. A lump formed in my throat at the memory of their deaths, at the memory of the little boy who'd been left behind.

"You think so?"

I felt him nod and gave in to a satisfied smile. "I wish I could've met them."

"I wish that too. And I would have liked to have known your mother."

I laughed at that. "She probably would've tried to kill you, Samael. She always warned us away from demons. I guess, knowing what I know now about my father, it made sense."

"Why did she not take your sister with you?"

"I don't know. I've wondered the same thing every day since she dragged me away. Once we were in Austin, all she would say was that it was too dangerous for Evie to leave. She said splitting us up had saved our lives."

"Interesting." Samael said. "And she never explained why?"

"No. Every time I got mad and demanded to know, she'd just get this sad, frustrated look on her face. I was a teenager, and I missed my sister. By the time she left me in Austin and came to Durham, we were barely speaking. I'd told her I hated her, and if she didn't let me visit, I was coming back myself."

"And then she was murdered."

"Yes."

"I'm sorry."

"So am I. The hardest part was not knowing why we had to leave. Why Evie and I were separated. And why we were never warned. That day… we were just kids, and we were suddenly told that mom and I were leaving. The coven stood by and did nothing. No, worse. They used their magic to *help* separate us. They were our family. I trusted them."

A tear had slipped from my eye, and it dropped onto Samael's chest before I could stop it. His whole body tensed and then he pulled me even closer, wrapping me in his warmth.

"One day," he promised. "You will have your answers."

Chapter Thirteen

DANICA

Samael reached for me again and again throughout the night, and my hands always reached for him too. I'd probably only had a couple of hours of sleep total. He leaned over and kissed my forehead. I grunted, and he chuckled, the sound much too delighted for this early in the morning.

"I need to shower, little witch. Join me."

I kept my eyes closed in an effort to avoid some of the temptation he presented. "Not on your life." I was so sore I ached.

Samael laughed again, sounding far, far too pleased with himself. As soon as I heard the bathroom door shut, I opened my eyes, staring down at the gold mark on my arm.

I was an idiot. A stupid, horny idiot.

The shower started, and I sat up, slowly rolling until I could inch my foot out of the covers. I swung my legs over the side of the bed and winced.

Ouch. He'd ruined me. And it was taking every ounce of my self-control to not march into his bathroom and push him against the tiled wall. He'd lift me in his arms, slide his hand down and—

No. No fucking way. I needed to get

out of here so I could think with a clear head. I was tempted to visit Samael's healer on my way out of the building but what would I tell him? *"Your boss fucked the life out of me and now I'm not sure if I can walk properly?"*

My cheeks heated. "Stupid, stupid, stupid."

I managed to make it to my feet. I pulled on my jeans and t-shirt, not bothering with a bra, and collected my weapons. Then I hauled ass toward the elevator, practically sprinting as the sudden silence warned me that the water had turned off.

The elevator doors opened immediately, and I blew out a breath, stepping inside and pressing the button for the lobby. Samael stepped into the living room, stark naked. Drops of water ran down his skin as he placed his hands on his hips, and I went suddenly mute.

"Leaving so soon?" he purred.

I was weak. I took a step toward him, but the elevator doors began to close, jolting me from my lust. Samael raised one eyebrow, then turned, and walked away, the muscles of his butt flexing enticingly.

He wouldn't beg me to stay. And I wouldn't step out of the elevator. We'd finally rolled between his sheets, and hopefully, this was just residual lust. Now, we could both get on with our lives and no longer have to fight against the insane chemistry that urged us to rip off each other's clothes.

The lobby was half empty this early in the morning, but plenty of heads turned my way. My walk of shame had been noted. Awesome.

I drove home, refusing to think about Samael. I didn't

think about the way he touched me, the way he breathed my name, or the way he made me feel more pleasure than I'd ever imagined I could. And I certainly didn't think about turning my car around, walking back through his lobby, into his elevator, and climbing back into his bed.

I'd finally bought Lia an automatic cat food dispenser, but she still ignored me when I walked in.

"Wow, if only I had a friend, I'd be sure to share these yummy treats," I said, shaking the bag.

She was curled on the sofa, her tail twitching back and forth as she steadily pretended I was invisible. I shook the treats harder.

"Yum, yum. Tuna flavored. Delicious."

She opened one eye.

"Come on, cat. Be my friend. Please?"

I took a step toward her, rattling the bag some more. She yawned, bared her sharp kitty teeth and sat up, staring at me. People said cats were fiercely independent. That they didn't need you around. But Lia liked to punish me for my absences.

Languidly, she jumped off the sofa, strolling toward me. She twined around my legs, and I grinned. "So, we are friends again? Shameless bribery for the win." I gave her a handful of treats and slunk into the shower where I lathered myself up with a vanilla shower gel which was the opposite of Samael's scent in every way.

Then I sat on my sofa and Googled the names on the list of human cleaners Mariam had given me. Nothing jumped out at me, so I took a photo of the list and sent it to Steve. If I had time today, I'd go to their office and interview the manager. I needed to know who was usually assigned to Mariam's floor. For now, I had my hands on Gary's calendar.

Halfway to the hospital, terror slammed into me, my pulse racing. I choked on my breath. Holy shit I was about to die here, at a red light in my car.

My breaths came in pants, and the world sharpened. Time slowing to a crawl.

A feeling of intense doom swept through me. I was hanging on the side of a cliff, my hands barely holding onto the rock. I was freefalling through the air. I was…

Someone was laying on their horn. The light had turned green, and now yellow. The truck swerved around me and shot through the intersection, flipping me off, and I shivered, sweat dripping down my body.

I managed to pull over to the side of the road. Someone was suddenly next to my door and I jolted, a throwing knife in my hand.

Don't kill the demon, Danica.

Inferus. Still following me around. And witness to my sudden, debilitating panic attack.

"Are you okay, ma'am?"

"Don't call me ma'am," I said automatically, through numb lips. "I'm fine. Please leave me alone."

He merely nodded and lifted off, back into the sky where he'd watch me some more.

Fear climbed back up my throat. I knew what this was about. Just because you choose to ignore the things that send earthquakes through your world doesn't mean that they don't simmer away in your subconscious and rip the feet out from under you as soon as you think you're making it through the day.

I was half demon. Half demon and bonded to Samael. My mother had slept with a demon at some point, and I needed to get control of my powers before I hurt someone. Bad.

I was also unemployed. I'd attempted to push that sad fact out of my mind, but the Mage Council was all I'd known since the moment I got to Durham. Now I was on my own. And I would be on my own for the next however many centuries while everyone around me died.

I focused on taking deep breaths, counted to one hundred, and waited for my hands to stop shaking. Then I turned the key and kept driving. I didn't have time for this today. At some point, I'd have to unpack the baggage I'd inherited from my mother. I'd have to figure out who I was, and what I was going to do with my life. But that wouldn't be today.

Today I had to help Gary.

I parked, strode into the hospital, and took the elevator up to his floor. The demons on the door had been replaced and I nodded at them when they greeted me.

Gary's status was still the same, and the healer gave me another one of her sympathetic smiles when I stepped into the room.

Where was the mother of his kids? I'd never asked him, figuring that if he wasn't with her, he probably didn't want to talk about it, but maybe she should know what had happened.

Although Gary hadn't told me to get the boys to her. He'd specifically told me to keep them safe myself.

"Did Gary have anything in his pockets when he came in?"

The healer hesitated. "We're not supposed to give that information out. Patient privacy."

I forced myself to blow out a long, slow breath. Then I held up my arm. The light glinted off the gold and her eyes narrowed on the demon mark before they moved back to my face. "Very well."

She turned and unlocked a drawer in the small table next to Gary's bed. Then she left me to it.

I studied the items. A set of keys, Gary's wallet, and a small planner. Searching through his stuff felt like a violation, but if it led me to his attacker, I'd do it a thousand times.

I rifled through his wallet, swallowing around the lump in my throat at the picture of him with his boys, all of their faces lit up with laughter as they posed in front of a human amusement park. There were a few parking stubs from last week, and I noted down the addresses, but that was about it.

His planner on the other hand… who knew Gary was so organized? It made sense, given that he was a single dad running a business and raising two kids, but I hadn't expected his neat handwriting to detail every moment of every day. From his work schedule to his plans to take the boys to the park, all of it was in here.

The only meeting he'd noted down was with someone he called "The Bladesmith." I jotted down the date and time. They'd met at Meredith's. Hmmm.

I whispered goodbye to Gary and left the hospital, heading back toward Main Street and Meredith's Bar.

Mere was polishing glasses when I arrived, her long hair curling around her face. I scanned the place, but there were only a few patrons dotted here and there, most of them drinking alone. I sat down at her scarred bar, shaking my head when she reached for a glass. "I can't stay. You probably heard about the attack on Gary, right?"

"Of course. Are you looking into it?"

"Yeah. He met someone here last week. A guy called The Bladesmith. Do you know who that is?"

Her hazel eyes narrowed. "I do. Just so happens, you're in luck." Mere jerked her head toward the far right corner, where a guy who looked to be in his late forties or early fifties was drinking alone.

It was a small stroke of luck, but I'd take it. "Thanks."

I'd seen him around before, I realized. He was one of the regulars who often drank here during the day. So not luck then.

He blinked blearily up at me when I approached. "Can I buy you a drink?" I asked.

His eyes sharpened. "Well now, a young, beautiful woman offers to buy an old man like me a drink? I'd be a fool to refuse that, wouldn't I?"

I took a seat as one of Mere's waiters approached. The Bladesmith ordered another whiskey, I ordered an ice water, and we both sat back in our chairs.

"I have an ulterior motive," I admitted. The Bladesmith gave me a tiny smile.

"I figured."

"I'm investigating the attack on Gary." He nodded again. "And Merrill's murder." Surprise flashed across his face, followed by sadness. "Ah, he's dead is he? It would've happened sooner or later, but I'm sad to hear it." His eyes met mine and his expression tightened. "You hit me hard with that to see if I knew of the murder or not."

I shrugged. "I figured word would've gotten around, but it helps to take you off the suspect list."

He gave a low chuckle. "I've been out of town for a few days. But you don't truly think I did it. Why are you talking to me, Danica Amana?"

I raised my eyebrows and he nodded toward my arm. "Even I've heard of the bounty hunter bonded to Samael himself."

"What's your real name?" I asked, curious.

He held out his hand. "David McKenna."

"And you make blades?"

"I make anything with a sharp edge. My 'Da was a smithy, and his 'Da before him. Only unlike them, I occasionally partner with paranormals."

I'd figured. "So you create weapons of power."

Not just illegal, but stupid. If the wrong person picked up one of those weapons…

He shook his finger at me. "Now listen here, Missy. I only take commissions from those who have power themselves."

I raised one eyebrow. "And I suppose Gary was going to wield a magical weapon in between serving customers and taking his kids to the park."

A dull flush worked its way up his cheeks. "That was different," he ground out. "I owed Gary a favor."

"I'm not here to judge you, honestly. I just need to know

why you were meeting with Gary. And if you know anyone who might've wanted Merrill dead."

The waiter approached with his drink and David finished his whiskey and reached for his fresh glass.

"Gary wanted a few throwing knives. He'd been teaching his kids how to wield them, and one of them was hopeless at hitting the target."

"So he thought an enchanted knife would help him."

He nodded. "He figured it was a confidence thing. If the kid got used to hitting the target, his skill would naturally increase."

"How much magic would it take to make one of these knives?"

He waved his hand. "He only wanted a small charm. I know a witch who occasionally works freelance with me. The trick is infusing the blade with power while it's still being forged. Too much power and you'll snap the blade."

"How long would the charm last for?"

"A few months."

I took a sip of water. This was a dead end. No one would've attacked Gary for a low-magic throwing knife.

"I wouldn't have expected anyone to target old Gary," David said. "He kept to himself, he did. Didn't go sniffing around places where he shouldn't."

I raised one eyebrow. "And Merrill did?"

David snapped his mouth shut and I gave him a hard stare. "The man is dead. Anything you tell me could lead to whoever killed him."

"My 'Da had a saying… a gossip's mouth is the devil's postbag."

"It's not gossip if it could lead to a murderer."

"I haven't stayed alive all these years by poking my nose into other people's business."

I slid my gaze slowly down his body. "You're carrying at least six knives— seven if you have one tucked in your boot. I'd bet that at least half of those knives are charmed. You can stay alive just fine."

He gave me a wide grin. "I like you, girl. Okay, fine. Merrill had recently taken up with some of the more… morally destitute residents around here. I heard a rumor that he was in attendance at an auction he shouldn't have gone near."

"What kind of auction?"

He heaved a sigh. "Every Tuesday at the old train station."

The old train station was a rehabilitated warehouse, built by the American Tobacco Company in the late eighteen hundreds. The building had stood for over a hundred and twenty years until the portals opened and a group of fleeing citizens used it for shelter. A pack of rampaging werewolves knocked down a wall, killed the humans, and then pulled up most of the tracks.

The building was falling to pieces and most people gave it a wide berth. A perfect place for an illegal auction.

For a fae artifact to be stolen and sold, multiple people had to be involved. Someone had to steal it, someone needed to authenticate it, and someone else had to calculate its value. Only then, if a private buyer wasn't already lined up— or if the seller knew for sure it would result in a bidding war, the artifact would be sold at auction. Mariam's missing fae artifacts needed to be passed onto a buyer quickly. I was betting at least some of them were being sold at that auction.

"What time does it start?"

David lowered his brow and leaned closer. "You don't want to go near those people, missy. They'll kill you as soon as look at you."

I gave him my best ass-kicker stare and he heaved a sigh. "Your funeral. Starts at midnight. But you need a ticket to get in, and something tells me you'll be noticed."

"I'll take care of that."

CHAPTER FOURTEEN
DANICA

By the time I was finished speaking to the bladesmith, the cleaning company was closed. Movement darted across my peripheral vision and I scanned the empty sky.

That was it.

I drove back to Samael's, spurred on by sheer rage. My vision had narrowed, and I double parked, threw the keys to the valet, and stalked into the lobby.

"Where is he?"

Bael was deep in conversation with a dark fae who looked amused by my obvious wrath. I ignored him, waiting until Bael raised his eyebrow. "His penthouse."

Good. I wanted privacy for this conversation.

I took the elevator up, strode through the living space, and pushed open the door to Samael's office.

He was sitting behind his desk, his sleeves rolled up, a pen in his hand. The king of the demons did paperwork. The sight made me choke on my words for a moment.

He lifted his head, surprise and pleasure flickering across his face for the barest second before his expression went blank.

"Danica. I didn't know you were planning to visit."

"This isn't a social call."

He unfolded himself from behind his desk, slowly stretching out his huge frame. He reminded me of a panther getting up after a nap.

"What is it I can do for you?"

"I want you to stop having your people follow me around."

"It's for your own safety."

"I'm serious, Samael, I want them gone."

He stared at me silently for a long moment. I threw up my hands. "Why do you care so much, anyway?"

He took a step closer. I took a step back. I didn't need his cedar and citrus scent winding around me.

"I find that the idea of you being hurt... discomforts me."

I stared at him. He met my gaze, expression inscrutable. Maybe he could be reasoned with.

"Samael–"

"And I am bigger than you, older than you, and more powerful than you. You have no choice but to accept my wishes in this."

Forget reasoning with him. I had to kill him at my first opportunity. There was no other option unless I wanted to go insane.

I ground my teeth. Samael needed a lot of education when it came to things like personal freedom, autonomy, and privacy. Unfortunately, I was no longer amused, and having someone witness the way I'd fallen to pieces today...

unacceptable.

"I appreciate the thought, truly I do," I said sweetly. "But the next time I see a demon following me around, I'll throw my knives first and ask questions later."

His eyes turned to silver ice, and I sighed, holding up a hand. Threats didn't work with Samael. Unless *he* was the one making them. I cleared my throat, shifting on my feet. "From the time my mom took me on the run, I was taught to take care of myself. I've worked hard to be independent, Samael, and I'm perfectly capable of keeping myself safe. When you have demons follow me around, it undermines my credibility, steals my privacy, and damages my reputation."

"Your precious reputation," he ground out. "Half of the people in this city believe you're a traitor."

Low blow. The gloves were coming off. "Yes. And the other half know damn well what would've happened if those witches managed to take your power. They know I'm bonded to you, and I still chose to save innocent lives over regaining my freedom. They know I'm fair. That's the reason why Mariam asked me to work for her. And when you have demons following me around, it impacts my ability to do my job effectively."

He heaved a frustrated sigh and his expression turned calculating. "If I do this for you, you will do something for me."

How was this my life? How was I being blackmailed with my own freedom?

"What do you want?" I attempted to keep my voice neutral, but it came out as a growl.

"You will allow me to take you on a *date*."

I blinked at him. He'd said the word 'date' as if it was a foreign language and he wasn't quite sure of the pronunciation.

I angled my head. "Would you like to repeat that?"

His low snarl communicated that no, he wouldn't like to repeat it at all.

"You heard me."

"We don't date."

"We do now."

I raised one eyebrow. Someone had told him that this was a good idea. That this was what humans did. "What kind of date?"

His expression hardened and he stayed stubbornly silent.

I studied his face. "I go on a date with you, and you promise to stop sending your demons to follow me around?"

"Yes."

This seemed strangely out of character after the way he'd insisted they were there for my safety. But I wasn't about to look a gift demon in the mouth.

"Deal."

He smiled. I smiled back. I had no doubt that he'd make me wear an exquisite, yet much too expensive dress, shoes that made me want to cut off my feet, and make up. He'd take me somewhere public, so he could demonstrate to everyone that he had a pet bounty hunter under his control. I'd resent him even more than I did now, and he'd be confused by the fact that I somehow still didn't want him in my life.

Lies, a little voice said in my head, and I scowled. Fine. There were certain aspects of Samael that I didn't hate, but they were always overshadowed by the things he did to make me wish I'd never met him.

"Our date starts now."

"Excuse me?" Every time I thought I had a handle on the demon, he blindsided me. The satisfied expression on his face told me he knew very well that I'd expected him to trot me out in public and make me wish I was anywhere else on our 'date.'

"Are you reneging on our deal?"

"Of course not. But I need to go to Merrill's and check out his store." He folded his arms, his body language nothing but stubborn, arrogant male.

Fine. If this was what it took to get my privacy back, I'd visit Merrill's store later. I rolled my eyes. "Let's go."

I let out a yelp as he leaned down and I was suddenly in his arms.

He strode to the balcony, pushed the door open, and leapt. A chunk of my hair found its way into my mouth and I spat it out as he shot into the sky, invisible wings taking us high enough that I shivered. He immediately dropped lower, where the air was warmer, and I watched the city fly by beneath us. Within a few minutes, we landed behind what was once a human university.

Wait…

I squirmed in his arms as he approached the portal. "Samael," I said warningly, and he ignored me. The portal was lit with every color of blue, the center so light it was almost white, while the edges gleamed a blue the color of the night sky moments after the sun had gone down.

The last time I'd gone through this portal, my body had

rebelled. It was evident that we were going through again, and the way Samael's hands tightened on my body made it clear he wasn't allowing me to change my mind about this little "date."

I wrapped my arms around his neck and buried my face against his throat. My nose brushed his skin and he stiffened in surprise, but he'd already steered us into the portal.

Pain ripped through me like sharp teeth. I sucked in a breath, but surprisingly, even as though it made me lightheaded, it wasn't as agonizing as the last time I'd entered it.

Either it was easier to enter with Samael's arms around me, or I was leveling up. I had a suspicion it was a little of both.

Samael took to the sky again. The sky was a rust-orange in this realm, and the sound of water crashing over rocks would have been soothing if it didn't mean that we were flying in the direction of Samael's dragon.

I froze. Was he planning to feed me to the beast?

The last time I was here, I'd snuck through the ward guarding his hoard. To get into the cave, I'd used a look-away spell to hide myself— and my scent— from the dragon. But the moment I'd picked up Misty, that spell had disappeared until the sentient dagger decided it had a better chance of getting out into the world if I was alive.

I had no doubt that the dragon would have memorized my scent.

"Listen," I yelled over the wind. "I know you and I have had our differences, but surely we can talk about this."

No reply. I could have a dagger at his throat in a couple

of seconds, but he'd probably drop me in retaliation.

The cave entrance loomed, and my mouth went dry. Samael landed outside the cave and strolled through his ward. I slid my Nim Cub out of the lanyard around my neck— yes, I was wearing Samael's gift, and yes it did look ridiculous with my t-shirt. By the time Samael let me down, I had my knife in my hand and my eyes were adjusting to the dim light.

I had no desire to hurt a dragon, but if it thought I'd be a tasty snack, it was game on.

Samael let out a low growl and I jumped, shooting him a look. He shook his head at me. "You don't need to be armed, little witch. This is a *date*."

I raised one eyebrow. "I think your definition of the word 'date' could use some work."

He ignored that, striding past the welcoming collection of old bones on the right side of the cave. I kept my feet planted and gazed up toward the massive stalactites hanging from the high ceiling. It was dark up there.

"Hello, Scylla," Samael murmured in a low, caressing tone. I was almost jealous of the dragon, hearing him murmur to her so intimately.

"Wait, she has a name?" I forgot my terror enough to take a few steps toward him, and he smiled over his shoulder at me.

"Of course."

My gaze was stuck on the huge beast. The dragon was a deep indigo, her iridescent scales darkening to black on her back and lightening to violet near her claws. She was slowly getting to her feet, and every muscle in my body tensed as her bright gold eyes landed on my face.

Recognition gleamed in those eyes. She yawned, displaying teeth longer than my fingers, and I took a step back.

"Relax," Samael murmured. "Scylla won't hurt you. Will you, darling?"

Darling? Are you kidding me? The dragon seemed to read my mind, a low snort escaping her throat as a curl of smoke drifted up from one nostril.

"Come closer, witchling. Or are you afraid?"

I rolled my eyes. If Samael wanted me dead, there were many, many ways he could achieve that without needing to bring me all the way here. I took a step closer, and the dragon watched me.

Her back arched as she stretched, her tail swiping across the dirt floor like a cat's. The last time I was here, she was hugely pregnant. Now, her belly was flat.

I shifted my gaze behind her, and my mouth dropped open.

"That's a dragon egg."

Samael nodded. "Scylla has passed her egg and will now stay in this cave until it hatches. She spent her pregnancy eating more food than she needed so she can stay with her baby until it has hatched. Come, Danica, introduce yourself to the dragon you tricked."

I glowered at him, and he merely raised his eyebrow back. Fine. I took a few steps closer, until I was within touching distance of the dragon.

"Hi," I said, shifting awkwardly on my feet. "My name is Danica."

She stared at me for a long moment and then lowered her head. I went exceedingly still as she inched her head closer, watching me out of gold eyes.

She nudged at my hip, and I nodded. "Yeah, that's the dagger. But Samael said I could have it."

She blinked at that, her gaze shifting to Samael. He nodded at her and she let out a low growl. A drop of sweat slid down the back of my spine.

"Your hoard is still more than large enough," Samael soothed. "If you like, I can bring you some more rubies. I know you enjoy them the most."

Scylla let out a sound like a purr and I pinched my arm. Ow. Okay, so the dragon *could* understand everything we said. Great.

I glanced at Samael. His smile said he was very pleased by how this date was going. He should be. Screw a fancy dinner or a night at the movies. The way to this girl's heart was through meeting a dangerous beast that could tear me into pieces.

"Would you like to stretch your wings?" Samael offered. "We will stay with your youngling."

Scylla went still. She surveyed the egg, and then her eyes turned longing as she shifted her attention to the cave entrance. Torn between her responsibility to her kid and her desire for a few moments of freedom. Mom life in a nutshell.

She stared at me. That stare said that she wouldn't hesitate to turn me into small pieces if I dared step any closer to her baby.

"I won't go near your egg," I promised. She shifted her

gaze to Samael, and he nodded. He raised one hand and stroked along her neck, smiling as she closed her eyes. I was not jealous of a dragon, Goddamnit.

With a final warning look at me, Scylla ambled toward the cave entrance. The cave was much, much larger than it looked from the outside, but she still had to duck her head and tuck her wings in close to her body.

"She must trust you a lot to leave you with her baby."

"Scylla and I have been bonded for centuries. She knows I would not harm her young. Come with me."

He turned and I followed him toward his hoard. The first time I'd seen it, I'd nearly swallowed my tongue. The benefit of knowing what was coming hadn't dulled my shock.

Demons bonded with dragons by offering them a hoard to guard. And Samael had been alive for more than enough time to build incredible wealth. He likely considered this to be little more than a few trinkets.

It was definitely more than a few trinkets.

I'd seen it once before, but I'd been desperate to get Misty and get out of here. Now, I took a moment to simply stare.

Last time, I'd seen one small section of the hoard and nearly swallowed my tongue. I'd seen the strands of Persian pearls, dangling from hooks along one stone wall, the luminous glow muted against the fiery flash of rubies.

Loose diamonds spilled from a muslin bag on the floor, and gold coins the same color as Scylla's eyes were stacked in at the back of the cave.

The sword I'd admired was still here. It looked like the

kind of sword a mythical knight had taken into one of the great battles. Crowns, brooches, rings, bracelets, it was all here. And it was a sensory overload.

Samael was silently scanning his hoard. I was too busy staring at an antique letter opener to pay him any attention.

"The diamonds around your neck are tiny."

I frowned.

"Diamonds?" I dropped my gaze but all I could see was my lanyard. Oh no, he wouldn't have...

Now I was paying attention. "Please, please tell me I'm not wearing diamonds."

He tutted at me, turning away to browse his hoard. I stared down at the sparkly stones around my neck. Not cubic zirconia then. Ugh.

I was guaranteed to lose or break this lanyard at some point. What was he thinking?

He reached for one of the larger diamond necklaces, offering it to me.

"No fucking way."

He scowled, obviously put out. I let out a choked laugh. The demon had taken me on a date, introduced me to his pet, and now was trying to give me a token of his affection. And I wasn't cooperating.

"Samael–"

"If I thought you would accept it, I would give you my entire hoard."

I swallowed. "You'd lose Scylla."

"I'd replace it within days. This will look stunning around your delicate neck." His gaze dropped to my throat and I swallowed.

"I have nowhere to wear it," I tried.

His slow smile told me he knew exactly where I'd wear it if it were up to him. In his bed, naked.

"Just out of curiosity, why do you think you should be giving me what is likely a priceless diamond necklace?"

He scowled. "Why must you be so difficult?"

I waited him out. He didn't blush— I didn't think such a thing was possible for Samael. But for a single moment, he couldn't quite meet my eyes.

"You have only seen the downside of being bonded to me. You've seen demon murders and the stares of people who believe you are a traitor. You've seen formal events you didn't want to go to, and your life has changed in countless ways."

I read between the lines. The demon felt bad and had wanted to do something to make up for all the shit he'd put me through since bonding me to him against my will.

I sighed. He wouldn't break the bond. That hadn't even occurred to him, and I doubted it ever would. I would still have to figure out a way to do that myself. In the meantime, this was his attempt to show me that life with him wasn't all bad.

"I don't need your diamonds, Samael. Although, I can admit I'm partial to the lanyard and sheath you gave me. If you were hoping to give me something incredible, you did that when you let me up close to your dragon."

His jaw tightened. "You don't want jewelry, you won't move into my apartment, you refuse my protection. What is it that you want, Danica?"

To be left alone. To go back to my life before I met him.

Even as I thought it, instant denial ripped through my chest. Samael's face went blank at my silence, and I had a feeling he knew where my mind had gone.

Once again, it came down to a deal.

"Okay, if you really want me to accept something from you, bring me back here when that egg hatches. If it's okay with Scylla, of course."

His gaze turned shrewd. "You want to see the baby dragon."

"Of course."

He glanced from me to the egg, his expression calculating. "Fine. As long as Scylla agrees, I will bring you back here on another *date*. And then you will have dinner with me."

Hold up, what?

I opened my mouth, but Scylla was already returning. She cast a suspicious look my way and I spread my hands wide. "I didn't go near your baby, I promise."

She snorted and turned away, the picture of disdain. Even the dragon thought I was inadequate.

CHAPTER FIFTEEN
DANICA

Samael landed next to my car, and I stepped back from him, turning to unlock it.

He let out a rough laugh, caught my wrist, and pulled me against him. My mind went blank as his mouth crashed down on mine, and I let out a sigh that he caught with his mouth, echoing it back to me.

"Come to my bed, witchling."

He was temptation incarnate. Unfortunately for him, I was wise to his ways.

"Can't. I need to go to Merrill's."

His expression darkened but he stepped back, watching as I got in the car and drove away. I checked my rearview mirror and my stomach twisted as he gazed after me.

By the time I got to Merrill's, the sun had already gone down. Since I was going to be snooping through a crime scene, that suited my purposes perfectly.

Merrill's store was several blocks west of Gary's, closer to what had once been the campus of a human university.

Like Gary's, Merrill's store had been ravaged. His shelves and tables were lying on the ground, spells, potions, and weapons mixing freely. My gaze lingered on the blood decorating most of his store and I swallowed.

Whoever had killed him had been enraged. Goblins didn't have a ton of magic, but he would've had more than enough if he'd been attacked by a human.

He hadn't had a chance. I poked around until I found his calendar in a drawer in his back room. I pulled it out, flipping through the last month. There were no mysterious meetings noted, just various auctions, which was likely where Merrill got his hands on some of the more illegal weapons I'd spotted in his back room.

Compared to Gary's store, Merrill had a much larger back room, with a door which opened to the alley outside. I poked my head out, but sadly, there were no security cameras perfectly positioned and aimed at the alley.

I took the calendar with me, making a note to check out the auctions. Then I stopped by all of the stores surrounding Merrill's.

"Didn't hear 'nothin,'" a human woman in her fifties stuck out her chin. She'd introduced herself as Bettie, smiling welcomingly at me until the moment she realized I was in her store to ask about Merrill— and not as a paying customer.

I scanned her antique store, pointedly letting my gaze get stuck on the wide window which looked out onto the street— and directly across to Merrill's store.

"Cameras?" I asked.

She shook her head and I just looked at her.

"Goblin," she spat. "Why do you care?" Her gaze

dropped to my arm. "Demon whore."

"That's real nice. How about you hand over your recording before the Mage Council gets an anonymous tip about a human dealing in magical items?" I jerked my head to a collection of brass lamps. "That looks like a djinn lamp to me."

She spluttered. "I'm a god-fearing woman. That's no genie lamp."

I bared my teeth in a grin. "There will still be an investigation. Your store will be closed while the council checks it out. Hand over the footage and you'll never have to see me again."

Bettie decided it was in her best interest to give me the footage and I went on with my day. Short of threatening her with pain, she wasn't going to tell me what she'd seen or heard, and torture was where I drew the line when it came to people who hadn't actively harmed me.

Hopefully, we'd get more from the camera outside Bettie's store than just the guy in the cloak. Frustration twisted like something alive in my gut. I was continually a step behind this guy. I didn't know what he wanted and why, or who he planned to target next. Both Gary and Merrill were lesser unseelie. Was this a hate crime?

I made my way back to Merrill's, searching fruitlessly for anything that could lead me in the right direction. In the back room, I pushed one of the shelves off the floor, cursing under my breath at its weight. When it was standing, I had a little more room to move, and I raised my eyebrows at the weapons strewn around.

The huge silver shield looked like a hex shield. That

meant it could block magic attacks, bullets, and even a werewolf if the wielder was powerful enough. Merrill also had a collection of antique daggers which gleamed dully in the light, strewn near a long spear which was leaning against the back wall. All of the weapons looked old, powerful, and illegal. Merrill had taken up fencing stolen objects in his free time, and it had likely gotten him killed.

As much as I'd like to poke around and explore his weapons, I needed to get moving.

I took a step toward the door. Then I froze. Something shiny glinted on the ground and I crouched down and examined it.

A glittery blue marble. I reached into my utility belt and plucked the gold marble out. A perfect match. I needed to talk to Cil and Zip. I turned, and the door to the alley slammed open.

Turning back cost me half a second. I dove for the floor as I caught a glimpse of a black, hooded figure, and a bullet slammed into the wall inches from where I'd been standing.

Son of a bitch. I ducked. The shooter let out a high-pitched laugh and I leapt across the stockroom, taking cover behind a steel shelf.

I'd gotten the barest glimpse of his gun, but I was pretty sure it was a Smith and Wesson Model 29. Humans loved the firepower, but if I was right, he only had six rounds to play with.

He'd fired three. Whoever had sent him after me hadn't told him who he was dealing with. He should've bought a fucking semi-automatic, because I was betting I could stick my knife in his throat before he could reload. As long as the next three rounds didn't kill me.

"Come out, witch, and I'll give you an easy shot in the head. Otherwise it'll be a gut shot."

Yeah, yeah. Unfortunately, I wasn't in a great position, frozen behind one of Merrill's overturned shelves. If I could get to the shield, I might have a chance. Of course, I could use my power, and the thought made it slam against my shields. The problem with that was that I was liable to kill the shooter. Even attempting a ward was risky. I needed to interrogate him.

But first, I needed to get closer. Without getting gut shot. No problem.

I gritted my teeth and army crawled along the floor, cursing whoever had knocked so many shelves over. While they gave me cover, the weapons and spells littering the ground made it difficult to move.

I peered through a gap in the shelf closest to me. The idiot had thrown off the hood of his cloak and I memorized his features. Wide mouth, yellowing teeth, dark, squinty eyes. His face was twisted in a mixture of rage and pleasure. He thought he had me pinned, and he was already celebrating. Idiot.

A long scar twisted down his neck and disappeared, covered by the robe.

I crawled faster and knocked over a painting. A bullet smashed against the wall, and I dropped to my stomach, hugging the floor. I hated being on the defensive.

Two rounds left.

An explosion spell glittered at me from a few feet away, tied to a piece of rose quartz. Tempting, but I couldn't risk killing this asshole before I interrogated him. The crunch of footsteps on broken glass made the decision for me. He was walking toward me.

I picked up the stone, coaxed it awake with my power, and threw it past the plates and into the wall.

"You bitch!"

Bet that made him piss his pants. I laughed silently and took the opportunity to move a few more feet. He'd be expecting me to head toward the open door leading into the main room of Merrill's store, so I did the opposite, backtracking toward where I was crouched when I found the marble.

Smoke filled the room from the exploding spell. I sure didn't think that one through. My lungs seized with the need to cough.

Oh crap. They itched, every breath tickling down my throat. But if I gave into it, that last bullet would hit me. He was shooting like he'd used that gun many times before.

Use your ward, dummy.

Yeah, because I could definitely trust my power enough to protect me from a guy who wanted to blow my head off without instantly killing him.

I slipped my hand toward my utility belt, slowly unzipping a pouch as sweat rolled down my back. The shooter stalked toward me, kicking a path through the rubble of Merrill's back room as he went.

I threw one of my throwing knives at the shield. It clanged against the metal, bounced off, and Scar-face jolted, swinging his gun wildly toward the shield.

"You're a dead whore!" He shot in the shield's direction,

and I jumped to my feet. Our eyes met and his face drained of color as he pulled the trigger. The click sounded loud in the sudden silence and his hand trembled as he cursed and reached beneath his robe for a magazine.

I smiled at him. "I'm a what?" I pulled my Nim Cub and he gulped, turned, and ran, slamming the door to the alley behind him.

I hauled ass through the wreckage, threw the door open and sprinted after him. He was heading southeast, and I grinned savagely. I'd bet I knew that neighborhood better than him.

He crossed the street and I cursed as I was forced to wait for a truck. He disappeared for a moment, and I growled under my breath as he appeared in my line of sight. The asshole was holding his gun on a human guy, forcing him out of his car.

Fuck interrogation. If I couldn't catch him, I'd kill him. His body would be plenty of evidence. I dropped my shields, lifted my hand, and something slammed into me, dropping me like a rock.

I rolled, instantly pulling my knife again as I held it against a throat.

A human teenager's throat.

He stared at me, stunned. Packing away my power took everything in me. I rolled off him and cursed soundly. The asshole in the cloak was long gone, and the teenager looked mighty pleased with himself as he brushed himself off and got to his feet. He offered me his hand, which I ignored, still fighting my power, which wanted to explode some shit. My shield held steady. Just.

I got to my feet and took one step closer to the kid, my voice very quiet. "Is there a reason you just did that?"

He nodded. "The guy in the cloak paid me fifty bucks. Said you were practicing for an audition for a play." His gaze scanned my face and he took a step back. "Not auditioning. Uh, sorry dude."

"Dude?" My power slammed into my shield and I gritted my teeth, holding it back with sheer willpower. The teenager took the opportunity to sprint in the opposite direction.

Of course, this had to happen directly after I'd convinced Samael to stop having his demons follow me around. If I hadn't, Scarface would be in demon custody right now.

The thought pissed me off. My phone vibrated and I fished it out of my pocket, forcing myself to stalk away from the kid.

"What?"

"Uh, are you okay?"

"Cara?" I was so mad I hadn't even looked at my screen. "Sorry. What's up?"

"I heard a little something through the grapevine."

I pushed the alley door back open and stepped into Merrill's back room. "What kind of something?"

"That rowan wood in your arrow? I did a little poking around, and the demons keep rowan quiet, putting a stop to anyone who grows it. But there's a seller in town. You could go talk to him and see if he knows anything about your arrows."

I sure could. "Can you send me his details?"

"Yup."

"Cara, I really appreciate this. Thanks."

"No problem."

CHAPTER SIXTEEN
DANICA

The next morning, I threw on a load of laundry, played with Lia, and then dropped by the tower, where I handed over the footage I'd collected from Merrill's neighbors to Steve.

He grunted at me, guzzling coffee, and I left him to it, heading to Selina's for a quick lesson.

She'd had me raising and lowering my shields every hour for the past few days, and I was officially convinced— I'd do whatever it took to learn how to wield my power without needing to lower them. After half an hour of intense focus, I could slowly eek out a trickle of magic from beyond my thickest shield. It felt like forcing syrup through a sift, but it was something.

My homework this week was to keep my shields up but use my power to see each person's magical 'signature.' Selina had shown me how I could use my power to measure other people's power without dropping my own shields, but it was easier said than done. I'd had a glimpse of Samael's power a few weeks ago. It was a crimson so dark it was almost black.

The practice seemed to help, and by the time we were done, I didn't need to concentrate on holding my power back. It was no longer pressed up against my shields like it was just waiting for me to lose control.

I thanked Selina and strode out her front door. Vas was waiting on her porch.

I scowled. "This seems like deja vu."

He grinned. "You know, I was recently thinking that we don't get to hang out enough. I'm always busy working for Samael, you're usually bounty hunting. Now we get to spend some solid time together."

I wasn't buying whatever he thought he was selling. "Samael said he wasn't going to have anyone follow me around anymore."

"He's not. I'm your partner."

For fucks sake. "I want some privacy. Is that too much to ask?"

Vas' face hardened. "Yes. Yes it is. Want to tell me what's got you so pissed?"

I turned and walked toward my car. Vas followed, and I scowled as he reached out and turned me back to him.

"I'm just struggling with a few things. I don't want people watching me break down."

"Ah. That."

"What?"

Vas' expression went blank and fury unfurled in my chest. "That son of a bitch reported my panic attack?"

"Not in that many words. He merely reported that you pulled off to the side of the road and seemed incapacitated."

"That's just fucking great. And Samael wonders why I want nothing to do with him."

"Samael ripped him a new one when he found out that had made it into his security report."

I shook my head. This was why Samael had been so remarkably cooperative and when I'd asked him to stop ordering his demons to follow me around. He'd already decided to replace them with Vas.

"I get that this sucks," Vas said. "But look on the bright side, I've already seen you at your worst, and whatever happens, you can trust me not to report it to anyone."

"Anyone except Samael."

"Only if he asks me a direct question."

It was our deal from the last time we'd worked together. I attempted a smile, but the whole situation sucked. Vas and I had the beginning of a friendship, but Samael just kept coming between us.

It wouldn't surprise me if he'd sent Vas for this exact reason. He knew we were friends, and the possessive demon was jealous. He was likely hoping I would take my frustration out on Vas.

Asshole.

"Fine. I'm going to interrogate some humans. You can stand around and look suitably intimidating."

He rolled his eyes. "Cramped elevators and bigoted humans. Two of my favorite things."

"Hey, why should I be the only one having a sucky day?"

Vas scooped me into his arms with a sigh. "Where to?"

I almost protested but flying would be faster than driving. Instead, I rattled off the address and closed my eyes as he leapt into the sky.

He flapped his wings harder, then caught a draft and soared. I stared into space, still pissed off about losing the asshole who'd shot up Merrill's back room last night. I'd given his description to the demons and light fae, along with the human authorities, so I had to believe that someone would recognize him and bring him in soon.

Vas let out a disgusted sound and I frowned at him. He was staring down at the bone bracelet wrapped around my wrist. He wrinkled his nose, his dreamy eyes narrowing.

"You're still wearing the bracelet from that witch."

"Her name is Hannah as you well know," I said primly. "And she said it would protect me."

"She's a *black* witch," he said patiently. "She's someone you need protection *from*."

I barely suppressed a smile. Vas had been thoroughly creeped out by Hannah. Completely offended by her existence. He sure wasn't going to like what was in store for him. Hannah was going to get me into that auction, and if Vas was glued to my side, he was going to need to play nice with her as well.

We landed with barely a bump, and Vas put me on my feet. Crystal Clear Cleaning's headquarters was a large garage attached to a duplex in Albright. The garage door was open, and a woman was sitting at a desk in the corner doing paperwork.

I heroically did not wrinkle my nose at the overwhelming scent of the cleaning products that were stacked throughout the garage.

"Can I help you?"

"Yes."

Crystal Moore had short brown hair which looked like she'd been running her hands through it. The short cut had the benefit of showing off her impeccable bone structure, and her face was makeup-free. She got to her feet behind her desk.

I'd spent some time online stalking Crystal Clear Cleaning last night. According to my research, Crystal had started her company ten years ago, and had fought hard and long to work for as many paranormals as possible. Not only did her employees clean Mariam's building, but they also cleaned a variety of dark fae businesses, a werewolf bar, and a small spell store owned by a witch in Brightleaf.

"I need to ask you a few questions."

"And you are?"

"Danica Amana. This is my… colleague, Vassago."

Crystal ran her gaze over us, and Vas gave her a charming grin. He was likely appreciating the fact that he hadn't needed to get in an elevator for this little talk. Strangely, Crystal didn't look entranced with him.

"You're the woman bonded to Samael."

"Yup." I popped the p and she shrugged. For a woman who had gone after as many paranormal contracts as possible, she sure wasn't impressed with the demon by my side. Curiouser and curiouser.

She sat back down and gestured to a couple of forest green plastic outdoor chairs in front of her desk. "Take a seat."

I sat. Vas shook his head and I didn't blame him. It'd likely be impossible to get comfortable with his wings. He leaned against a wall instead.

"Do you recognize this man?"

I'd worked with a sketch artist last night after the shooter escaped, and I handed over a copy of his face. Crystal took the time to study it and finally shook her head.

"No."

According to the dagger on my hip, she was telling the truth.

"A priceless fae artifact has gone missing from the fae representative's office. Your employees were the only ones who had access."

That wasn't completely true, but I wanted to see her reaction, and the blood drained from her face. For the first time, real fear flashed through her eyes.

"Wh-what?"

"I have a list of your employees who were working in that building, but I'm going to need you to give me some more information. Have any of them mentioned fae objects before?"

"No, of course not."

Misty stayed inert. "I need to know anything you can tell me about the people who have been working in the fae representative's building. Anything you think may be helpful."

Crystal nodded and turned to the thin gray laptop on her desk. "Give me a moment."

I'd already run a check on her employees, looking for anyone with a criminal record. Nothing had popped up. But maybe something Crystal knew could help.

"I should be asking you for a warrant," she muttered as she typed.

"If any of these people are involved in stealing from paranormals, me finding them before the fae do could very well save their lives."

Something whirred, and she pushed away from her desk, wheeling her chair toward the printer. She scanned the printouts, shrugged, and handed them to me.

"I don't know if this will help, but it's the roster for that building. If you look here, you can see who was scheduled on that floor each day."

"Have any of your employees stopped showing up to work since the theft?"

She nodded and printed out another few sheets of paper. "There are quite a few." Her mouth twisted. "A lot of people consider cleaning beneath them. They consider this a temporary gig and leave me short staffed while they interview for other companies."

I took the papers and nodded at her. "Thanks. Just one more question."

"Yes?"

"You wanna tell me why you're going after every paranormal contract you can find?"

The look on her face told me she thought I was a special kind of idiot. "Paranormals pay the most."

Well, that made sense.

My phone vibrated in my back pocket as we walked away from the garage. I pulled it out. Steve.

"Hey."

"I'm sending you a picture."

I rolled my eyes. Steve wasn't known for his pleasantries. "Okay." I put him on speaker and opened the picture as soon as it came through.

The footage was grainy, but Steve had done something to make it clearer. He'd zoomed in on something.

"You're going to have to tell me what I'm looking at."

He sighed. "It's a belt."

Once he told me, my eyes were suddenly able to make sense of the twisted strands on the screen. It was threaded leather. I showed the screen to Vas and his eyes hardened.

"The belt of Thor. Whoever attacked Gary and Merrill was wearing it."

I thought only a paranormal could've done that much damage to a gnome and a goblin. It hadn't made sense that they'd be using humans to do their dirty work for them. But the belt changed everything.

"I got a slight face shot," Steve said. "I'm sending it now."

I clicked into it. The cloak was obstructing most of his face, but I could see enough to pick out a few features. White male, beefy, double-chinned. I compared it to the sketch in my hand and held them up so Vas could see.

"No scar. This isn't the guy who shot at me yesterday."

"Nope."

"Thanks, Steve." I hung up and paced toward the car, turning to pace back as I thought it through.

"The attacks against Merrill and Gary are somehow connected to Mariam's missing fae artifacts."

Of course they were, because nothing in my life was ever easy.

Vas nodded. "What could humans want with fae artifacts?"

"It's a little-known fact that the fae keep hush-hush, but some of these artifacts hold enough power that they can be used by humans."

I turned back to the garage. Crystal let out an audible sigh as she watched us walk back toward her. I held up my phone.

"Recognize this guy?"

She frowned. "He looks familiar." She held out her hand and I gave her my phone, watching as she zoomed in. Frustration warred with annoyance as she narrowed her eyes. "Maybe one of my employees dated him briefly or something? I feel like I've seen him before, but I can't put my finger on where. Sorry."

"Thanks anyway."

Vas stretched, and his wings rustled behind him. "Where to now?"

"Now we find out how Hrunting was stolen."

CHAPTER SEVENTEEN
DANICA

Vas flew above me as we headed to Hope Valley. The fae who'd owned Hrunting lived close to Mariam.

I gave my name at the gated entrance and it slid open, revealing a long drive. Through the trees to the right, I could see a tennis court and a pool, and I couldn't help but gape as the house itself came into view. The drive circled around a huge fountain, and I parked my car, taking in the ivy creeping up the house, the expansive entryway with its double doors, and the multiple balconies above me.

Wow.

Strangely, it didn't feel ostentatious. But maybe that was because I was subconsciously comparing it to Mariam's monstrosity.

A butler opened one of the main doors and nodded as I gave him my name. Vas landed behind me and the butler smiled at us both. "Right this way."

Aubrey was a light fae, and clearly he had some kind of affinity for plants and flowers, because his home smelled like lush greenery. Exotic plants sat in pots in every corner, and on almost every surface. It should've been too much, but walking through his house was like walking through a secret garden.

Vas sneezed. I glanced over my shoulder at him and he shrugged.

"He's just in his weapons room," the butler said. "He instructed me to bring you straight up."

We climbed a flight of stairs, and I couldn't help but reach out a hand to stroke the purple vine that twined around the banister. The butler caught my hand.

"That is extremely poisonous to mortals," he said apologetically.

"Sorry. I'll keep my hands to myself, I promise."

"Well, I wouldn't say you have to keep *that* promise," a voice said silkily from the landing above us. My gaze slammed into stunning lavender eyes, which laughed at me as I stared. I barely managed to keep my mouth from dropping open as I ripped my gaze away from his eyes to take in the rest of the perfection that was Aubrey's face.

His hair was silver, and the pale eyebrows on his fair face should've washed him out, but they merely highlighted the stunning color of his eyes. His cheekbones were high enough to give him a slightly feral edge, while his jaw looked like he could take a punch or two.

"I appreciate the glamor," I told him as I reached the landing, "but it's not necessary."

He laughed again, and despite myself, my lips wanted to quirk. He just seemed to be having so much *fun* with life.

"I'm not using any glamor," he said. He pointed to the tiniest scar on his chin, half of it buried in the silver scruff growing along his jaw. "See?"

I leaned closer and he went very still. Behind me, Vas cleared his throat. Wow, I was far too close to this guy. I took a careful step back, and the fae reached out a hand, grabbing my arm before I tumbled down the stairs. With my luck, I'd probably take Vas unaware and we'd both end up in a heap on the floor.

"Careful now," Aubrey purred.

"Apologies. I'm not usually clumsy." I shook his hand off and he stepped back.

"So if you were using glamor, you'd have no scars at all?"

"No. Right this way," he turned and led us down the hall. "Glamor is designed to demonstrate beauty. It takes more power than most have at their disposal to still allow imperfections to peek through."

"Interesting."

"It is, isn't it?" he grinned at me and stopped at a door near the end of the hall. The door was covered with the same purple vines, and he waved his hand, clearing them away. Then he held that same hand up and his ward glowed a poisonous green before it disappeared.

The door swung open.

"Wow."

Weapons were mounted on three walls, taking up every inch of space, and yet the room was large enough that it didn't seem cluttered. The fourth wall held shelves and lockers. My hands itched to explore, and I forced myself not to touch. This was the one place in the house I'd seen so far that was plant-free.

"I'm glad you approve." Aubrey shifted his attention

to Vas, who was silently following me. "Your bodyguard?"

I frowned at him. "My friend."

Feathers tickled my cheek. Vas showing his appreciation.

"I meant no offense. Humans who are precious to paranormals are often guarded like the prizes they are."

"I'm not human." I was finally admitting it. "And I'm no prize."

He stared at me for a long moment, and his power reached toward me. I allowed it. He didn't mean me any harm. Aubrey dropped the jovial act and his eyes narrowed, and then widened at what he found.

"Not human," he agreed. "But a prize... definitely."

I didn't know what to say to that, so I turned back to the weapons room. "You have quite the collection."

"It's something of a hobby," he said modestly. He stepped to the side and I took in the huge room.

Other than the weapons, the room was sparse. The small table and chairs in one corner were plain, almost utilitarian. This wasn't a room used to many visitors.

The walls and shelves held almost every gun and knife imaginable, but my eyes were drawn to the ancient weapons, kept in impeccable condition along one wall.

"You can touch," Aubrey breathed, and I jumped. I'd been so obsessed with the weapons, I hadn't noticed him stepping closer. The rustle of Vas's wings told me he wasn't happy, but he stayed silent and let me handle it.

I took a careful step away, and, to his credit, Aubrey stayed put. If he'd attempted to stalk me in his territory, I would've had to shove a knife somewhere he really didn't want a blade. But thankfully, he was clearly taking no for an answer.

His gaze dropped to my arm and he shot me a half-smile. I let out a low growl. The flirting suddenly made sense. Paranormal males couldn't help but stroke their own egos, and Aubrey saw Samael's claim as a challenge. These jackasses needed to be put in their place.

I opened my mouth to do just that, and my gaze caught on a hooked blade behind him. The sickle sword was about 20 inches long, with an inside curve that was used to pull a shield aside or trap an opponent's arm.

"A khopesh," I blurted out. My trainer Edward had been something of a history buff, and he'd taught me everything he knew about weapons through the ages.

He smiled. "This is a very special khopesh... but I won't bore you."

"I'm not bored."

He grinned at me, dropping the flirtation. I got the feeling his flirtatious act was automatic for him, and now that he knew I wasn't interested, his boyish smile was so compelling I couldn't help but grin back.

"My cousin was obsessed with the boy king Tutankhamun. She had grown bored in the light fae realm and the portal she slipped through took her to Egypt, where she grew enamored with the child, planning to heal him of his ailments.

"It is... difficult for light fae to bear children. My people had begun looking to mortals to help grow our numbers, but my cousin had recently lost a child."

Old grief twisted his face and I reached out and squeezed his arm. "I'm sorry."

He placed his hand on mine. "You're very kind," he told me. "Her child was to be a boy, and something about the young king softened her heart. She had petitioned our king to heal him— back then, the fae did not have the same freedoms we have now."

I knew a little about King Tut. He'd been a sickly kid, likely because of so much inbreeding within the Egyptian royal family. When he died, he'd had malaria, and his left leg had been broken and infected.

"What happened?"

"Our king did not often give permission to meddle in the lives of mortals— unless of course, it was to kidnap them for our own population growth." He gave me a wry smile.

"The king said no?" Vas stepped closer, obviously intrigued despite himself.

Aubrey gave a languid shrug. "My cousin is very persuasive. She had managed to convince the seelie king that she could make it look as if the sun god Aten had performed the miracle. He finally agreed, but it was too late. The boy king died.

"My cousin was furious, and she learned that this khopesh was one of two that were to be entombed with the king. She infused the blade with her power, so that any who disturbed the boy king would be cursed. When the tomb was once again opened a few decades ago, I had to step in, or the results would have been disastrous for the mortals involved."

"How did you get through the portals, if you don't mind me asking? They weren't open at the time."

Aubrey smiled. "Those portals have always been open to those with enough power and the key to unlock them." He turned and took the khopesh off the wall, handing it to me.

I barely breathed as my hands clutched the weapon. Aubrey threw his head back and roared with laughter as I stood, frozen with the ancient sword in my hand. Even Vas sniggered, and I glared at them both.

"Relax," Aubrey chuckled. "The protection wards on that thing have lasted for centuries and they'll last for centuries more."

I swallowed, ignoring the guys as they bonded over my deer-in-the-headlights reaction. Instead, I slowly brought the khopesh up to my face. Wow.

"You are a lover of blades," Aubrey said.

I smiled at him. "They get the job done."

He shot a pointed look at my hip, where Misty was covered with my t-shirt, and raised one eyebrow. Maybe he could feel the dagger's power. I tensed, and his eyes sharpened. Then his gaze dropped to the khopesh in my hands.

"Keep it," he said.

I gaped at him. "Excuse me?"

"You've been a delight. It's not often I get to ramble about weapons to someone who isn't merely humoring my interest. My cousin has been considering visiting me, and if she found that sword, it would upset her."

"What about the curse?" Vas asked.

Aubrey waved one hand. "That has long been lifted."

"Wow, are you sure?" My hands tightened possessively

on the khopesh and Aubrey's wink told me he'd noticed.

"I'm more than sure. It'll clear a space for something I've been seeking for a long time."

I opened my mouth to ask what exactly that was, and Vas cleared his throat. Right, we had work to do.

"Thank you, I appreciate this."

He waved his hand again. He'd been alive when this was buried with the king and was older than the weapon I considered ancient. To him, it was likely as mundane as one of my throwing knives.

"Okay." I forced myself to focus. "So Hrunting disappeared from this house, is that correct?"

He nodded.

"Was it in this room?" I glanced around. Between the poisonous vines and the ward, it seemed impossible that someone could have slipped in here without warning the fae.

"No," he said. "I brought you here to show you that I have many weapons in here that are much more powerful than Hrunting. If whoever had stolen the sword had targeted me specifically, they should have found a way to get in here."

This was torture. My mind was immediately on the ancient weapons behind him. Which ones were the most powerful, and why? I opened my mouth to ask, and a feather tickled my cheek again.

Right. I needed to stay on task.

"So where was Hrunting when it was stolen?"

Aubrey led us out of the weapons room and to a large office a few doors down. A white vine curled toward me as

I stepped through the doorway, and I froze.

"She's not poisonous. Just curious." He gave the vine a hard stare and it slowly curled back along the top of the doorway.

He gestured to the desk which took up half the room. More plants and flowers dotted the desk, the scent heady and Vas sneezed again behind us.

"The blade was on my desk," Aubrey said.

I closed my eyes briefly and he let out a humorless laugh. "Yes, I know, it was stupid. However, I had just removed the blade from my personal collection because my king had asked for it to be brought back to him."

There was only one reason why the seelie king would want this sword. "He's going after the sword that killed Grendel's mother."

Aubrey shrugged. "I had arranged for a friend to take Hrunting to our realm. He was due to arrive that day." For the first time, Aubrey's perfect face turned cold. Lavender eyes burned with retribution. "Someone had either been watching for that exact moment, or it was a crime of opportunity."

"Who has access to this office?"

He shrugged. "Myself and my staff."

"I'll need the names of your staff."

"My staff are above reproach. We are a family."

Uh-huh. "Any humans in that family?"

He frowned. "I'm unsure what you're asking."

"You've heard about the other missing artifacts," Vas said. He sneezed again and I had a feeling he was attempting to hurry this along so he could get out into the fresh air.

"I have. You believe they're connected?"

I shrugged. "Mariam does. It seems a little too convenient that three artifacts— that we know of— have gone missing within the same couple of weeks."

"That *is* too convenient. Mariam didn't tell me her suspicions when we spoke."

She was likely covering her ass. Whoops, sorry, Mariam. "When I asked for a list of people who had access to her office, she left the human cleaning company off the list."

"You believe it could be humans who have done this?" his brows raised as if the idea was preposterous.

I sighed. "If I hadn't reminded you that any humans with access to your home should be placed on the list of suspects, would you have thought of them?"

"No," he said slowly. "It wouldn't have occurred to me, and that's likely to my own detriment."

"Humans are invisible to you," I said.

He studied me. "Not all humans. Certainly not the half-blooded ones." I rolled my eyes and he laughed. "Fine. I will have my assistant make a list."

"Do you use a human cleaning company here?"

"No. The house is self-cleaning."

Man, what I wouldn't give to be able to say the same about my apartment. I peered out the window. "What about the grounds?"

"The grounds?"

"You obviously have an affinity for greenery. Do you also take care of all of the plants and flowers outside? Who mows your lawn?"

"I travel constantly. When I am here, I walk the grounds

and coax sluggish plants along, but when I'm away, I have a groundskeeping company... I hired the humans a few years ago at one of the light fae king's advisor's urging. He hounded most of the high fae in this realm. Apparently, it would be good for *optics*." Aubrey snorted. Obviously, he felt the same way about that idea as I did.

I strode over to the window and glanced down. We were on the second floor, but a collection of patio furniture occupied the paved area directly below us.

"If someone worked outside, would your plants allow them access to this office?"

His face went blank as if he'd never thought about it, and then his shoulders slumped.

"If I've given them access through the main ward, my plants know they are not to be touched. The plants share one... hive mind, I guess you could say. They would recognize the intruder as someone who was allowed access to my territory."

I opened the window and leaned out. With the help of the patio table, I could scramble up here in about twenty seconds, and I was betting anyone who worked a physical job outside could do the same.

Aubrey's expression was mournful as I pulled myself back into the room. "I let my guard down."

"It's normal. This is your home. You've never had anything stolen here."

"You're kind. Hopefully my king will show a sliver of the same understanding. I will get you that list."

He whirled and strode away. Vas sneezed again and I frowned.

"What's going on?"

"He has demon bane throughout the house."

"Demon bane?"

"It's a mild allergenic. More annoying than anything else. If slipped into food it'll cause weakness and unconsciousness."

I hadn't noticed anything. It was beginning to appear that, despite my half demon blood, I was more human than demon.

Aubrey reappeared with a stack of papers in his hand. "My assistant took the liberty of collecting this data earlier today." Aubrey shrugged one shoulder. "Apparently she was able to see the obvious link between the people who work here and the theft."

"I'm not saying that anyone who works for you is responsible," I cautioned him. "In fact, if I were you, I'd question all your staff."

"I already have. They are incapable of lying to me— they signed a writ when they began working for me which prevents such a thing. If they attempted it, my power would spark."

Welp. It was looking more and more likely that a human on the list Aubrey had just handed me was my prime suspect.

"Thanks for your time," I said. "I appreciate you answering all of my questions— and the history lesson."

He smiled. "You're most welcome. I find so few people who care about weapons as I do. Come back anytime."

I studied his face. Any hint of flirtation had been wiped away. I grinned back at him. "I may just do that."

Vas waited until we were standing next to my car before

he arched one eyebrow. "Samael's probably going to have a stroke if he finds you with that blade."

I stroked it. "My precious," I whispered. Samael could pry it out of my cold, dead hands.

Vas rolled his eyes. "Where to now?"

"Home. It's late, and the kids will be sleeping soon. I'll talk to them in the morning. I think they saw something that can lead us to whoever is behind these thefts."

CHAPTER EIGHTEEN

DANICA

The kids were sweaty and grinning when I arrived the next morning. I raised my eyebrow at Samael and he shrugged. "They played basketball with Bael and Sitri."

Cil pumped his fist in the air. "And we beat them!"

Evie sent me an amused look from across the room. She looked fresh and pretty in a floaty white skirt and turquoise tank top, and she grinned at me as I came to terms with the thought of the demons playing basketball. With lesser fae kids. And letting them win. Wow. I glanced at where Bael was leaning against the window, and he raised his eyebrow at me, face blank.

I turned back to Cil and Zip. "Okay guys, I need you to help me out here. When you were hiding from the man who hurt your dad, the man was talking to him, right?"

Both boys nodded, all excitement draining from their faces. I was an asshole for ruining their good moods, but it had to be done.

"I need you to tell me anything you can remember that the man said."

Cil shivered. Evie reached out

an arm and cuddled him close. She hated seeing anyone hurting, especially if she could do something about it.

Samael cleared his throat. "I have a suggestion."

The boys blinked up at him, their wide eyes reminding me of baby owls. There was more than a little hero worship going on and it was cute as hell.

"There is a spell that can allow us to hear what happened that day."

I opened my mouth to refuse, and he gave me a quelling glance. "It isn't painful and there will be no ill-effects. But my witch is well versed in getting information that would otherwise be lost."

For a moment I thought he was talking about me. But no, he was talking about Gloria, the witch who he kept on retainer for all the times he needed witch magic. He used that spell for torture.

I slowly got to my feet. "A word."

He gave the boys a quick, charming grin, and walked with me to the corner of the room. His hand raised briefly, and a dull pop hit my ears.

"What was that?"

"A silence ward. Gnome children have exceptional hearing."

"I don't want your witch to terrify the kids."

His nostrils flared almost imperceptibly. Had I offended him? "Give me some credit," he bit out, and I narrowed my eyes at him.

"Tell me you don't use Gloria for torture."

He gave me a patient look. "Of course I use her for torture. She feeds on pain and suffering, and I sometimes need information that people are reluctant to share."

Ask a stupid question.

"Okay. Tell me she's not going to do anything that will scare them."

"She won't. I will watch her carefully, and she knows not to cross me, no matter how delicious she finds the terror of children."

I scowled. He was fucking with me now. He smiled and reached out slowly, giving me enough time to knock his hand away if I wanted to.

I allowed his touch, and he tucked a strand of hair behind my ear. "I miss you," he murmured.

"What do you mean? I'm right here."

"I miss the sight of you in my bed. The feel of your skin against mine. The noise you make when I–"

"Samael!" I shot a look over my shoulder. Evie was stretched out on the couch, but she gave me a knowing smirk as my face turned red.

"So recalcitrant when it comes to admitting that you want me too. Do you never get tired of fighting this thing between us?"

All the time. "I'm not talking about this now."

He lifted his hand and magic tinged my skin as he broke his ward. "If you have your way, you'll never speak of it," he said. "I've called the witch. She is on her way."

"How did you call her?"

He gave me a look and I swallowed. He could speak in her head. Could he speak in mine?

Of course I can, he said, and I jumped, backing away. On the sofa, the kids turned, watching me curiously.

Did you just read my mind?

Your face, witchling. I choose not to speak to you this way because I know you loathe any intimacy between us.

I swallowed. He was right. It *was* intimate.

Good. Keep it that way.

I turned my back on him, ignoring his low laugh, and narrowed my eyes as Gloria walked in.

Samael's hand stroked along my lower back as he walked past, and I attempted to ignore what his possessive touch did to my stomach.

"I heard you have need of a spell," she said, smiling at the boys.

Gloria had to be in her seventies or eighties, but she walked with a spring in her step. Her gray, curly hair was braided back from her face, and she wore a gray pantsuit and sensible heels. Gloria was a black witch, and her power crawled through the room, raising the hair on the back of my neck.

I hadn't liked her when I found out Samael had allowed her near my unconscious body— I hadn't much liked him either— and I still didn't like her. Unlike Hannah— another black witch who'd helped me in the past— there was something about Gloria that rubbed me the wrong way. While Hannah made no secret of the fact that she was a black witch, Gloria had the innocent old lady act down.

She smiled at me and I bared my teeth. If she hurt the kids, scared them in any way, she was dead. My power felt like an ocean of lava as it lapped against my shields, and Samael sent me a warning look.

I walked over to the sofa and sat next to Zip. He grinned

at me, shooting Gloria a suspicious look. Cil eyed her with interest.

"Which one of you boys is the bravest?" she asked, and I scowled at her. I opened my mouth, but Evie was on it.

"They're both brave. They stayed silent while someone was attacking their dad because they knew he wanted them to be safe."

Gloria ignored Evie, her gaze on the kids. I turned to them and attempted an encouraging smile.

"Did Evie explain how the spell works?"

They both nodded. "Okay, great. You don't have to do this, and no one will be disappointed if you choose not to."

"Will it help you find out who hurt our dad?" Zip asked.

"It might. But he wouldn't want you to do anything that makes you scared, and we have plenty of other ways we can investigate, okay?"

"I'll do it," Cil said. "I'm not afraid."

He *was* afraid. His little body trembled, and Evie reached out and grabbed hold of his hand. He held on so hard his knuckles went white. To Gloria's credit, she didn't appear to be feeding on his terror, and I shot her a look that told her clearly that if she attempted to, it would be the last thing she did.

She rolled her eyes at me and knelt next to the long wooden coffee table, her knees creaking. She pulled a candle out of her purse, along with a few herbs I couldn't identify. Samael was watching her intently, and my eyes met his for a single moment. He leaned against the wall and raised one eyebrow. I either trusted him to make sure the kids were safe or I didn't.

I chewed on my lip. His eyes darkened, his gaze falling to my mouth, and I turned my attention back to where Gloria was chanting.

She reached out one hand, holding it against Cil's forehead. He stiffened, his eyes rolling back in his head, and my hand tightened around the hilt of my throwing knife. I hadn't remembered pulling it.

"If you kill her, you will regret it."

I scowled at Samael. *"Stay out of my head. Also, is that a threat?"*

"A fact. You could kill her in the blink of an eye, but you would traumatize the children and terrify your sister. And you would feel bad about killing an old woman for the rest of your life."

"You think you know me. You don't. Don't speak to me this way again."

"I find I enjoy speaking to you like this," Samael smiled at me from across the room. He'd found another way to get under my skin, and knowing him, he'd use it ruthlessly. I turned my attention back to Gloria, who was murmuring an incantation. Samael was right. I didn't *want* to kill the witch. Black witch or not, she was still human, and an old woman. But he was wrong about me carrying it with me for the rest of my life. I had too many other regrets that pressed on me. This one would barely add to the load.

Cil made a strangled noise and Zip turned white.

"I don't have what you're looking for. Get out of my store." Gary's voice came from Cil's mouth and I shuddered.

"Stupid gnome. Did you think you could hide it from us?" The voice was deep, trembling with borrowed power, but it sounded familiar in a way that scratched at my memories. I'd heard it before. I knew I had. Frustration roared through me. Was it someone I'd met recently? A cop? One of the mages?

"I don't know what you're talking about." Gary sounded legitimately confused. Whatever he'd had, he hadn't expected anyone to come after it.

"See these?"

The sound of retching. Something the guy had been holding had made Gary sick to look at it.

"What the fuck are those?"

"Werewolf eyes. You know what that means? I can *see* that the artifact has been here. Hand it over, and I'll kill you quick."

"You're out of your damn mind. Get out." Gary's voice trembled. It wouldn't be perceptible to most people, but I knew him. He'd been afraid. My hands fisted.

"Your choice. I'll kill you, destroy this sad excuse for a store and take it from you."

Gary growled, but the sounds he was making quickly turned into screams. A pained moan escaped Cil's throat, and I shot to my feet.

"End it. Now."

Gloria didn't argue. Cil jolted and his eyes lost their distance. I crouched in front of him.

"You were very brave. I'm sorry you had to hear that again. Is there anything else you guys want to tell me?"

Cil glanced at Zip and then back at me. Then he shook his head. I sighed. The kids knew something else, but they weren't saying. All I could do was give them time and keep asking.

"What will you do now?" Evie's voice was low as I got to my feet. Samael was by the door, murmuring to Bael, who'd entered at some point while Cil was under Gloria's spell. The witch packed up the last of her things and left without another word.

"If what that guy said is true, the werewolf alpha has a dead werewolf on his hands, and that werewolf is missing his eyes." The wolves had their own morgue and prosecuted their own crimes. "I need to talk to him and see if that werewolf can lead us to his murderers."

Evie got to her feet. "I'm going with you."

I frowned. "I thought you'd want to stay with the kids."

Evie shrugged. "I have to go. I can't explain why, but I just have a feeling."

We'd both been raised not to ignore our gut instincts. "Okay."

Samael finished up his conversation with Bael and stalked over to me. He leaned close while Evie packed up her things, his breath warm on the shell of my ear. I shivered.

"When you speak to the alpha, remember how it felt when I was deep inside you, bounty hunter."

Bounty hunter. He was pissed. Pissed and… jealous? I eyed him.

"Don't be gross, dude. Do we need to have an awkward conversation?"

He merely reached for my hand. I allowed it, until he had the audacity to run his hands over the gold mark his bond had etched into my skin. I stiffened and yanked my hand back, giving him my death glare.

Unsurprisingly, he didn't curl up in a ball and beg for mercy. He simply gave me a long look. "Remember who you belong to."

I opened my mouth but he was already walking away.

DANICA

"Remember who you belong to," my sister made her voice low and gruff. Then she gave an exaggerated full-body shiver. "Now, that was sexy."

I took my eyes off the road long enough to glower at her. We were driving toward werewolf territory, and she'd been teasing me the entire time.

"It's not sexy. He says shit like that because he knows it annoys the hell out of me. It's a game he plays."

She tutted. "If you think that's a *game*, you're crazy."

I shook my head and took the turnoff toward Duke Forest. The wolves lived less than fifteen minutes from downtown, but out here, it was like a whole different world. A howl echoed through the forest as we got closer to Nathaniel's house, and Evie shot me a wide-eyed look.

"That'll be a sentry. Last time I visited, Nathaniel knew I was on the way. I'm surprising him this time."

"Of course. Because why wouldn't you surprise the territorial, paranoid, deeply distrustful werewolves? Sounds like a good plan."

"You know the rules. Try not to meet their eyes if you can help it. Sometimes, you need to make it clear they can't push you around, but there's no point playing power games if we're hoping for cooperation."

"And what do you do if they decide to play power games?"

I shrugged. "I've visited before. Nathaniel knows I'm not a threat."

I cursed as a werewolf dropped out of the sky and onto the hood of my car. My foot fumbled for the brake and Evie let out a yelp as the car slid. I wrestled with the steering wheel, my heart pounding like a drum, and we finally came to a stop.

I stared at the werewolf. He stared back at me. Movement out the corner of my eye drew my attention and I gaped at my sister as she popped a magazine into the Glock in her hand and aimed at the wolf.

"Where the fuck were you hiding that?"

"In a thigh holster under my skirt."

"Since when do you carry?"

Her lips curled, although she kept her attention on the werewolf. "There's a lot you don't know about me."

"We're going to talk about this."

"Yeah, yeah."

Jesus. It was like talking to a more stubborn version of myself.

I returned my attention to the man currently crouched in front of us. He'd landed lightly on my hood, legs spread, arms crossed, face hard.

"I think he wants us to get out," I said.

Evie snorted. "You think?"

My guns were in my safe in the trunk, but I wasn't planning on needing them. I just had to refrain from making any fast movements near the pissed-off werewolf.

"Stay in the car," I said.

I palmed my Mark II and slowly opened the door.

On the other side, Evie opened her door and got out. Because of course she did.

The werewolf jumped off my Toyota and I scowled at him.

"That was unnecessary," I said. He just stared at me, and I reached for patience. "I need to talk to Nathaniel. It's important. One of his cases may be related to one of mine."

He pulled a phone from his pocket, muttered a few words, and nodded.

"Drive toward Nathaniel's. Don't veer off-course unless you want to die."

I nodded and glanced at Evie. Her face was hard, her gun still aimed at the werewolf. He ignored it and stepped back, his eyes glowing yellow as he watched us. I got in the car and Evie did the same, her face pale.

I cleared my throat. "Sorry about that," I said. "I guess I should've made an appointment after all."

She tucked her Glock away under her floaty skirt and burst out laughing. "I guess so."

Nathaniel had been the alpha of the Triangle's werewolf pack since the portals first opened. He'd managed to gain control of his wolf after the shock of transforming, and had forced the other wolves to fall in line. He lived down the end of a cul-de-sac, in a ranch-style house with floor-to-ceiling windows. His home seemed to melt into the forest around it, and Evie let out a low whistle as we parked.

"This place is huge."

"I guess it has to be since the pack is so big."

Tobias opened the door as we walked toward it. Like last time I visited, he was wearing a suit.

"Ms. Amana," he said. "It's nice to see you. However next time, you may want to–"

"Make an appointment? Yeah, I got that. Why are you guys so jumpy?"

He clammed up and gestured for us to walk into the sitting room off the entranceway. Nathaniel was already waiting, and he didn't look pleased.

The ice-blue color of Nathaniel's eyes warned me that his wolf was close to the surface. I dropped my gaze, hoping my sister knew to do the same. Last time I was here, I'd used my power to keep myself from succumbing to his dominance, but something told me that Nathaniel wasn't in the mood to play. I'd get more cooperation if I treaded carefully.

I studied Nathaniel's face. His gaze had left me, and he was staring at my sister. There was something in his eyes that I didn't like.

He got to his feet. "Ms. Amana. And who is this?"

"My sister, Evelyn," I said.

Nathaniel took a step closer, and I stiffened. He seemed to catch himself and stood eerily still, his attention on Evie's face.

"Look at me," he demanded, and his dominance spread through the room.

Evie had listened to my instructions on the drive here, and her gaze was glued to the floor. She didn't have a hope against the demand in Nathaniel's voice though, and her gaze jumped to his. My hand wandered toward my lanyard, but I forced myself to relax as Evie stared at the alpha.

He wasn't hurting her. But something was going on.

"It's nice to meet you," he purred, and a faint blush hit Evie's cheekbones. She shivered, and Nathaniel took a step closer to her.

I was distantly aware of another werewolf entering the room, but when Nathaniel decided to tamp into whatever power made him dominant enough to hold a pack of werewolves, I didn't have a hope of pulling my attention away unless I reached for my own power.

I managed to clear my throat. Nathaniel continued to gaze at Evie in apparent fascination for one more moment before he turned his attention to me.

"Ms. Amana," he started, and the werewolf next to him let out a strangled sound. We all looked at him, but he was focused on Evie.

"Evelyn?"

Her mouth dropped open. "Liam?"

They stared at each other, and then the werewolf moved toward her, wrapping her in a hug. He was obviously dominant enough to be able to move while Nathaniel's displeasure radiated throughout the room.

Liam was taller than my sister and lanky for a werewolf. He had green eyes which were currently lit with joy, and a sprinkle of freckles across his face. From the look of his wide shoulders, he was still growing, and when he filled out, he'd be a force to be reckoned with.

"What the hell are you doing here?" Liam asked.

Evie grinned. "Um, shouldn't I be the one asking you that?"

Nathaniel turned and sat back down, closing his eyes. I'd seen him do this before, and I was unsure whether he was counting to a hundred or attempting some kind of werewolf meditation.

Evie turned to me. "Liam went to my high school," she said. "We were close for a few years, and then he moved away." Her face shuttered and my heart ached for her. Story of Evie's life. People loved her, but they always left.

Nathaniel let out a low growl. He kept his eyes closed and my eyes met Liam's.

"We can smell emotions," he said, with a quick glance at his alpha. Then he turned back to Evie. "I'm sorry I left."

She attempted a smile. "Don't be silly. Your parents moved away. But how did you end up back here?"

Liam swallowed. "A feral wolf broke into our house and killed my parents. I survived. I guess I had the right DNA or gene or whatever, because a few days later, I woke up furry. A neighbor came to visit and peered in the window. They called the local pack."

Evie choked out a gasp. "I'm so sorry."

"Thanks. It's been a rough ride, but Nathaniel has helped. I was too dominant to join the pack in Florida— where my parents had moved. Their alpha had been killed and there was too much infighting. Someone told me to come here, and Nathaniel helped me control my wolf. The first few years were... hard."

I shifted on my feet. Werewolf dominance didn't always go the way human dominance did. I'd seen guys who blushed if you looked at them turn into powerhouses who became alphas once they were turned. Liam seemed cute and a little nerdy. But for him to be too dominant to join the Florida pack, he was likely high up in the hierarchy.

I watched Nathaniel. His eyes were open, and they'd darkened to his usual color. His face was blank.

"Take a seat," he murmured, and Evie automatically moved toward the sofa.

Liam let out a low growl, and Evie jumped. Strangely, she didn't jump toward me. She skittered toward Nathaniel, who had his eyes on Liam.

"Control your wolf or leave," he said. Liam closed his eyes and took a deep breath.

"Apologies. My wolf doesn't like it when you tell Evie what to do."

"Your wolf forgets who is in charge here," Nathaniel said silkily.

Last time I was here, I'd thought Nathaniel was a giant dick on a power trip. After witnessing one of his wolves teeter on the edge of control... and seeing the look in his eyes when he regarded me as a snack— and not the *cute* kind of snack, I understood the werewolf alpha much better.

Evie, however, did not. She narrowed her eyes at Nathaniel and he stiffened.

Disgust has a scent, he'd told me last time.

And we were way off course.

I stalked over to the sofa and took a seat, gesturing for Evie to do the same. Liam smiled at Evie. "Let's hang out soon," he said.

"Sure."

He turned and walked away. I glanced at Nathaniel and he nodded at me. "Liam has enough control that he has full freedom of his movements. He isn't bound to this house. Now, why don't you tell me why you arrived with no warning?"

I flushed. "I'm sorry. I was hoping to talk to you about a

case that might involve one of your werewolves."

"Which case?"

I explained what had happened to Gary. When I got to the part where Cil talked about the werewolf eyes, Nathaniel stiffened. He slowly got to his feet, fury emanating from him. I'd spent enough time with Samael that I was getting used to enraged, powerful, dominant males, but Evie stiffened, her hand drifting toward the bottom of her skirt.

If she thought she could flip that up and pull her Glock before a werewolf could leap, she was dreaming. I made a mental note to give her some speed drills later.

Nathaniel collected himself and his voice was gentle as he addressed my sister.

"Forgive me," he said. "I did not mean to scare you."

She swallowed and nodded. They stared at each other for a fraught moment and then Nathaniel turned to me. "Please follow me."

He led us back out the front of the house and gestured for us to get into the black SUV in the driveway. The back of my neck itched. The werewolves were clearly keeping a close eye on us while we were with their alpha.

I sat in the front. It was only a few days until the full moon, and I had a feeling Nathaniel would find it more difficult to control his wolf if he knew I was heavily armed and sitting behind him. The flicker of gratitude in the alpha's eyes told me he appreciated it.

Nathaniel was famed for his control. He'd managed to clean up the Triangle and stop a pack of rampaging werewolves within a couple of weeks. But something was making it difficult for him to keep that control.

We drove deeper into the forest, passing the occasional house. Most of the pack lived out here, and I gawked at the huge homes.

"Wow," I said.

"Werewolves like a lot of space," Nathaniel murmured.

"It's beautiful out here," Evie said, gazing out the window. Nathaniel gave her a hint of a smile in the rearview mirror. Then his face went blank as we rounded a corner, and a steel building came into view.

Evie was pale as we got out of the car. "This is our morgue," Nathaniel said. "Would you like to stay in the car?"

She shook her head, and he didn't linger on the subject, leading us through the front doors. The woman working at the front desk nodded at him and he nodded back, taking us through double doors.

His nostrils flared and I shuddered. I could already smell far too much. This place must be hell with a werewolf's nose.

The corridor we entered was white. White walls, white floor, and steel doors. Nathaniel stopped at the first door and raised his hand to the ward. It briefly glowed green, and the door swung open.

I shivered as we stepped into the temperature-controlled room. The smell of morgues always made my stomach roil—antiseptic and the sickly-sweet scent of death. I glanced at Evie. Her face was ashen, but she narrowed her eyes at me. She'd followed her intuition here, and she was determined to see it through.

Fair enough.

Nathaniel stalked over to a long row of metal coolers and opened one of the doors. The body slid out, and a muscle ticked in his jaw as he gazed down at one of his wolves.

"The eyes are missing," I stated the obvious, and Nathaniel nodded. He kept his gaze on the wolf for a long moment. I leaned closer, examining the body. No obvious sign of injury. What the hell could take down a werewolf so easily?

"Cause of death?"

"We're still unsure. My coroners have reached out to a forensic technician from a pack in New York. She's agreed to travel here to take a look. So far, cause of death is heart failure."

Werewolves didn't have heart attacks. Nathaniel's eyes were a winter's frost, and I shifted my attention back down to the body.

"I know someone who's good with stuff like this."

He stayed silent and I sighed. "She was able to find a suppression spell on my magic, and she helped me narrow down my suspects in the demon murders."

"Fine. Call her."

I ground my teeth. Evie reached over and squeezed my arm, and then she stared at the alpha.

"Call her, please," Evie said.

Nathaniel's eyes darkened, and his face lost some of its rage. "I apologize," he said solemnly, his gaze on her face. Then he turned back to me. "I would very much appreciate if you could call your contact. Please."

Evie looked away, her face turning pink.

I raised one eyebrow but pulled my phone from my

pocket. "Selina? Hi. I was wondering if you could do me a favor. The wolves are looking for someone of your skillset." I smiled at Nathaniel. "They've got money to spend, and they need answers."

Amusement flickered across his face, but he nodded.

I lifted the phone away from my face. "She says she can come out tomorrow and take a look. Does that work for you?"

He nodded. I thanked Selina and hung up.

"I need to ask you a question."

He nodded again. I shifted on my feet. "Could cutting out a werewolf's eyes allow someone to see where a fae artifact has been?"

His eyes turned so light they were almost white. Evie and I both froze, and I dropped my eyes, waiting as he got his shit together. He let out a low growl.

"Yes," he said hoarsely. "The myths are correct, at least in that. But it would require a black witch with knowledge of the most ancient spells on this earth."

"How long would it last for?"

"Until the eyes decomposed enough that they were no longer usable."

I winced. We both knew that there were plenty of ways— both magical and non-magical— to keep the eyes from decomposing.

CHAPTER NINETEEN

DANICA

I dropped Evie at home and sat in my car outside the coven's house for a few minutes as I pulled up my notes. I needed to look into the amulet. According to the email Mariam had sent me, the amulet had disappeared from the light fae realm. I had no plans to visit that realm unless I absolutely had to, especially since she couldn't even pin down when it had gone missing.

I lifted my head as movement darted across my peripheral vision. Evie was striding down the porch steps. I wound down my window.

"Where are you going?"

Evie narrowed her eyes at me. "What are you still doing here?"

"Reading my notes. What's going on, Evie?"

She bared her teeth. "I have revenge to accomplish. And then I need to do some laundry and head back to the tower." She was holding something in her hands, and I leaned over and pushed the passenger door open.

"You want some help?"

"I don't need help, but you can come for the show."

I was officially intrigued.

"Where are we going?"

She buckled up and gave me directions. The target of her wrath was just a few minutes away in Walltown.

"Who are you gunning for?"

She sniffed. "His name is Vic. He's a human. We had a thing all winter, and then a few months ago we had the 'where is this going' talk. We agreed to be exclusive."

Uh-oh. "And he wasn't exclusive."

"No. He's been cheating on me with a light fae girl. I confronted her and she had no clue who I was. She was *pissed*. So we created a little something to make him regret messing with us. I have to video the whole thing for her cause she's out of town." She slid me a look. "You can be the videographer."

"Um. What did you create?"

She held up the bag. "You'll see."

This wouldn't be good.

I pulled up outside the house. "No, park further down," she hissed. "We'll need a quick getaway."

"How are you planning to stay hidden, exactly?"

"I've been practicing a bastardized look-away spell. It'll only hold for a few minutes, but that's all we need."

I drove further down the street and we hopped out of the car. Evie's delicate face was hard with determination, and I almost laughed. It was the same expression she'd made when learning to ride her bike, standing up to bullies at school, and learning magic well beyond her years. Vic didn't stand a chance.

Evie turned toward his house, and I tensed as she gave another wet sniff. Beneath her fury was a deep hurt.

"You want me to beat him up?"

"No. This is better."

"Uh… you're not gonna kill him, right? Cause if so, we should probably wait until dark, and I'll need to put my tarp back in my trunk."

She sent me a withering look. "I'm not going to kill him. I'm just going to humiliate him a little. Maybe I'll send our little video to his friends."

Alrighty then.

Once we were within a few feet of his neighbor's house. Evie held up her hand and squinted in concentration. The dull pop told me the spell had taken effect.

I frowned. "Why am I going to a black witch when you can do this shit?"

She trembled, already panting as she held the spell in place. "I can only do it for a few minutes. And we'll talk about the black witch later."

She crept forward and I trailed after her until she was standing on his porch steps and I was waiting below her, phone held up and ready to record.

She opened the bag and showed it to me. I frowned at her, disappointed.

"A spring-loaded dick bomb? That's weak, Evie."

She smiled at me. "Just wait." She murmured a few words and the shape of the package changed, until it appeared to be nothing more than a small box.

It took power to mask an object like this. My sister was wasted on spells for her coven and pranks against her exes.

Evie turned, placed the package on the doorstep, and knocked on the door. Footsteps sounded, and I raised the phone.

The guy who answered was tall and lean, with shrewd gray eyes and the beginning of a five-o'clock shadow. His t-shirt clung to wide shoulders, and he had a surprisingly lush mouth. I could see why my sister had fallen for him.

Evie slowly backed down the porch steps as he leaned down and picked up the box.

I shook my head. Picking up an unmarked box was a good way to end up dead. The guy was clearly not just an asshole, he was also an idiot.

Evie stood next to me, her eyes narrowed as we both waited. Vic cast a glance around his front yard and shrugged. Then he opened the box.

Tiny, glittery cocks flew at him. A smile played around Evie's mouth as they grew larger until they were at least a couple of inches tall, and I gaped as they formed tiny mouths and sharp stingers. They hovered in the air for one long moment. Just long enough for realization to dart across Vic's face.

Then they attacked.

He screamed, swatting at them as they bit and stung. I looked at Evie and her smile widened as she met my eyes.

"Just enough to hurt, but not enough to leave a lasting mark," she whispered. "He's not worth ending up in front of the Mage Council."

We darted out of the way as Vic stumbled down the porch steps, waving his hands and yelling like a crazy person. His voice turned high-pitched, and I raised my eyebrow. Some of the glittery dicks had honed in on the bulge in his jeans, and he was smacking at them with one hand and attempting to keep them off his face with another.

I couldn't help it. I burst out laughing.

Vic must've heard me, because he froze, and then let out another squeal. This time, Evie chuckled.

"Evie, you bitch! I know this was you!"

We both froze. Evie waved her hand, and the dicks seemed to attack with a new determination. Vic let out a hoarse growl, but instead of running into his house, he ran down the street. Huh.

Evie grinned and the spell faded. We hustled back toward my car before anyone could identify us.

"I bet he's running to his friend a few blocks away," Evie said. "He's a low-level mage, but there's no way he'll be able to break my spell."

A low-level mage, huh? "What's his name?"

"Ben."

I grinned. "Any chance they'll attack him, too?"

"Nope." Evie studied my face. "You know, I'd be happy to repeat this little experiment."

"Don't tempt me."

A sharp scream came from down the street, and I threw my arm around my sister's shoulders.

"Feel better?"

"You know what? I do. Any man who can scream in that pitch isn't the man for me."

I laughed. "How long will they follow him for?"

"The spell will wear off in the next few minutes."

I dropped Evie back at her house and headed toward my apartment. I was halfway there when Steve called. I put my phone on speaker.

"I got a ping off that phone number you had me flag.

She's back in town."

My pulse began to race. "Thanks Steve."

Harriette had been a friend of my mom's. The light fae had warned me that she was going out of town for a few weeks, but she'd been gone for over six. The last time we'd spoken, she'd told me that my mom had left some things with her, and she had information for me.

Now that I knew what I was, I had more than a few questions for Harriette.

Steve had messaged me her address, and I headed toward Hope Valley. Halfway there, I got stuck in traffic, my car crawling toward the intersection.

Vas dropped down from the sky, hands on his hips. He ambled toward me, as if he had all the time in the world. The lights in the intersection turned green and the guy in the Tesla behind me laid on the horn.

Vas merely shifted his gaze behind me, and the Tesla ducked out of the line and took off.

Demons.

He opened the passenger door. I'd thought he'd just stick his head inside, but he folded his entire body into the cramped space. One of his wings whacked me in the cheek and I scowled at him.

He raised one eyebrow. "Hey, you think this is comfortable for me?"

"What are you doing in my car?"

"Thought you were going home, partner. This isn't the way to your apartment. Also, I liked the dick thing. Your sister is scary, you know that right?"

I sighed. Of course, he'd seen that. I drove through the

intersection as the light turned green once more.

"You remember that woman who was outside the tower before Ramiel attacked me?"

His expression turned somber, and he nodded. "You said she was a friend of your mom's."

"Yeah. She's been out of town ever since, and now she's finally back. She said she's got some information for me."

I turned onto Lakewood Ave, feeling Vas' eyes on me. "What?"

"I thought you didn't care who your father was."

"I didn't. Then I learned I was a demon." I scowled.

He nodded. "So now you want to know who he was?"

"I'm a freak, Vas. Demons don't have babies with human women. Or witches."

He sent me a slow smile. "Times are a-changing, Dani."

"Don't call me Dani. There was no dating app for paranormals in my mom's day. Whoever my father was, he got her knocked up and left her with the responsibility of raising a half-demon, half-witch kid."

I pulled up outside Harriette's stately home. At the sight of the white stucco walls, my memories began to trickle into my mind, piling on top of each other. I remembered walking up this path right after mom had taken me from my sister. She hadn't trusted me alone in the car in my distraught, defiant mood.

"Do you want me to come with you?"

I shrugged. "I don't mind. Just... please don't tell anyone what we talk about."

"I won't."

Harriette opened the door as soon as I knocked.

"Danica. What a surprise. And this is?"

"This is my friend Vas."

Harriette had a strange fear of demons, given that she must've come into contact with them numerous times over her long life. She gave Vas a tight smile and he nodded gravely back at her.

"You mentioned that you had some information for me."

"I did. But listen, I just got into town–"

"I know what I am."

She froze. "How?"

"Did you think I could be bonded to a demon and not find out?"

"I suppose that makes sense." She heaved a sigh. "Come in, then."

Harriette's house smelled a little musty, and she'd thrown open the windows. She was obviously using her magic, because while the fresh air streamed in, there was none of the heat that had made sweat dampen my hairline all day.

Stained glass windows attracted the light, throwing rainbows onto the marble floors. We followed Harriette into a sitting room off the main entrance and she gestured for us to take a seat on her white sectional. Vas appeared to make himself at home, arranging his wings while I took in the high ceilings with exposed beams and let my gaze drift to the stone fireplace.

It had been winter when we left. I'd sat in front of that fireplace, staring into the flames while my mom murmured to Harriette, hiccupping out the occasional sob.

"Wait right here," Harriette instructed. She returned a few minutes later with a tray of cookies and three steaming cups of coffee.

"I wasn't sure if you preferred coffee or tea."

"Coffee, definitely," I said. I reached for the coffee just as Vas reached for his, and his arm knocked into mine. "Shit."

The coffee spilled, arching toward the cream sofa. It was as if time rewound as the liquid froze in the air, then streamed back into the cup.

I hadn't done that for a while. And my shields had been up. Selina would be proud. I glanced at Harriette. She gave me a watery smile. "Your magic is so much like your mother's, you know. All instinct. Your witch magic, anyway."

Vas leaned back on the sofa, his cup in his hand.

I sighed. "I know you placed the suppression spell on me, Harriette."

Her eyes widened. "And what makes you think that?"

I hadn't been sure, but the cagey look on her face confirmed it. "Light fae can sometimes suppress demon magic. You're the only one with motive and the only light fae I remember being around when I was a kid."

"I wasn't powerful enough to do it alone," she said quietly. "I had to ask a friend to help."

I stared her down. "Why?"

"There are many reasons why children of your blood are dangerous. One of them is the power swings that occur, especially during puberty. Your mom had no one to help her. She was going on the run. It was the best solution."

I sneered. "My power was suppressed when I was too young to remember it. She didn't know she would have to run then."

Betrayal. It was betrayal that was creeping up my throat and choking me. My mom had left me powerless in a world where power meant safety.

Harriette heaved a long-suffering sigh. "She always knew she'd have to run at some point."

"And you never helped her? Instead, you magically neutered me! It wasn't just demon power that you suppressed— I couldn't access witch magic either. I couldn't even set a fucking ward."

"You could set a ward. You just needed to use your blood."

"And how would I know to do that?" I asked through my teeth.

"We both know you weren't interested in using your power."

"Because I had none to use!"

She laughed. "Would you truly have used your power as an adult? You loathed the witches with every fiber of your being."

If she knew that, she'd been watching me more closely than she'd wanted me to know.

"I loathe the witches because when my mother ran to them for help, they convinced her to leave my sister with them and take me on the run. That coven was one of the most powerful in Durham and they left her alone. And yes, if I'd known I had enough magic to keep me alive, I would've used it."

She merely raised one eyebrow. I put my coffee back on the tray so I wasn't tempted to throw it at her. "At the expense of becoming over-reliant on it? On never learning the skills you needed from Edward?"

I went still. "How do you know about Edward?"

She smiled. "Who do you think told your mother to take you to him?"

Great. She told my mother which direction to head in while she was obviously fleeing for her life. Good for her.

"Who is my father?"

"Nothing good can come of this, Danica."

"Who?"

"He was a high demon who was in the underking's inner circle. He was immediately entranced by your mother and they had an affair."

"What happened to him?"

Harriette shrugged. "He went missing. Your mom insisted he never would've left her, but it sure looked like he decided the responsibility of a baby was too much for him. Your mom was… fragile at that point. She'd had two relationships that had… imploded, and two little girls who were… different. She was all alone in a world where being alone made you a target."

"Why did she have to run?"

"You're a Nephilim."

I frowned and she clarified. "A child that is half demon, half human. Although in your case, you had the added benefit of being witchborn. It was forbidden to create such a child. It still is. When your father found out your mother was pregnant, he warned her that his enemies would eventually come for her and would try to kill the baby. She told me they were planning to leave together. Instead, he left and never returned."

"So when we left… it was because she was worried that someone connected to my father was coming for her?"

She lifted one shoulder again. Beside me, Vas was very still, but the way he held his head told me he had his listening ears on.

"She never told me. She was inconsolable, Danica. We'd been friends for years and she told me she needed my help and I couldn't ask questions."

I tried to put myself in my mom's shoes. Tried and failed. "Why leave Evie?"

"She said it was for your sister's own good. For her safety. She loved both of you girls more than birds love the sky. I can tell you now that leaving her baby behind… it nearly killed your mother. She became a shadow of herself the moment she realized she needed to run."

Harriette reached for her cup. "If you like, I can find a way to redo the suppression spell."

Vas snarled. Harriette's eyes went wide as he leaned forward. "Just fucking try, seelie."

I gaped at him. He let out a low growl at whatever he saw on my face. "Don't let them tell you you're broken, Danica."

I smiled. "You're a good friend, Vas." Then I turned back to Harriette. "No thank you."

She wasn't surprised by my answer. She simply gave me a nod. Then, with a wary glance at Vas, she got to her feet and hurried out of the room with a muttered "be right back."

"You wanna tell me what that was about?"

Vas sipped his coffee as if nothing had happened. "She never would've told you what she did, you know that right?"

I nodded. "I could've killed someone. If I hadn't met Samael, and then Selina, I probably would have some day when the spell failed. And it probably would've been someone I cared about. I can maybe understand suppressing my magic as a child. But to never tell me about it… to never give me a choice as an adult…"

"They stole that from you."

"Yeah. And now I have all this power that I can barely control."

We both went silent as Harriette's footsteps on the wooden floorboards warned us she was entering the room. She held a small, mother-of-pearl box in her hands and she set it on the table in front of me.

"Your mom ran with little more than the clothes on her back. She asked me to keep a few things for you girls… in case she didn't make it."

Frustration roared up from deep within my soul. Mom had known there was a high chance she would die. Why had she left Durham? And why had she come back? What would make her risk returning to the same place she'd fled?

I ran one finger over the lid of the box, imagining my mother doing the same. "Evie should be here for this."

Harriette smiled at me and sat back down on the sofa. She'd regained her composure when she left the room and was now choosing to pretend Vas didn't exist. The demon stretched out his long legs and watched us both.

"I'm sure she won't mind," he said gruffly. "Maybe you could keep a few things for her."

I nodded. Evie and I continued to dance around the subject of our mother. While she seemed willing to pretend the past between us didn't exist, I had my doubts about whether she would ever forgive our mom for leaving her behind.

Truthfully, I couldn't blame her.

I opened the box. Mom had worked for the coven, selling a few of her more powerful spells on the side when the coven didn't need them. She'd created charms, but we'd never had much money to spare. Her jewelry was mostly costume, but she'd worn it with pride.

"I'd forgotten she loved these earrings."

They were a simple design. Four glass beads hung in various shades of blue. Evie had made them during the brief period she'd become obsessed with jewelry making. Gemma had worked on them with her, and mom had worn them almost every day. I put them aside for my sister.

It hurt, seeing these things. They reminded me of a safe childhood when mom had kept her jewelry box beside her bed and occasionally let us play dress-up. There was the necklace she wore each Christmas, with matching Christmas tree earrings she insisted were cute. There was the silver bracelet she'd worn as a baby, tarnished now, and still sized for a child's wrist. There was her grandmother's wedding ring, which Evie and I had fought over each time we'd played dress-up. Water dripped into the box, and I frowned, swiping at my face. I hadn't realized I was crying.

I froze as I stared down at two pairs of tiny diamond

studs.

"When did she buy these?"

Harriette shrugged. "I don't know. I get the feeling she meant to take them with her. We spoke once after she left, and she asked me to make sure they were safe."

I reached for one of the studs. Mom had charmed them. Without any contact with human skin, the charm hadn't faded, so it had lasted all these years. I could *feel* her. Feel the love she had for us, the spell of protection she'd wound carefully into each earring.

I popped one of them out and shoved it into my earlobe. I hadn't worn earrings for a while, and I winced as I pushed the posts through the holes that always wanted to heal back up.

I'd take the other pair to Evie. No matter how deep her hurt ran, it was evident in these earrings that mom had loved us both equally. The spells were exactly the same, infused with a mother's need to protect.

I haven't forgotten about you, Mom. I'm going to find who killed you. And I'll make them pay.

CHAPTER TWENTY

DANICA

As soon as someone knocked on my door the next morning, I threw it open, blinking at the empty hallway. "Let me in before this spell drains all my magic."

I stepped aside and my sister popped into existence.

Lia hissed at her from the sofa, clearly perturbed. Evie hurried over to pet her. "She's so cute! Look at her little white paws."

I smirked as she cooed over the cat. Lia ate it up, nuzzling into her and purring. Evie's gaze landed on the wall behind me. "What, exactly is that?"

"A khopesh. It's an ancient Egyptian weapon. It looks great on that wall, right?"

"Normal people decorate their homes with art."

I laughed. "I really appreciate you doing this."

"Anytime. I have to say, I love the idea of messing with the demons. Are you going to tell me why this is so important?"

"There's a rowan seller in town."

Evie's blank look told me she had no idea what I was talking about, so I filled her in.

"Wait, so you're saying whoever was killing those demons you were interrogating was using rowan wood?"

"Yeah. And producing the wood is highly illegal. If there's a seller in town, he might be able to point me toward whoever was buying it."

"And then what?"

"I dunno. There's something else you should know."

She sat down. "Whenever you get that look on your face, I know it's not going to be good." Lia climbed into her lap, and I took a deep breath.

"I'm not half unseelie like I thought. I'm half demon."

Evie froze. Lia meowed, and my sister absently began stroking her again. "Would you like to tell me how the fuck that happened?"

"I'm not sure. I've been trying to figure out who my father could be, but apparently creating someone like me was forbidden." And I hadn't realized how depressing that thought was until right now.

Evie narrowed her eyes at my tone. "Yeah, forbidden because you're such a badass. The world couldn't handle having more of you around."

I had to laugh. When my sister loved someone, she was all-in. Even when we were fighting as kids, she was always my biggest cheerleader.

"Either way, I don't think whoever is shooting these demons knows what I am."

"Why?"

"Because it seems like a lot of work to kill the demons to stop me from asking questions. After all, shooting rowan wood through my heart would kill me too."

The blood slowly drained from Evie's face. "Jesus, Dani."

I hadn't meant to scare her. "All I'm saying is, I have a chance to find out who's silencing anyone who recognizes the photo of Mom."

She nodded. "That's good, I guess."

"I have something else to tell you." May as well get it all out now.

"Oh god, what is it now?"

"As a half-demon, it's likely that I'll have a longer-than-normal lifespan."

It took Evie a moment to understand what I meant, and then her mouth dropped open. "Jesus, you'll be around for centuries."

"I'm sorry."

"You should be. How am I going to end up old and wrinkly while you'll still look like that?"

Guilt flowed through me, and Evie burst out laughing.

"I'm a homebody, Danica. You spend your time going up against insane witches and fighting paranormals. If I had to put my money on who would live longer, it'd be on me."

I smirked. "You know, that's basically what Vas said."

"I knew I liked him. It'll be fine, Danica. I promise."

"You can't promise that. There's one other thing."

Evie slumped back on the sofa and rolled her eyes. "Oh god, make it stop."

I couldn't help but laugh at her dramatics. I walked over and sat next to her, stroking my hand down Lia's silky head. "When I was at the coven's house the other day, I noticed something weird."

"Weird in what way?"

"When I lower my shields, I sometimes see magical signatures. They occasionally look like colors, although sometimes it's just a feeling. Did you know the coven's house had power?"

She nodded. "Yeah, hundreds of witches have added their power into wards and protection spells over the years. It's not sentient or anything, but it now requires less and less power to sustain the wards."

"The power looks like yours. No one else's."

She frowned. "I've never adjusted the wards. I've never needed to."

"Hmmm. Weird." My phone buzzed and I glanced down at it. "Vas just messaged, asking when I'm planning to leave."

Evie grinned, gently placing Lia back on the couch. She pulled a piece of paper out of her pocket, closed her eyes, ripped up the piece of paper, and I gaped as her hair slowly began to darken.

She lost a couple of inches and her skin turned slightly darker, matching mine. Her hair lost its curls, and while she'd never pass as my twin, from the back, hurrying toward my car, people would see what they expected to see.

I took a moment to marvel. "God you're good. Hold on, let me grab some clothes."

My sister was wearing a white sundress, and I handed her a pair of my jeans and a t-shirt. She pulled her gun from her purse. "Do you have a spare holster?"

"You know your gun's not doing you much good in your purse. By the time you reach for it–"

"Dani. I've got approximately half an hour before this spell wears off and I need a nap."

I winced. "Point taken."

She pulled on my clothes, and I handed her a holster. "Okay," she said. "I'm ready. So, I'll just drive around?"

"Yeah. I've told Vas we're heading back toward Hope Valley. Once you get there, circle for a while if you can, but make sure you get home before that spell drops."

I felt bad tricking Vas, but if he found out that I was researching rowan, he'd be forced to tell Samael. As loyal as he was to me, not passing on that little information to Samael would get him in deep shit. And I didn't want it on my conscience if he kept it from Samael and the demon found out.

This way, Vas would be oblivious, and I could head to my meeting in peace.

"Okay. How do I look?"

"It's scary how well you can do that." We swapped keys, and Evie gave Lia one last pat before she sauntered toward the door.

"What, exactly, are you doing?"

"What? This is how you walk. You think I should swing my hips more?

I let out a low growl but we didn't have time to bicker. By the time Evie got downstairs, I was wearing her sundress and a large hat. I peered out the window, careful to stay out of sight just in case Vas happened to glance in my window.

My sister climbed into my car and drove out of the parking lot. A figure shot into the sky behind her and I grinned. Vas had been hanging out on my roof, waiting for me to leave. I'd been lucky he hadn't decided to simply knock on my door.

Hopefully my luck would hold.

I hauled ass out of my building and into Evie's car. Except the residual magic told me it wasn't Evie's at all, which I should've remembered, since her car was destroyed. No. This was Gemma's car.

Ugh.

I put the car in drive and headed southeast toward the Durham Green Flea Market. The market was closed, but the rowan seller had told Cara he would meet me in the parking lot.

Distantly, I wondered if I was heading into a trap. But I trusted Cara. Besides, just because I was wearing a sundress didn't mean I wasn't armed.

I'd rather be preparing for the auction tonight, but, according to Cara, the seller was leaving town in a few hours. He hadn't wanted to meet with me at all, but she'd managed to convince him. I couldn't waste this opportunity.

I circled the lot and parked. Within a few minutes, a human guy appeared. I watched as he strode toward me. The slight bulge on his hip told me he was carrying at least one gun. I gritted my teeth. My Colt 1911 was tucked into a thigh holster under Evie's sundress. Pulling up the dress would slow me down.

I hopped out of the car and leaned against it, ensuring no one could come up behind me. The rowan seller nodded at me, his sunglasses covering his eyes.

I let my gaze scan him. I'd put him in his sixties, although he looked healthy and fit. He was a white guy, but the tan line that poked out from beneath his t-shirt and the freckles on his forearms told me he spent a lot of time out in the sun.

"You're not what I expected," he said.

I raised one eyebrow. "It's the dress, isn't it?"

A smile danced around his mouth. "I don't have long. Ask your questions."

"Name?"

His mouth firmed and he gave me a dark frown. Okay then.

"Cara filled you in about my arrows?"

"Yes."

"Is there anything you can tell me about whoever has bought rowan from you recently? Maybe someone who would be happy to target a demon?"

He shrugged. "The thing you gotta know about rowan, is it's about the most illegal thing you can sell in this realm. Once the high demons arrived through those portals, one of the first things they did in this realm was eradicate the tree in almost every country around the world. They burned them to the ground with demon fire, so they would never grow again."

Knowing Samael as well as I now did, none of this surprised me. He'd never tolerate a potential threat to his people. "So how did you happen to get your hands on it?"

"It grows in the dark fae realm. It's a guaranteed prison term if you bring it through the portal, but lesser unseelie have to make a living somehow."

"Uh-huh. So, someone brings it through to you and you sell it off?"

He shook his head. "No. My contact brings it across, and my supplier sells it on. Deals are done via email and payments are encrypted."

"How do the buyers get the rowan?"

"It's left in a different pickup spot every time."

I pinched the bridge of my nose. Then I turned and opened my car door, pulling out the arrow. "So there's nothing you can tell me about who might've made this?"

He frowned. "They'd have to be wealthy. That doesn't look like a lot of rowan, but it's probably worth half a million dollars."

I gaped at him. He nodded. "Anyone caught selling or buying rowan will have to deal with either the high unseelie or the high demons. The price has to be worth it."

"Okay. Is there anything else you can tell me?"

"No. I'll let you know if I think of anything." He shifted on his feet, and I reached into the pocket of my sundress for the cash I owed him and handed it over. Three hundred dollars, gone just like that. And I was no closer to whoever had been killing my marks. It pissed me right off.

Selina called when I was halfway home.

"Hi Danica, listen, I examined the body."

"What did you find?"

"Hold on, I'm putting you on speaker."

Nathaniel's deep voice came over the line. "Danica."

"Nathaniel."

He chuckled. Glad I could amuse him.

"I examined the body," Selina said. "Whoever killed this wolf was a black witch. The magic is so dark, I've never seen anything like it."

"Cause of death?"

"Some kind of spell. You told me the McCormick coven had one of the black books. If I had to guess, I'd say something like this could've been found in one of those grimoires."

Son of a bitch.

"Okay. Nathaniel… tell your wolves to be careful. If this witch knows her spell worked, she could decide she'd like to get her hands on more werewolf eyes."

"The wolf was feral, Danica. My wolves can handle themselves. But I appreciate your concern."

I had no idea what that meant so I shrugged and hung up.

Vas was waiting for me in the parking lot when I arrived back at my apartment. His feet were spread, hands on hips. Uh-oh.

I got out of the car. Where was my sister?

"What were you thinking?" Vas snarled. I gaped at him.

"I was thinking I had something to do. Something that definitely didn't need to involve Samael."

"So you let your sister pretend to be you."

"Well, yeah."

"Do you know where I found her?"

"In Hope Valley, I'm assuming."

He flashed the edge of his teeth. "Curled up in the drivers' seat of your car a few streets from Mariam's."

I froze. "What?"

"Yeah. She's obsessed with making you proud and helping you out, she sucked herself dry."

The thought made me shudder. My sister was beautiful,

and I could just picture her after the spell had dropped, looking weak and vulnerable in the car.

"I told her to head home before the spell dropped."

"Yeah, well she didn't listen."

Jesus. I could've gotten her kidnapped or killed. I'd told her to go straight into fae territory, for fuck's sake. The thought made nausea sweep through me.

I was so focused on figuring out who'd killed my mother, that I'd risked my sister's life.

Vas shook his head at me. "Now you're getting it."

"How did she get home?"

"I drove her."

"Thank you."

Vas studied my face. "Was it worth it?"

I swung my leg back and kicked the tire. "No."

He was silent and it was my turn to examine him. "Do you ah… have a thing for my sister?"

He threw his head back and laughed. "No. Not that she's not beautiful, but I'm focused on someone else right now. I just know what it's like to try and live up to the heavy hitters in your family," he said. "I don't want Evie to get hurt trying to make you love her."

I flinched. "I do love her."

"Yeah, but you also left her. Now, she's probably thinking that you could do it again at any time. She's probably hoping that if she can prove herself to you, you'll want to stay with her, instead of abandoning her."

I froze. "What the fuck, Vas?"

He shrugged. "I call it like I see it."

Was my sister really doing everything she could to win

my approval? I frowned, my head aching at the thought.

"My sister knew you were above her, Vas. If she let the spell drop, it was because she knew you'd land and find her, and it would distract you. You insist on believing she's helpless, but she's much more powerful than she appears. She's also sneaky as hell, and she can think on her feet better than most bounty hunters I know."

"Maybe. But what if something had happened to me and I couldn't get to her?"

I pinched the bridge of my nose. "You've got a point. I'll talk to her."

Vas frowned. "Fine. Now that you've decided I'm trustworthy enough to hang out with, where are we going now?"

I winced. Vas was already in a terrible mood. Learning where we were going next wasn't going to help.

CHAPTER TWENTY-ONE

DANICA

"I don't see why we have to use *this* witch."

I sighed, shifting on my feet. "Because she's performed a look-away spell for me once before. And because I trust her."

Vas snorted and I held back a growl. "It's happening. You don't have to come, you know."

He sneered and I let out a low growl. I was not having a good day. I'd spent the night tossing and turning, my dreams plagued with memories of my mom's body, cold and lonely on the ground. Then I'd had zero luck with my only lead into rowan wood, and found out my sister was willing to hurt herself to earn my approval.

I was in a pissy mood.

So was Vas.

We stood and hissed at each other in front of Hannah's mint-green bungalow. Vas had his feet planted, hands on his hips, and I'd bet his wings were spread in sheer rage.

"Who else do you suggest I use, Vas?"

"Gloria?"

It was my turn to sneer at that, and Vas raised one eyebrow.

"Oookay."

I put my own hands on my hip and lowered my chin. "Let me make one thing clear. You guys let her near my unconscious body ever again, and we're going to have problems."

He was silent for a long moment, then he heaved a sigh. "Fair enough." His gaze swept past me and settled on Hannah's house and his lips pulled back from his teeth once more.

I'd thought Vas was a kid when I first met him, falling for his young face and dreamy eyes. But if I'd seen this side of him, he would've scared the shit out of me.

I wasn't budging on this, and I waited for him to come to terms with it. I needed to get into that illegal auction tonight.

"Are you coming in?" Hannah was standing on her porch, her hands on her hips as she examined us. Her gaze landed on Vas.

She smiled. He bristled. I groaned.

Then I threw up my hands and stalked toward her front door. Hannah stepped to the side and let me enter, and I shivered as her ward swept over my skin.

Vas snarled behind me, and I turned. Hannah was waiting for him to walk past her. I could've told her he wouldn't trust her at his back.

She tutted and shuffled toward me, allowing Vas to shut the front door behind her.

"Please," she said, gesturing for us to move into the kitchen. "Have a seat."

Hannah's home was crowded with antique furniture

which had been dusted and polished until each piece gleamed. She instructed me to head into her kitchen and I took a seat at the scarred wooden table dominating the room. Vas leaned against the wall, his eyes dark. Hannah ignored him and moved toward her stove. I cleared my throat.

"Last time we did this, I needed some of Samael's hair."

Hannah kept her eyes on the spell she was stirring and nodded. "His ward was set to recognize only his magical signature. The place you are going must, by nature, allow the entry of multiple people. Their ward will have been created to prevent exactly what you're planning. I added a little something into the look-away spell to help you get through the ward, but ultimately, that'll be up to you and your power."

My mouth went dry. Hannah smiled and glanced over her shoulder at me, inhaling deeply.

She was totally feeding on my fear. I scowled at her.

"Tone the creepy down a notch, Hannah."

Her face fell. "You're no longer scared of me." Anyone else would have been pleased. Hannah's voice was heavy with disappointment.

I rolled my eyes. "So how do we know I can get through their ward?"

"They may be good, but I'm better."

I raised my eyebrows at that and she smiled. "If there's one thing I was born to do, it's break through wards. They so often contain the things that I want."

"Alrighty then."

She poured her potion into two mugs, handing one to me and one to Vas. Mine tasted like lemon and ginger. From the look of disgust on Vas's face, his tasted like a potion from a black witch. I gave Hannah a look and she smiled at me.

"I have to get my pleasures where I can find them, and the young demon has been mean to me."

Vas gulped his potion down. "I don't like black witches."

Hannah shrugged, apparently unconcerned. "I don't like bigoted demons."

Vas bared his teeth, and I shook my head at him. I'd never seen him act this way with anyone. Something was going on.

"You prey on the weak, witch. It's not bigotry."

Hannah's face turned hard, the wrinkles around her mouth deepening as she narrowed her eyes at him. Her hand clenched on the wooden spoon she was holding, and I prepared to jump between them. Something was going on with Vas's power, and I didn't know if he could take down a black witch of Hannah's power level.

I cleared my throat. "Cash or Venmo, Hannah?"

She finally pulled her gaze away from the demon. "Cash. I don't need any transactions connecting us. You know how it is."

Yeah, I knew how it was. If I was caught, anyone who helped me was at risk. Hannah was covering her ass.

She opened her mouth and muttered a word I couldn't catch. A dull pop sounded, and I felt the spell smooth over my skin. Vas shot me a questioning look and I nodded. We were now invisible to everyone but each other.

Vas stalked behind us as Hannah led us out of her home. I turned to her once we were on the porch. "Thank you."

She nodded in the direction of my voice. "You're welcome, halfling. Happy hunting." She turned, walking slowly back into her house. I glanced at Vas as she closed the door. When they'd first met, Hannah had teased the demon. Now, she seemed almost lost.

"I think you hurt her feelings."

He cursed and prowled down the porch steps, holding out his arms. "Let's go."

I gave up. I had enough problems of my own. If he wanted to be pissy because we were working with a black witch, that was his prerogative. In the meantime, we needed to get to the auction.

DANICA

The problem with being invisible was that you forgot how many tiny sounds you made without even noticing. Well, I did, anyway. Vas moved soundlessly through the night, shooting me the occasional dirty look as I scuffed my foot, breathed too loudly, or brushed up against a wall.

If I was half-demon, why didn't I get any of their natural abilities? Their penchant for prowling soundlessly through the night would've come in pretty damn handy over the past few years.

We were standing outside the train station, watching as people approached from all angles. A few of them were wearing cloaks, while others wore balaclavas, or hats and sunglasses. Even knowing I was invisible, I had to fight the urge to cower behind the rubble.

The werewolves had ripped up most of the train tracks while they were rampaging through the station, and no one had bothered to move them away. They were sprawled around the station like stitches pulled from the wound of that day 72 years ago.

The old train station was just around the corner from Meredith's. Given the location, it was surprising that the remains of the building hadn't been knocked down so the space could be used for something else. But a witch claiming to see ghosts had come out a few years ago and insisted that the spirits of the humans who'd been slaughtered by the werewolves were here and had declared that anyone who built on this spot would be cursed.

The pararnormals didn't seem to need the station, and most humans had believed the witch, although she'd later been found to be low on the power scale. It took serious power to see a ghost.

Still... this would be an incredible space if anyone ever fixed it up.

More people were arriving, and I slunk closer to the chairs that had been set up in neat lines close to a small stage. Vas shadowed my footsteps.

"Creepy place," a voice muttered. "Why'd we have to come here, anyway?"

"It's the best place for something like this," a guy next to him explained patiently. "Now quit whining and help me carry these."

I watched as they carried several paintings into the train station. My shoe scuffed along a broken brick and both men jumped, glancing around.

"I *told* you it was haunted," the smaller guy said.

"Haunted or not, we need this auction so we can sell this shit."

My breath caught as I gazed at the paintings. They'd obviously been painted in another realm, because I'd never seen colors or flowers like those before. I could stare at those paintings for days.

The items being sold tonight were all being placed on the crude wooden stage, and I took a few steps closer as the men leaned the paintings against the wall.

Along with the paintings, there was an obviously priceless bracelet— dripping with glimmering stones I'd never seen in this world. Next to the bracelet sat a pair of brass knuckles which radiated power, a handful of old scrolls written in a language I didn't recognize, and a stack of books which looked suspiciously similar to the grimoire the witches had used to kill Samael's demons.

I tensed. "Are those books–"

Vas shook his head. "They're copycats," he whispered. "There are nine of the real grimoires, and Samael–" he cut himself off and I stared at him.

"How many does he have, Vas?"

He didn't say a word. I scowled at him, opening my mouth, but then he went so tense I jolted, glancing behind me at the stage.

"What is it?"

"That bracelet belonged to Samael's mother."

I gaped at him. "How do you know that?"

"I remember my uncle looking for it before we left. Samael had been missing for centuries at that point, and everyone assumed he was dead. But Ag knew Samael's mother and remembered how she'd adored that bracelet. He'd hoped to find it one day." He pulled his phone out of his pocket and showed me a picture of what looked like an ancient sketch. I studied both the sketch and the bracelet. They sure looked the same.

"How do you think they got their hands on it?"

He shrugged. "Enterprising humans can get their hands on almost anything. Likely, one of the underking's men looted Samael's mother's jewelry when they took power and then they sold the pieces off when it was safe to do so." He glanced at me. "I don't like the look on your face right now."

I ignored him, my gaze glued to the bracelet.

Eight-year-old Samael's pain was branded in my memory. His little heart had broken as he stared at his mother's body. I *would* leave this auction with that bracelet.

I could feel Vas's gaze on me. I gave him a wide smile and he shook his head, turning back to the auction. People had taken their seats and were giving each other the side-eye, scoping out who was here.

"Clint's just arrived," a couple of late-comers were striding in, moving so quickly that Vas had to yank me out of their path before one of them rammed into me.

One of the women laughed. "You know it's going to be a good night then. He's almost as magical as the artifacts he peddles, he's so skilled at getting his hands on them."

Was that so? We'd be having a little talk then, wouldn't we?

The auctioneer arrived. The room went silent and the last of the people gathered took their seats. I scanned the room. There must've been fifty people waiting to bid, or simply curious enough to see what was on offer.

A hushed silence fell over the crowd as the auction got started.

The paintings sold for six million dollars. The two men who'd been hauling them in looked both shocked and triumphant. But the guy with the beard looked consideringly at his partner and I suppressed a snort. I had a feeling he wasn't planning to split the money.

"Next we have a bracelet from the underworld. While its origins are unclear, there's no doubt that this is an incredible piece."

I snorted. Origins unclear my ass. If people knew it was in any way connected to Samael, they'd think twice before buying it.

"Bidding will begin at nine hundred thousand."

My mouth dropped open.

No one bid. The auctioneer looked surprised and began to rattle off information about the bracelet.

Silence.

The seller's face was grim. I barely suppressed a chuckle. The people here would do almost anything to avoid attracting the demons' wrath.

The bracelet was the only thing that didn't sell. Everything else was snapped up with bids that made me let out strangled gasps. Vas sent me an amused look as I recovered from the sale of a two million dollar book.

"That's some serious money," I whispered.

He shrugged "Many of the buyers of these illegal artifacts will be paranormals who have had a millennia to build wealth. And human groups will definitely be well-funded if they have access to these kinds of auctions."

"Clint seems like our best lead. Regardless, I'm going after that bracelet."

Vas let out a long-suffering sigh. "Of course you are."

CHAPTER TWENTY-TWO

DANICA

"It's risky," Vas said.

"But worth it."

We were huddled in the shadows, keeping an eye on the auction as I attempted to convince Vas of the benefits of my plan.

"From what those dickheads with the paintings said, Clint is also our most likely lead into the artifacts that Mariam is missing. Two birds and all that."

Vas rolled his eyes at me in a way that told me he wasn't buying it. Whatever.

We split up, both of us staying close and eavesdropping as buyers and sellers mingled after the auction. My skin began to tingle, and I made wide-eyes at Vas from across the room. He nodded at me. We needed to get out of here before the look-away spell dropped completely. There were a few high fae in this room, and if they caught us, we were in big trouble.

Vas jerked his head toward the exit and I stared at Clint, memorizing his face. Sharp, pointed nose, small eyes, receding hairline. His eyes were an almost otherworldly shade of blue, but they glinted with fury. Clint was having a bad night, and while he was being pleasant to the people he came into contact with, he was *pissed*.

Good.

We ducked outside and waited for him to leave. My skin tingled some more and I cursed. If the spell fell while we were still snooping around this auction, we'd never get our chance at the guy.

Vas grabbed my elbow and steered me away from the door and further down the street. I hissed at him, and he ignored me until we were standing in the shadow of a building, next to a black Bugatti.

"This is his car," Vas told me, looking mighty pleased with himself.

I gaped at him. "How do you know that?"

He held up a keyring with an obnoxiously large logo on it. "Picked his pocket. He'll be coming this way."

"Maybe I'll keep you around after all."

Vas lifted his lip at me and I grinned. We leaned against the concrete wall of a thrift store where we'd be in the shadows. Hopefully, between the shadows and the remnants of the spell, Clint wouldn't see us waiting for him.

Within a few minutes, the clomping sound of his footsteps reached us. Well, they reached Vas far before me and he shot me a warning look, his superior hearing tipping him off.

We crouched and waited. Clint was muttering to himself, and once he was within a few feet of his car, he slid his hand into his pocket, clearly looking for his keys.

"Fuck."

He turned to stalk back toward the auction, and I leapt at him, taking him down to the ground. The box with the bracelet clattered onto the pavement and Clint's eyes went wide. Then he had a knife in his hand.

I hadn't seen him pull it. This guy was an idiot for walking to his car with a priceless bracelet in his hand, but he was an armed idiot.

"Uh-uh," Vas said, crouching next to me. Thanks to the way we'd rolled, I was straddling Clint, and Vas shot me an amused look as he pulled the knife from his hand. "Naughty naughty," he said.

"Demon," Clint stated the obvious. He opened his mouth to scream, and I slapped my hand over it. Within a minute, we had him gagged, tied, and in the trunk of his car. The Bugatti didn't exactly have much trunk space, and Clint looked miserable.

Served him right.

Vas handed me the guy's wallet after taking a good look at his drivers' license.

"You want to drive, or shall I?"

Vas slid me a look. I shrugged. "You found the car."

He didn't argue. He settled himself into the car, cursing as his wings clearly impeded his movement. I held back a smile at the put-upon look on his face.

It was clearly worth it for him, because when the car let out a low rumble he grinned like he'd won a prize.

"You could afford a garage of these," I said. "Why don't you buy one?"

He shook his head as he pulled out, heading back toward the tower. "Too uncomfortable to be in a confined space like this for long. But for a few minutes… worth it. I wish we could open her up."

There were few people on the roads at this time, and Vas wound down the window as we arrived at the tower, sticking his head out to chat with one of the demons guarding the garage entrance. The door rolled open and Vas pulled in, parking near the elevator.

Being tied up and stuffed in his own tiny trunk had clearly dampened Clint's fury, and it had shifted to pure terror. I pulled out the box we'd thrown in next to him and opened it. Samael's mom's bracelet glinted at me, and I slipped it into my pocket.

Clint let out a strangled shriek behind his gag.

"Oh I'm sorry, did you think you'd be brought to the tower and we'd let you walk away?" I snorted and he fell silent as Vas pulled him from the trunk.

I'd always known Samael had cells beneath his tower, but I'd never checked them out. His dungeon wasn't unlike the Mage Council's basement, with a long corridor lined with cells stretching out before us as the elevator doors opened. Unlike the Mage Council, however, there was no one to check the prisoners in— just cells and interrogation rooms waiting. And the corridors here were more than wide enough for wings— three high demons could likely walk side-by-side.

Vas pushed Clint down the hall. He shrieked, putting up a fight, and Vas merely wrapped an arm around his neck and dragged him along as if he weighed nothing. He stopped at the sixth door on the left and raised his hand, breaking the ward. I pushed the door open, revealing an empty room which held nothing but a steel chair. The floor angled down toward the back of the room, where a gutter waited for any… fluids that would need to be collected.

As far as interrogation rooms went, it was creepy. Vas grinned at me.

"Even Danica doesn't like this place," he told Clint. "You should probably just tell us what we want to know."

I shot Vas a look and untied Clint's gag. Vas strapped him into the steel chair, and I closed the door as he began to scream.

He didn't bother with threats. Being stuffed in his own car and dragged into the tower cells had obviously done a number on his tough-guy image. He went straight into begging.

"Please, please don't kill me. You got the bracelet, just let me go and I'll never sell anything related to the demons again, I swear."

He didn't bother begging Vas. He kept his eyes on me. I rolled my eyes. This type of asshole always thought women were the ones with soft hearts. He should've known better.

Clint flinched at whatever he saw on my face. And then he started crying. His shoulders shook with full-fledged sobs. I rubbed at my temple. Vas wrinkled his nose.

"Listen," I said, since Vas was clearly wrestling with his disgust. "There's still a way for you to live through this. Just tell us everything we want to know. I've got places to go, things to do tonight. I don't have time for torture. And if you make us drag this out, it's really going to piss me off, you know?"

Clint's breath hitched and he shot me a look of betrayal

before turning to Vas. If he was expecting the demon to play good cop, he'd be waiting a while. Vas kept his face blank and simply nodded. "What she said."

The door opened and Sitri walked in, handing me a file. I raised one eyebrow as I opened it. Vas had clearly passed Clint's info onto Sitri when he checked his license and Sitri had already done his background checks.

"Says here you're a bad guy, Clint. Looks like you served some time. For sexual assault." I raised my head and watched the blood slowly drain from his face. I pulled a throwing knife and flicked it through the air, throwing and catching it as I smiled at him.

Then I let out a low whistle as I read the rest of his file. "Out on good behavior, huh? I bet your parole officer would be unhappy to learn what you were up to with these auctions."

He stared at me and I closed the file. "Why don't you just go ahead and tell me what I need to know."

He cleared his throat. His eyes glistened with tears and snot dripped from his nose.

"Okay," he said.

I slipped my phone from my back pocket and pulled up a picture Aubrey had sent me of Hrunting. "See this sword? I want to know everything you know about it."

His mouth dropped open. Then he swallowed. "I can't talk about that. They'll kill me."

Vas dropped whatever magic hid his wings from view. The cell was just wide enough for him to stretch them out slightly, although not to his full wingspan.

"Ooh," I said. "Pretty."

He shot me a look and I realized my hand was poised in the air above his left wing.

"I have a feeling Samael won't be pleased if you touch another demon's wings." He eyed the camera in the corner of the room. I showed whoever was watching my teeth and stroked a hand down Vas's wings.

I didn't know why I was so obsessed with demon wings. Maybe because they were always hidden from my view. Maybe because I was half demon, but I hadn't exactly won the genetic lottery, and I would never fly on my own terms.

"Soft," I said, "and deadly." I turned to Clint and wrinkled my nose as the sharp smell of urine hit me. "Tell me you didn't just piss your pants."

Clint's face was ashen as he stared at Vas. I had a new appreciation for the demons' torture methods. Shove their suspect in one of these cells, show them just how otherworldly they were, and they'd be willing to sing like terrified little birdies. I bet they hardly ever had to clean these cells after interrogating humans.

Other than the piss, of course.

"Okay, I'll tell you," Clint burst out. "I have a friend– a guy who works for the fae. He heard they were moving some important sword. He hates the fae— his wife left him for some light fae dude and he wanted to make them pay."

"So he stole the sword."

Clint nodded.

"What's your friend's name?"

He clamped his mouth shut. I stared at him and waited.

"Look, he's not a bad guy, okay? He just kind of snapped."

"Name."

"Mike Brown. I don't think he knew quite what he had taken, he just wanted to get rid of it."

The name was familiar. He'd been on Aubrey's list— one of the guys who hadn't turned up to work for at least a couple of days in the past week."

"So you helped him with that."

He nodded. "I know a guy who authenticates these kinds of things. His name's Durin and he's seelie— barely any power, but he can read artifacts. He said it was the real thing. I was going to sell the sword at auction, but then this woman got in touch with me. I guess Durin ran his mouth."

"Who was she?"

He shrugged. "Said her name was Cassie. She offered me more money than I could ever dream of, even splitting it with my buddy."

"Then what?"

He gave me a 'duh' look. "I sold it to her. She told me to keep an eye out for anything similar. Said it would be worth my while." He wrinkled his nose. "She got all creepy. Wanted to know who else had known about the sword. I told her to mind her business."

"And the bracelet?"

"Durin had a deal go wrong a few months ago. This guy brought the bracelet to him. Durin told him the bracelet was the real thing, and then the guy tried to kill him. Obviously, he didn't want anyone who could tie him to the bracelet. Durin may not be powerful, but he's strong. He killed the bastard and took the bracelet, then handed it off to me to sell." He sniffed. "I was going to leave the country after the auction tonight."

"Life's tough. Tell me about Cassie."

He let out a weak growl. "I don't know nothin', I swear."

I shifted my gaze to Vas. He stretched his wings and took a single step closer to Clint. He let out a shriek and cringed away from him. "All I know is she's into some bad shit, okay? I asked around."

"Last name?"

"I don't know.

"What does she look like?"

"I dunno, Jesus, don't hurt me!"

Vas took another step closer and Clint flinched. "Okay, okay. I might've gotten a picture of her face."

"You might've? You're pissing me off, Clint."

"Okay, I did."

"Where is it?"

"On my phone."

I did not want to fish his phone out of those jeans. Vas gave me a look that said there was no chance in hell he was doing it.

I sighed. Luckily, Clint's phone was sticking mostly out of his back pocket thanks to all his writhing around on the chair. I popped it out and unlocked it as Clint rattled off the combination.

I scrolled through his photos. "You fucking perve."

He'd obviously set up some kind of camera in his bathroom, and this Cassie woman was pulling off her blouse. She had another shirt on the counter in front of her, and her top half was only covered by her bra.

A paranormal would've likely found the camera, but as

a human, she'd had no idea.

I looked up from the phone and my power exploded.

CHAPTER TWENTY-THREE

DANICA

Power poured from me, darkening the room as I clamped my hand around Clint's throat. I'd kill him for daring to think he could record a woman— any woman— without her permission. I'd skin him alive with my power, and hang him from Samael's tower as a warning to any other man who thought they could fuck with the women of this city. *My* city.

"Danica. Danica, you're killing him. He might have more information."

I focused on one finger at a time, slowly loosening them. Clint's eyes were bloodshot. "Please," he mouthed.

I managed to let go, but I couldn't pack my power away. It tangled around Clint, eager to make him pay.

"Talk."

He could barely speak. Vas folded his arms and we both watched as he attempted to get the words out.

"Contacted me," he finally mouthed. "Recent calls."

I scrolled through the phone, holding it up until he nodded. I added the number to my own phone, and then

I checked his messages.

He'd shared the photo of Cassie with several of his friends. They'd started a message thread, filled with lewd jokes.

"How'd you get her to take her top off in your bathroom, Clint? You spill something on her?"

Clint stared at me, his expression resigned.

"Tell me."

"Yes, okay! It's just a harmless prank!"

His body lifted from the chair, straps snapping as I held him in the air. Fury blinded me, and I slammed him into the closest wall, again and again and again.

Sexual assault. He'd gone to *prison* for it. And now he was violating women again.

"Danica. Danica!"

I raised a hand and Vas was suddenly on the other side of my ward as I stepped closer to the piece of shit I was holding against the wall with my power. I palmed my knife and slid it down his cheek, opening his skin up as he let out a low moan.

"You fucked up, Clint." I breathed. I couldn't even recognize my voice. "And I want you to think of all the women you've traumatized throughout your useless life. Because I'm your karma, baby."

Men who preyed on women had a history of it from the time they first learned what sex was.

Clint cried out and I laughed as I stabbed into him with my power, rummaging through his guts. I'd disembowel him slowly, and then I'd release the video from the camera in the corner of this room as a warning.

"Little witch," a voice was crooning in my ear. When did Samael get here?

"Leave, demon."

I could feel his amusement as he brushed up against me. When had he slipped beneath my ward? Had I dropped it?

"He's almost dead, witchling. If this isn't what you truly want, let him go."

I slammed Clint into the wall again, and he let out a low groan, his eyes rolling up into his head. He bled from numerous wounds all over his body. The ropes of his intestines gleamed at me as I dropped him.

"That's it," Samael breathed. "Now pack your power away. I'll help you."

I turned. I'd dropped my ward at some point, likely because I was so focused on killing the worthless piece of shit at my feet. I wiped at my face and my hand came away red. I gazed down at it and then raised my head, my eyes meeting Samael's.

Something like sorrow flashed across his face. "It's okay," he told me gently. "You're okay."

Vas was very quiet in the corner of the room. He nodded at me. "We have enough to go on. I'll send the photo to Steve and Sitri for facial recognition."

Power swept through me once more, only this time, Samael raised a ward between me and Vas.

"I'll share her face, and nothing else, Danica," Vas said carefully.

Of course he would. Vas was a good man. I needed to get control of myself somehow.

"We need Mike Brown, too."

Vas nodded. "I'm on it."

I turned back to Samael. He stepped closer. "Just close your eyes and visualize your power. That's it."

His voice was calm and confident, and I focused every ounce of my attention on his instructions, until my power was finally behind my shields where it belonged.

Clint choked once, and then went silent. I'd killed a man. It certainly wasn't the first time, and it wouldn't be the last. But when I made a decision to end a life, I used cool, calculated logic. I didn't lose control and disembowel people with my power.

The smell of death hit me. Clint's blood was sticky on my skin. I leaned over and heaved.

When I'd regained control, Samael wrapped his arm around me and walked me out of the cell. He turned left instead of right, and I allowed him to steer me like a puppet as he opened a door which led to a set of concrete stairs.

He gestured for me to go ahead of him, and I climbed the long staircase until we were around the back of his tower. Then he swept me into his arms and jumped into the sky, hauling me up to his penthouse. He let me go as soon as we landed on the balcony, and I stared down at the glowing lights of the city below us.

He didn't make me talk about it, merely took my hand, and led me inside, walking me through his rooms and into his bathroom, where he turned on the shower.

"Do you need help?"

I shook my head. I needed to be alone. He read my answer on my face and merely nodded, although his jaw tightened. Then he turned and laid a fluffy white robe on the chair close to the shower.

He walked out. I stripped my shirt off, refusing to look in the mirror. I could feel blood caked in my hair, on my cheeks, along my neck and throat. I stepped out of my shoes and peeled my jeans off, leaning down as something clinked onto the floor.

I picked the bracelet up and slipped it into the robe's pocket. Then I stepped into the shower, letting the water pour over me. I washed my hair twice, conditioned it, then washed and conditioned it again, unable to resist the urge. I took Samael's shower gel, breathing in the scent of cedar. I rubbed it everywhere, rinsed, lathered up again, and then sat on the floor of the shower under the stream of water and cried.

It wasn't that I'd killed that man. It was that I'd killed him so brutally and taken such pleasure in it. Sure, he was a piece of shit, but I'd been completely out of control. What happened next time someone pissed me off and my power decided they had to die, slowly and painfully?

What if it was someone I cared about?

I couldn't even recognize who I was anymore.

Strong arms surrounded me and I jumped. I hadn't heard the demon come in.

"Your shower is oversized. Is it because of the wings?"

Samael ignored my rambling, picking me up and placing me on the bench. He was still wearing his clothes, expensive Italian shoes included. He crouched in front of me.

"Tell me what I can say to make it better," he said.

Tears filled my eyes again, and his face twisted. "There's

nothing you can say," I said. "I'm a m-monster," I wailed.

To his credit, Samael didn't laugh at my dramatics. Instead, he pushed my hair off my face and nuzzled at my neck.

"You're *my* little monster," he purred. "And while you may be having some... issues with your power, it won't always be this way."

My lower lip trembled and I bit down on it as he pulled me to my feet. "Promise?"

"Promise." He reached for a towel and wrapped me in it, keeping his gaze on my face. There was a ginormous bulge in his wet pants, but he cared for me tenderly. I didn't know what to do with that. I picked up the robe and darted out of the bathroom, leaving him to strip off alone.

By the time he reappeared, wearing nothing but a towel wrapped around his waist, I'd managed to pull myself together. Mostly. Samael's robe swallowed me, and his lips twitched as he took me in, standing in his bedroom.

"You look very young," he said. "Almost innocent." I shot him a look and he laughed. "And there you are."

I reached into my robe pocket. "I have something for you."

Nerves danced through my stomach. Losing his family the way he had... I couldn't think of anything more traumatic. I hoped he liked it. Hoped it carried good memories for him.

Samael's eyes lit with a curiosity I hadn't seen before. I stepped closer, pulled the bracelet from my pocket, and handed it over.

He went still. Then he lifted his head, gazing between me and the bracelet.

"Where did you get this?" His voice was hoarse.

"From the piece of shit in your cell. I saw it come up at the auction. Vas said it belonged to your mother…"

"So you decided to get it back for me."

I nodded. He returned his attention to the bracelet, stroking one finger slowly along the stones, linked together by a metal that gleamed with a dull fire.

"What are they?" I asked him.

"Underworld gems."

They were stunning. They put diamonds to shame, glinting with a rainbow of colors which danced in the light. Samael held the bracelet gently in his hand and pure, exposed grief settled deep into his face. I didn't know if it was from the bond between us, or my own memory of him losing his entire family, but I could *feel* his grief.

"You have given me a priceless gift," he said, his eyes glittering. "How can I repay you?"

I shook my head. "Not everything needs to be a bargain or a deal, Samael." Although, if he was serious about repaying me, maybe I could convince him to break our little bond.

He let out a low laugh at whatever he saw on my face. "If you were hoping to convince me to free you, you have erred, little witch. This just proves that you are a woman like no other, and I am right to guard you like a dragon guarding his hoard."

I frowned at him, but I couldn't feel much indignance. His obvious pleasure in the gift, and the way he stroked the gems, his eyes distant as he remembered his mother… it was worth it.

"Stay here tonight," he ordered. I opened my mouth to decline, and his voice softened. "I prefer my women conscious," he purred. "We won't do anything except sleep in the same bed."

I eyed him. It was a bad idea. The demon was doing his best to give me an innocent look, but I was pretty sure he didn't know what innocence actually was. I sighed. My clothes were covered in blood, I was so tired I was dead on my feet, and truthfully, I wanted nothing more than to bask in the heat of Samael's body.

"My cat–"

"Will be fine. If you moved her into my tower, she would be even better."

I blinked at him, and my mouth hung open in a way I was pretty sure wasn't a good look for me. His silver eyes gleamed.

"Since when do you like cats?" I managed to get the words out.

"I've always enjoyed tiny felines. They're independent, territorial, and live their lives on their own terms. Why wouldn't I like them?"

Well, when he put it like that. I shook my head. "There's no need for me to move my cat in here. The amount of time I've been spending at your tower is an outlier. Once the kids are safe, my life will go back to normal."

He shook his head as if I was being stubborn for no reason and I gritted my teeth. I *hated* it when he gave me that look. He was as transparent as the window we stood in front of, and I knew damn well that he planned for me to "come to my senses" and move in with him.

He was dreaming.

I strode past him, effectively ending the conversation, and hopped into his bed, robe and all. He frowned at me. "You'll overheat."

"I'll be fine," I said sweetly.

He shrugged and dropped the towel. I slammed my eyes closed. "Samael!"

"I sleep naked," he informed me, sliding into bed next to me. "As you well know."

He ignored my half-assed struggles and pulled me into his arms.

"I'm lying on your wing!"

"It can take it."

I indulged myself long enough to stroke one hand over the feathers beneath my body.

"Samael–"

"Sleep."

To his credit, he kept his promise. He dropped a kiss onto the tip of my nose, molded his body to mine, and closed his eyes.

"Goodnight, witchling."

I didn't know what to do with that. I closed my eyes and dreamed that my power tore me apart.

DANICA

"I'm serious Samael. Take me home or I'll get a Lyft."
I could always ask Vas to take me, but threatening Samael
with that didn't seem like a good idea.

The demon let out a low growl. If he'd made that sound
when I first met him, I probably would've had a heart attack.

I'd woken up tangled in his arms, the long length of him
nestled right up against where I needed him the most.

He'd already been awake, his face carved out of stone
as he stayed very still.

He'd promised not to touch me, and I'd been grinding
up against him in my sleep. Mortification swept through me
and I hurriedly untangled myself and stalked into his closet,
where I found a pair of sweatpants and a t-shirt that came
down to my knees. I rolled the sweatpants up until I could
walk in them without falling on my face.

Then I'd made my way into the bathroom, gathered my
weapons, and strapped them on.

Now, the demon was stubbornly glaring at me, wearing
nothing but a pair of sweatpants that I'd thrown at him.

"We need to talk about your living situation."

"Now is not the time." It would never be the time. This
was the problem. Give the demon an inch, and he attempted
to take a hundred miles. "Forget it, I'll take the elevator."

I turned and Samael cursed. In the blink of an eye he'd
pulled me onto the balcony, where he launched into the air
and silently flew me home.

The silent treatment. Great.

I studied his face, but his eyes were fixed on the distance, his expression remote… almost cruel. Then he looked at me and his face softened for a split second— so fast I almost missed it— before he shifted his gaze away.

We dropped into my parking lot.

Samael watched me walk toward my car, his eyes dark. I unlocked it.

"Bounty hunter."

There was a chasm between us that we could never quite cross. I turned toward him. "You know what? You–"

The world exploded.

Heat seared me and I flew through the air. I had a single moment to recognize that this was going to hurt, and then I slammed into an SUV. I hit it with my face and crumpled to the ground.

Samael was suddenly next to me, face twisted into a vicious snarl. I flinched away from him but his hands were exceedingly gentle.

"Stay still, witchling. I need to check you for injuries."

Vas appeared next to us. "The healer is on his way."

"I'm okay."

He ignored that. I blinked, and I was suddenly surrounded by demons. Had I passed out? Samael's brow was creased in concentration as he gently ran his hands over every inch of my body and Vas looked worried as he held his phone up to his ear. I glanced behind them where Bael stood next to my burning car. The demon lifted a hand and the flames went out with a whoosh.

"Whoa."

"Don't move," Samael snapped.

I blew out a breath. "Anyone ever tell you you're a mother hen?" His face was whirling around me and I wanted to puke. A concussion. Great.

"This is good news," I mumbled. "It means I'm getting close and they're scared." My head gave a vicious throb that radiated into my face. Ow.

"Shhh." Samael cupped my cheek and pressed his lips to mine in an achingly gentle kiss. Tears inexplicably burned my eyes. I attempted to blink them away but one of them escaped out the corner of my eye.

Panic darted across Samael's face and the breath left his lungs in a whoosh. "Don't cry."

I let out a laugh that sounded suspiciously like a sob and Samael turned and roared for the healer. "You're going to be okay," he said, turning back to me.

"I know."

"What's wrong?"

You're wrong. We're wrong. The fact that you touch me with this tenderness and yet steal my freedom at every turn is wrong.

"Nothing." Another tear slipped out and he sucked in a sharp breath. If I didn't know him better, I'd say the expression on his face was frantic.

"I'll kill them all," he vowed, and I blinked up at him.

"Uh–"

"I'll make them beg as they die. They'll never hurt you again."

"Samael–"

"It's done."

My tears dried up. The psycho leaning over me looked

satisfied. He thought I was no longer crying because he'd promised to turn some people to ash.

"Listen–"

Eldan arrived and Samael let out a low growl. "What the hell took so long?"

I reached for his hand and squeezed.

The light fae ignored him and kneeled next to me. "What do we have here?"

I rolled my eyes. "I'm fine. I could get up, but Samael would probably have an aneurism."

"You're not fine," he snapped. "She has a head injury and a broken wrist."

I frowned at that. I'd been cradling my arm without realizing it. I was sore in so many places that I felt like one giant bruise.

I closed my eyes while Eldan checked me out. When I opened them, Sitri had arrived and was murmuring to Samael. Samael's hand tightened on mine, and his face went scarily blank.

Uh-oh. I'd seen that expression before. Samael had his murder-spree face on.

He wasn't going after the humans who did this without me. No way. Not just because he'd kill them all, but because I was sure this went deeper than it appeared.

"I don't want whatever it is you do that makes me fall asleep," I said to Eldan.

He raised his hands, shooting me a look. "If I could heal you and send you on your way, I would. But that's not how healing works on the body. Particularly human bodies. If I don't fully heal you, you'll be in a lot of pain."

Samael bared his teeth at me and returned his attention to the healer. "Ignore her."

I sighed and let my mind fixate on the explosion while the fae checked me over. Explosives in my car? That was a human MO. Paranormals would have no need to rely on that kind of technology.

"I suggest you find whoever is doing this before I do," Samael said silkily. I eyed him. Was he trying to distract me from the pain? Cute. Unfortunately, the retribution in his eyes made it clear the demon was officially out of patience.

"Don't do anything stupid, Samael. I mean it."

He merely glanced at Bael, who nodded.

I let out a low growl. Unfortunately, Eldan had just moved my wrist and it came out like a whine.

"Samael? I'm serious. *I* was hurt, which means *I* get to go after the bad guys. That's the rule."

He snorted. "I'm a demon. I was born to break the rules." His tone was wry and I gaped at him. Did he just make a… joke?

I needed to take another approach. Otherwise, ash would still be blowing in the wind when I woke up from my little nap.

I shot Eldan a look. "Do whatever you can to get me back on my feet as soon as you can, okay?"

He frowned, but whatever he saw when he looked into my eyes must've convinced him because he shot a look at Samael and then nodded. Good. Now I just had to deal with the demon.

"Don't leave me," I grabbed Samael's hand with my good one and squeezed. "Please."

He narrowed his eyes, obviously confused, and I pulled out the big guns. I let my lower lip make the tiniest tremble as I gave him a mournful expression. "I don't want to be alone."

Samael stared at me. I sniffed and glanced over his shoulder. The look on Vas's face told me clearly that he knew I was full of shit. He shoved a hand over his mouth and walked away, his shoulders shaking.

I regarded Samael. His brow creased, a lock of dark hair fell over his forehead, and it made him appear almost boyish. "You want me to… stay with you?"

I would feel bad about my little 'woe is me' act, except that I was likely saving hundreds of lives.

"Yes." I blinked quickly, as if holding back tears, and he gave a slow nod.

"I will stay."

Excellent. You're welcome, good— and not-so-good— people of Durham.

My eyelids were already heavy and I cursed. On the bright side, thanks to the fae healer, I was likely to wake up in a much better physical condition than I was in right now. But I didn't have time to nap. I needed to find the coward who'd exploded my car and hurt them. When I woke up, I was going hunting.

CHAPTER TWENTY-FOUR

SAMAEL

Danica's eyes fluttered open and immediately caught on mine. A glimpse of relief flashed through them before she rubbed at them with her fists.

"How long was I out for?"

"One hour. You will still be bruised and sore. I advised the healer that you would not wish to sleep through the day."

And I had fought against all of my instincts to do so.

Surprise flashed across her face. "Thank you." Then she scowled. "You didn't go hunting without me, did you?"

"I gave you my word." I was well aware that her insistence that I stayed with her was pure manipulation. But I'd found myself unable to deny Danica. I'd *needed* to watch her sleeping safely in my bed, after seeing how close she had come to true death.

My little witch was only half demon, and she healed like a human. *Anyone* could kill her. Even hate-filled humans.

A cold sweat broke out on the back of my neck.

"Samael?"

I forced myself to regain my control. Her eyes saw too much, and she narrowed them on my face.

"Something else happened."

I raised one eyebrow. I kept our bond tightly closed, but perhaps my rage was leaking through.

"There has been an attempted attack on my tower."

Danica's mouth fell open, revealing her pink tongue. My mind attempted to veer in the direction of all the things I wanted to do with that tongue, but I forced myself to focus.

She let out a low growl. "This is why you don't let fae healers knock me out when I'm protecting two kids."

I waved my hand in the way I knew made her grind her teeth in annoyance. "Cil and Zip are fine."

She threw my covers off her, revealing her nakedness and yelped. I couldn't help the smile that hovered around my mouth, even as my body hardened.

Danica shot me an accusing look and searched for her clothes. They'd been laundered but were hanging over a chair a few feet from me.

"Your clothes were dirty," I said. "*Filthy.*"

"I'm not playing these games with you," she said, although I caught the flash of amusement that darted over her face. She'd never admit it, but she adored our games.

Danica covered herself with the blankets once more and leveled her gaze on me.

"What happened?"

"It was an attempt to hack our security systems. They likely were attempting to find out where the children were."

The little witch's face drained of color and then flushed

red as her fists clenched. She threw the covers off once more and stalked to her clothes. Gloria had muttered about wasting her power when I'd ordered her to spell all the blood out of the material.

I fisted my own hands to prevent myself from throwing Danica back onto my bed and rolling her beneath me.

She pulled on her clothes while muttering softly to herself. Her eyes cut to mine as she yanked her shirt over her head, the movement drew attention to her full, round breasts.

I forced myself to look away.

"What do you know?"

I smiled. "My people are better than their people. They didn't have a chance of breaking through. My IT team allowed them to get close enough that they could uncloak them, revealing their IP address. Bael and Sitri are hunting for them now."

Danica let out a low throaty laugh. She'd made a similar sound in my bed. I got to my feet and she held up one finger.

"I don't think so. Stay over there, mister." She began strapping on her weapons and I gave her my most charming smile.

"You don't want me to stay over here."

She slowly backed away. "I have people to hunt. Whoever blew up my car is going to regret it." Her delicate face twisted into a scowl and she cracked her knuckles.

I suppressed a chuckle. I had a feeling the bounty hunter would not want me to tell her how *cute* she looked while plotting vengeance.

She headed for the elevator and I watched her as she

stalked away. Danica was ephemeral. Every time I thought I had come closer to making her truly mine, she pulled away. In my quieter moments, I wondered why it mattered. Why I couldn't simply remove the bond and allow this mortal her freedom.

"And where do you think you're going?" I asked.

She glanced over her shoulder at me. "If you've found the IP address, that's great. But Steve sent me the full name of the woman who Clint was working with. Her name is Cassie Grant, and I'm going after her."

I waited for it to sink in. She took a few more steps and then paused, realization darting across her face, quickly followed by fury. "I forgot," she muttered. "My car is totaled. I'll get a ride from Vas."

I tensed at the thought of her 'riding' Vas, and Danica gave me a narrow-eyed stare that told me to tread carefully. I smiled.

"I took the liberty of arranging for a new car for you," I informed her.

She placed her hands on her hips. "Did I ask you to do that?"

My smile widened. "You didn't need to ask, bounty hunter. As usual, I am anticipating your needs before you even think of them."

I didn't know why I enjoyed making this woman scowl at me. Why I drank down the fury that radiated from her. Perhaps because she was one of the few people I knew who hadn't had centuries of learning to hide their true feelings behind a bored mask.

"Look, Samael–"

"Borrow it, if the thought of owning it makes you worry."

She thought about it. "Fine. Thank you."

The sour look on her face made me quirk my lips. "The picture of grace and manners. As usual."

"Yeah, yeah."

DANICA

Nice cars were wasted on me. Even if I could have afforded the smooth ride I was enjoying right now, it wouldn't have occurred to me to spend whatever insane amount of money Samael had spent on this car. And I'd seen his personal floor in the tower garage. This was just one of many.

And yet... this was a special kind of car. It was some European brand I'd never heard of, but the valet had raised his eyebrows when he'd handed me the keys.

The leather seat cradled my butt, the air conditioning actually cooled down the car, instead of giving a half-hearted attempt, blasting hot air in my face, and then shutting off. The interior was large and spacious, and the thing practically parked itself.

Say what you want about Samael, but working for him had its perks.

You're not working for him, idiot. You're bonded to him.

Yes. And then there was that.

He'd looked... distraught when I was hurt. And he'd tamped down all of his instincts, which told him to hunt—the instincts that *urged* him to make the problem go away—because I asked him to.

When I thought of Samael these days, I didn't picture the bone-chilling fear I'd experienced when he caught me in his club. I thought of him tenderly pushing my hair back from my face. I thought of him cracking a wry joke, entertaining Cil and Zip, and making sure my sister was okay, even after I'd told him to stay out of my life.

Every time I pulled away, he gave me that patient smile that told me he'd wait as long as it took. And I was worried that eventually I'd succumb, and I'd be in his bed for good.

Once that happened, I'd have no chance at breaking the bond between us.

And that was the problem. Samael still refused to break it. He either didn't see how much it killed me, or he didn't care.

If he wasn't a demon, he'd be the perfect guy.

My mood was dark as I pulled up outside Mike Brown's house. He lived in a small bungalow in Colonial Village. The garden was unkempt and overgrown, and the once-red car parked on the lawn was now a faded tangerine, speckled with rust spots.

Vas was meeting me here after he'd had a meeting with a few of Samael's other demons, so I sat in the cool air and waited until he landed next to me.

Heat punched me in the face as I opened the door. That was the problem with working A/C. It made it worse when you had to go out into the real world.

We walked toward the door and Vas froze.

"What is it?"

"There's something dead in that house."

They'd got to Mike first. Guilt drowned me and I attempted to suck in a breath. Would this guy still be dead if I'd come straight here after learning that he stole the belt?

"We need to check for evidence," I said. I'd already rifled through Samael's trunk, when he gave me the car, and I strode back to the car and pulled out the huge first aid kit.

I snapped on a pair of gloves and handed one of them to Vas as we made our way up the path and back to Mike's front door.

It was unlocked. Whoever had killed him had likely just strode straight in.

"Fuck." I slapped my hand over my nose and mouth at the putrid stench. The body was sprawled on the kitchen floor. Mike had been dead for at least four or five days judging by the bloat.

I couldn't have stopped this. They'd gotten to him too fast.

"They slit his throat," Vas said.

"Yeah."

I stared at the body and swallowed. "He was sitting at the table drinking. From the looks of that bottle, he wasn't exactly sober, but either way, he had his back turned to the killer."

I forced myself to take a step closer. "They were left-handed. Came up behind him probably." I pulled my t-shirt up and shoved it over my nose as I crouched next to the body.

"How do you know that?"

I frowned. "You must've seen a lot of dead people during your life."

He grinned at me. "Demons don't slit throats."

In my mind, a reel started. Samael exploded a guy's head in front of me, and then turned a coven of witches to ash.

"I guess that makes sense. See how the deeper part of the cut is below the ear on the right side, and it ends lower on the left side?" I got back to my feet and held my hand against my throat. Starting just below my right ear, I mimed cutting into my throat. "They pulled his head back, sliced his throat, and walked off. Probably didn't even get much blood on them." I sighed. "I need to call the human authorities but I don't have time to be questioned."

The murder came under the fae's jurisdiction anyway, since it was connected to the investigation. But the police wouldn't see it that way, and if the Mage Council got involved, it would be a giant pissing contest.

"I'll take care of it," Vas said. "We have secure lines at the tower."

"Thanks."

I gulped in the fresh air as we walked toward the car.

"Cassie doesn't live far from here," Vas said. "I'm guessing we're visiting her next."

"You guessed right."

Cassie worked in a bank in Duke Park. Her shift ended at five, so for now, we were going to poke around her house— and her life— and see what we could find. Conveniently, she lived just a few streets away from her work.

Her cottage was mint green with white trim, and I rubbed my hands together as we climbed the stairs leading to her front door.

"Breaking and entering, my favorite thing."

Vas laughed. "You know, it's making more and more sense that you're half-demon."

I ignored that. Slipping my tools from my utility belt, I crouched and went to work on Cassie's lock. It took a while.

"Hey, what are you doing?"

Nosy neighbors. Awesome. "This is a demon-sanctioned investigation," I said. I was half-demon, and I sanctioned it.

The neighbor, a bearded guy with a potbelly, scowled at me.

"Leave, or I'm calling the police."

I frowned. Did he not *see* Vas? I glanced at the demon, but he'd gone around the back of the house, likely looking for an easier entry point. Nice of him to let me know.

"Look, dude, this isn't your fight."

He snarled at me and stepped closer, brandishing a... rake? "We look out for each other around here. We don't need *your* kind." His eyes dropped to the mark on my arm and I gave him a steady look.

Vas appeared beside me, and the guy jumped back, moving further away and back onto his own lawn. He took one look at the demon next to me, made the sign of the cross, and disappeared without a word.

I glanced at Vas. He shrugged.

"I kicked a door open."

"Alrighty then."

I was having no luck with the lock, and we were drawing too much attention. We moseyed around to the back of the house and I stared at the door lying flat on the floor, completely removed from its hinges.

"You kicked the door down, not open."

"Semantics."

I rolled my eyes and walked over the door. Cassie's house was small, with two bedrooms— one of which she used as an office. I hit the office first while Vas went through the bedroom.

She kept the place neat, and I took her laptop for Steve to crack later. My gaze got stuck on a small filing cabinet under the desk. Why bother picking the lock when I had a demon with me?

"Vas?"

He appeared a moment later, his expression grim. "You need to see this."

I followed him into the master bedroom. I'd thought Cassie would keep anything tying her to the artifacts in that locked filing cabinet. But, like most people, she'd gotten lazy. Vas had emptied the drawer from her bedside table onto her bed, and I gaped at the flyers and stacks of paper.

The Federation for Human Separatism, the Human Freedom Union, the American Alliance for Mass Resistance, Portal Control for Concerned Citizens— there wasn't a hate group targeting paranormals that Cassie *wasn't* a member of.

We searched the rest of the house, including the filing cabinet, but there wasn't anything tying her to the artifacts. I handed the laptop to Vas.

"Can you take this to Steve? I'll meet you at the bank." Cassie would be getting off work soon.

He didn't look happy. I gestured at the car. "This thing is a tank, and I'll stay in the car. I need Steve to crack that laptop and help us find the other members so we can locate the artifacts."

"Fine."

I sat in the parking lot outside Cassie's bank until five. I watched as she got into her car and slowly followed her out of the lot.

Cassie was heading somewhere. If she was going home, it would be easier to take her in from there. Here, there were too many concerned members of the public.

But she didn't head toward her house. Instead, she was driving further west.

She pulled into the parking lot of a community center and found a spot. A guy got out of his car a few rows back and joined her, and they began walking toward the community center.

I parked my car on the road where I could keep an eye on anyone arriving. Another woman walked past the entrance to the community center, checked her surroundings, and then backtracked, ducking into the entrance. Smooth.

I called Samael. "Any luck with the IP address?"

"We've found six humans who were connected to the attack on my security."

"Yeah, well I've found a few more. You wanna help a girl out and send some demons?"

"Now you want my help?"

"I'm only one woman. I don't want to shoot them all, which leaves me with a few options."

"And where is Vas?"

The demon appeared next to my car, a wide grin on his face. I jolted. "Standing next to me."

"If I do this, you will owe me."

"You know what? Forget it."

I hung up, ignoring my phone as he rang back. Samael would loathe being hung up on. Served him right.

I couldn't find a parking spot, so I flicked my hazard lights on and double parked like an asshole.

Then I skedaddled to the other side of the street and crouched behind a car.

"What are you doing?" Vas asked.

"Shh, get down. I want to see how many of them turn up, and if they see me, they'll run."

Vas sighed but crouched next to me. Then he sniffed. "You know, you're starting to smell like Samael," he said.

"Not the time, bro."

A quick grin, and then he leaned forward. We both peered around the side of the car.

"I can barely see anything," I complained. "Holy shit, I know that guy."

"What?"

"You do too. That's Gas Station Bob!" Vas looked at me blankly. "I knew there was something familiar about the guy in the picture Steve sent through. He's the manager of the gas station in Brightleaf— the one where–"

"Tarel's body was left. The humans were spelled."

"Yeah. The witches used a mass spell of forgetting, and Bob was *pissed*. Pissed and terrified, which, as we can see, is a terrible combination."

We both watched silently, but it didn't seem as if anyone else was coming.

"Not gonna lie, I wish we'd had a chance to visit Hannah. A look-away spell would be real handy right now."

Vas sneered at me, and we both got to our feet.

"They've put Bob on the door. Makes sense, since he's wearing that fucking belt." That meant there was a pretty high chance either Bob, or someone he was close with was the one shooting at me in Merrill's store.

"I'll take him out," Vas said.

"I don't think so."

Vas glanced at me and I narrowed my eyes at him. "I owe Bobby a punch in the face. Don't get in my way with this."

"Fine. But if he kicks your ass, I'm going to spread your humiliation far and wide."

"That's just mean."

After a few minutes, it was obvious everyone else had arrived. Vas elbowed me gently. "Don't let him kill you. I'll take the back exit."

"I won't. Thanks."

I crossed the street, and Bob took a step toward me warningly. Then he froze.

"Oh hey, Bob. You fucked up when you targeted the people I care about."

Bob cast a glance over his shoulder and I let out a chuckle. "Gonna get your little friends to back you up? Can't even take me with the belt of Thor holding your pants up?"

His face flushed but he turned back to me. "I don't need their help," he said, his eyes wild.

I took one step closer to him, taking him in. Bob was my height, but he was much wider than me, and if he hit me while he was wearing that belt, I was screwed.

Good thing I had a lot of rage to work out.

Bob bared his teeth and ran at me. I stepped to the side and tripped him, but he managed to keep his feet, stumbling wildly.

So I kicked him in the ass and sent him sprawling.

"That's for threatening the kids, Bob."

He jumped up, his face flushing purple-red.

Then he lunged, his meaty fist swinging toward my head. But while the belt may have made Bob strong, it hadn't improved his speed.

I slid out of the way and shoved my knee into his gut. He roared, throwing another punch. The punch threw him off balance and I dodged, grabbed his right arm and introduced his face to my fist.

Bob roared, and I followed the punch up with a slap across his face. His mouth fell open and I took the opportunity to smash the side of my hand into his throat.

The knife-edge made his eyes bulge, and he choked, falling to his knees.

"Yeah, that can't be comfortable. Try and take deep breaths, Bob."

My power caressed my shields, craving more violence. It would be so easy to shove my knife in his heart right now. Or I could slit his throat. The satisfaction would almost be worth it.

No. I needed him to tell me what he knew.

A flap of wings, and I jumped about a foot in the air as Samael appeared beside me.

"I hate when you guys do that. What are you doing here?"

He gave me a look. Oh right, I'd invited him to help me take down the bad guys and then hung up on him.

This little hate group had blown up my car, and almost me with it. Of course the demon would be here, protecting what he saw as his property.

Samael gave me a dark look that warned me we'd be talking about me hanging up on him later. I ignored him.

Asmodeus landed next to us, his red hair gleaming in the sunlight. He reached down and pulled the belt off Bob. Bob groaned but didn't struggle when Asmodeus threw the belt to me.

"Thanks."

I was holding something that was once worn by a god. By *Thor*. If I thought about that too hard, I'd lose my mind.

The belt wasn't anything special. There was no gold to be found, no silver etching, no priceless gems. It was brown, woven, and could've been any old leather belt except for the power that radiated from it.

Misty let out a purr and I jumped. The dagger had been silent for a while now. If it liked the belt, it was a pretty good sign that I needed to give it back to the fae as soon as possible.

I folded the belt up and shoved it in my back pocket. Asmodeus hauled Bob to his feet. Bob swayed and the demon met my eyes.

"Where to?"

"The Mage Council."

Samael shook his head. "That is a mistake if you're planning to interrogate them."

"They're human, Samael. Like it or not, but they fall under the Council's jurisdiction. And I'd like to clear my name."

He studied my face. "Fine. I will, however, notify Albert that while the interrogations may take place in his territory, his people are not permitted to be involved."

I shook my head. "Is that your idea of compromise?"

He shrugged and looked at Asmodeus. The demon took to the air, hauling Bob toward the Council.

Samael had brought a few other demons with him. Bael, Mammon, and Sitri were moving around the sides of the community center, blocking off any other exits.

Samael stroked his hand down my hair and I glanced at him. "Thanks for coming."

He merely nodded and we walked toward the entrance and into the hall where the hate group had gathered.

There must've only been twenty or so humans sitting in a circle on plastic white chairs, and a few of them leapt to their feet as we walked in.

One of them looked at me, looked at the demon next to me, and turned to run. Vas had already moved inside from the other exit, and he raised one eyebrow as the guy desperately swung his arm.

"Alive," I called out. "We need them alive."

For now.

Vas shook his head at me. Then he snapped a fist into the guy's solar plexus and the guy hit the ground, gasping like a fish on land.

The humans were either attempting to run or pulling out weapons. I couldn't see the sword anywhere, but Cassie had armed herself with a blade the length of my arm. I pulled out my own knife. Hers may be longer, but I'd bet mine was sharper.

A beefy guy pulled out a machine gun and everyone froze. Well, I froze. Samael's wing pushed me off balance and I stumbled a few steps to the side as the demon casually took a step front of me. I ground my teeth. We would be talking about this later, that's for sure.

"Go on then," Samael said. "Shoot me."

The idiot did. Bullets bounced off Samael's ward. He held out one hand, and the gun flew out of the guy's hand. Everyone watched as it lifted into the air and melted until it was nothing but a ball of metal. Then it landed on the ground.

"Well?" Samael said to the room at large.

Everyone dropped their weapons and put their hands up. As much as Samael's overinvolvement annoyed me, there was no question that he and his demons got shit done.

I stalked over to the guy with the gun. "Not so easy taking down a paranormal who isn't half the size of you guys and taken by surprise in his own store, is it?"

"Fuck… you."

"Cool story." I slammed my foot into his face.

"Let's get them all back to the Mage Council," I said. "I've got a few questions I need to ask them."

CHAPTER TWENTY-FIVE

DANICA

"Alright, Bob, you know how this goes."

He glowered at me. "Why would I tell you anything? You're gonna kill me anyway."

I shook my head. "I brought you to the Mage Council for a reason. You cooperate, I'm happy to turn you over to the human authorities. They get pissed when you guys mess with paranormals, since they never want to start a war they can't win, but they'll just lock you up. Otherwise, I'm happy to have you transferred to Samael's tower instead?"

His eyes darted and I sat back in my chair as he considered his options.

Vas walked in and whispered into my ear.

"Let's get a drink after this."

I frowned and nodded solemnly. He turned and walked out.

"What?" Bob slammed his hands on the table. "What did he say?"

"He said Cassie is already telling us everything." I shook my head sadly. "She says she had nothing to do with it— you guys forced her to contact Clint and she feared for her life."

Bob's face turned a worrying shade of purple. "That lying bitch."

I shrugged. "You're bigger than her and you've been wearing that belt. I'd understand if she was terrified enough to go along with your plans."

The purple began to drain from his face. He was getting it now.

"I want a lawyer."

I burst out laughing. "You're lucky you're not getting ripped apart. What do you think would happen if we released you to the seelie king?" I shivered. "He may be the 'light' fae king, but the guy's not exactly known for being merciful. And that's if the fae representative doesn't make you beg for death first. You and your little friends made her look like an idiot."

Bob swallowed. "Okay, no lawyer. I get it. I was scared, okay. You were there when that demon was left at the station. We had our memories *wiped*," he spat. "I told my cousin and he let me know about an organization. They were fighting back against the paranormals."

"What organization?"

"Humans for Population Stabilization."

"And what does that mean?"

"Portal control. Those freaks are streaming through every fucking day. Before long, humans are going to be the minority in our own fucking world." He narrowed his eyes at me. "You're no better than us just because you're a witch. Luck of the draw gave you that power."

"I never claimed to be," I said mildly. If Bob knew I was half-demon, he'd probably have a stroke.

"Yeah, well we're sick of it. These other groups, they talk a big game, but all they're doing is writing letters to politicians. *Human* politicians. As if they can do anything. HPS was actually willing to do something about it."

I sat back in my chair. Now we were getting somewhere. "So you decided HPS could help you get rid of the paranormals."

"Right," Bob nodded, warming up now. His nose was broken, likely from my fist. From the way Bob winced when he talked, gently prodding the swelling around his eyes, I'd say he was regretting swinging at me.

"Look, if you don't have power in this world, you're screwed. Hard work doesn't count for shit anymore. Humans are invisible to these paranormals— we're only useful for cleaning up their fucking messes."

I mean, he had a point. Bob must've seen agreement on my face because he gave me a vigorous nod.

"You get it right? You may be a witch, but at least you're human. Can't you see things from my point of view?"

His voice had turned into a high-pitched whine, but now I could hear traces of the man who'd attacked Gary. I think I'd hear his voice— and Gary's choked moans— in my sleep for months.

"Pretend like I do see things from your point of view. No one else is going to. The best thing you can do for yourself is to spill everything you know."

Bob was silent for a long moment. I rolled my shoulders and let him think. Finally, he heaved a sigh.

"Okay. Here's how it went down. I joined HPS and went to a few meetings. For a while it looked like it was shaping up to be similar to the other groups— a lot of talk and no action. But then Cassie heard about this sword. At first we were disappointed, you know? There were rumors it was powerful, but it didn't do anything when we tried to use it."

"So Cassie got pissed."

"The organization has money. Lots of secret donations from human politicians. But we paid a lot for the sword. Cassie told everyone that our new mission was to find as many fae artifacts as we could. She said it was our turn to have power, and once we were a threat to the paranormals, they could no longer ignore us."

"Tell me about the belt."

His gaze dropped to his waist as if he was expecting to see it. His face twisted in what looked like longing.

"One of the women works for this cleaning company."

"Name."

"Crystal Clear Cleaning."

"Name of the *woman*."

"Oh. Ashley."

I eyed the camera, well aware that the demons were listening in. I'd bet Albert was observing as well. Either way, someone would be locating Ashley.

"Ashley stole the belt."

Bob laughed, the sound muffled as he winced and raised his hand to his nose.

"It wasn't even difficult. She said she worked for this fae bitch who treated her like garbage— wouldn't even reply if Ashley greeted her when she was taking out her trash. She walked in one day as the fae was putting it in a safe."

"And then she stole it."

"Like I said, it wasn't difficult."

"So Ashley gave the belt to Cassie."

"Yeah. Cassie was her best friend after that. Told us all that Ashley was an example of who we should all be." Bob's lips thinned. "Then Cassie put the belt on, and we realized it was the real thing."

"And the amulet?"

"This other guy Derek, he's been obsessed with the fae for years. He'd heard about this amulet that would give us all the information we needed to find other artifacts."

"How did you hear about the auction?"

Bob shifted in his seat. "This girl I work with is dating an unseelie." He sneered at the thought. "One day they drank too much fae wine and he told her about an auction they were trying to shut down. Apparently, the organizers had strong magic and they kept moving the auction every time the fae got close to them."

"You figured out it was at the old train station."

"Yeah. It wasn't easy, let me tell you. We had two hundred people looking for it–" Bob cut himself off, looking slightly sick. I made a note on my phone. We didn't have close to two hundred people in these cells. The meeting tonight was clearly just for Cassie's inner circle. We needed to crack all of their electronics and find the rest of the members.

"So you located the auction. How'd you get in?"

"Cassie got in touch with a witch friend who spelled her long enough to make her appear seelie to the wards and the paranormals. The amulet came up and she bid on it. But she got outbid by the goblin."

His dismissive tone made my hand twitch with the

need to punch him in the face again. "What happened when Merrill won the amulet?"

"Cassie told James to go talk to him. We'd managed to get our hands on more funding and James offered him a hundred grand more than he'd paid for it. The goblin told him to fuck off. Said he had a buyer lined up who'd pay double what he'd bought it for."

"So you killed him."

He winced. "That wasn't me, I swear. It was James. And he wasn't supposed to kill him— just find the amulet."

"Where is he now?"

"Uh…"

"Where?"

Bob hunched his shoulders and focused on the metal table between us. "We had to kill him, okay?"

"Why?"

"Once he saw how strong the belt could make him, he became obsessed with it. When you started poking around, he got convinced you were going to find us and steal it back. He attacked you where anyone coulda seen him." Bob snorted. "Shooting up the place was a fucking idiot move. If the Mage Council had caught him, he woulda squealed and told them everything about us. He was unstable."

Yeah, no shit. "And my car?"

The blood drained from his face. I wagged my finger at him. "That was you, wasn't it, Bob?"

"I didn't plan it. Cassie ordered us to do it, I swear."

"Uh-huh. So James killed Merrill. And Cassie realized she had a loose cannon on her hands. She gave you the belt, and you tracked the amulet to Gary's."

He shrugged. Behind me, the door opened. Samael walked in, and Bob began trembling.

I shot Samael a look. This was my rodeo. He simply smiled at me and leaned against the wall as if he was bored.

"How did you track the amulet?"

"Werewolf eyes."

"I got that. How did you spell them?"

"Cassie's witch friend. She's batshit crazy if you ask me. I never saw her, but Cassie told me a few stories that made me never want to go near her, if you know what I mean. Apparently, she cursed her ex-boyfriend pretty bad. He ended up killing himself."

"Name."

"I don't know. I don't, I swear! Cassie met her a while ago, and she just calls her L. I don't think Cassie knows her full name either. The witch is the private type."

"So you traced the amulet to Gary's store. Then you beat the shit out of him and ruined his life's work."

Bob closed his eyes and hung his head. "I didn't mean to," he whispered.

"His kids were hiding, Bob. They heard everything. And then I heard it too. I heard your creepy-ass voice threatening their lives."

Bob flinched, squeezing his eyes shut, as if he could make it all go away. "I didn't know the belt would do that to me. I didn't want to hurt him, I swear. I thought James went crazy cause he was just a psychopath, but once I put that belt on… I couldn't stop. It was… impossible to control myself."

"Magical artifacts weren't designed to be used by

people who have no magic."

He nodded. "I could hear myself say things and my voice came out all wrong. It was as if I was possessed. I told Cassie I didn't want to use it again. James wanted it back, and he figured he could get on Cassie's good side again. That's when he went back to the goblin's shop. Said he was going to find something that would lead us to the amulet. I guess that's when he shot at you."

"Yup."

"I only wore the belt tonight because Cassie said there was no one else for a job we had to do."

I'd bet money that job involved my death. After failing to blow me to smithereens, Cassie would've been pissed.

"Where's the sword and the amulet?"

Bob closed his eyes. "The sword is buried in a trunk in Cassie's backyard. We couldn't find the amulet."

I had a pretty good feeling I knew why. I was an idiot.

I left Bob sobbing and walked out. Samael followed me and I gave him a look. He can't have been comfortable walking down the narrow corridors in the Mage Council. I could hear his wings brushing against the walls on either side of us.

"I will stay silent, but these people attempted to take your life. I will be present for this."

"Fine."

I opened the door to Cassie's interrogation room. She looked younger than I'd expected, maybe Evie's age. She should've been hanging out with friends, complaining about her boss and talking about the latest guy in her life. Instead, she'd been killing multiple people. I had to remember that.

Cassie raised one eyebrow, her expression bored. And then Samael walked in behind me. Within moments, her face was sheet white, and her hand shook as she reached for the glass of water on the table in front of her.

I glowered at Samael. The demon was always stealing my thunder.

"I don't have anything to say," Cassie said.

"That's okay, Bob told us everything. We know you were the mastermind behind all of it. Right now, I'm more interested in your witch friend. It takes some serious black magic to kill a werewolf and make it look like a heart attack."

Black magic and access to a grimoire, according to Selina.

"I can't talk about her."

"Oh," I said softly. "You will."

"I mean it. I can't, okay? She spelled me."

Well, that was inconvenient. Samael shot me a look and I frowned at him. Then the door opened, and Gloria walked in.

Of course. I slid a look up to the camera in the corner of the room. I doubted the Mage Council needed to see exactly how Samael interrogated his suspects. The camera's red light flicked off and I glanced at Samael. He smiled at me.

"I was a practicing witch when your friend was a sparkle in her mother's eye," Gloria crooned to Cassie.

I scowled. What did that even mean? On the bright side, Cassie was trembling. It was probably small of me to enjoy her terror, especially when the expression on Gloria's face told me she found it delicious. But Cassie had tried to kill me. Twice. It was game on.

Cassie stuck her chin out. "Do your worst," she hissed.

"Oh, I will," Gloria said. She took out herbs, candles, and most importantly, a very familiar grimoire. I stiffened, and Samael raised one eyebrow.

I slit my eyes at him. *"Not only do you have a grimoire, but you're sharing it with Gloria?"*

"I knew you would eventually succumb to this method of communication, little witch. If only to berate me in private.

"I'm serious, Samael. What are you thinking?"

"Relax. Gloria is holding one of six grimoires that I own. She has used them before and always returned them to me."

I gaped at him and a hot, very male look slid into his eyes. *"Close your mouth, Danica. You're giving me indecent thoughts."*

My mouth snapped shut and I barely refrained from letting out a low growl. He had six grimoires. Six. *"We* will *talk about this later."*

"I look forward to it."

Gloria cleared her throat. "If you two are quite finished, I am ready to proceed."

I turned to face her. "How come you need the grimoire for this, but you didn't need it for Cil?"

"The child is young and wanted to tell us what happened. This woman is stubborn and has been spelled to do everything but tell us what we want to know."

Cassie began shaking. "Wait, please don't do this." She turned and faced me. "Don't let her do this to me."

I shook my head at her. "Even if you hadn't planned

to murder me multiple times, the fact remains that you were hunting the kids. I know you paid someone to set that magical bomb, which means you could've killed my sister too." I let her see how I felt about that, and she flinched. Now she was getting it. There would be no mercy from anyone in this room.

Gloria began humming in a way that made the hair stand up on the back of my neck. I had the strongest urge to burrow into Samael's chest, to wrap one of his wings around me and close my eyes, shutting out the world like a child.

I took a careful step away from him so I wouldn't do anything stupid.

And then Gloria stopped humming. Cassie's eyes were blank, as if she was a puppet, a shell of herself.

"Tell me the name of the witch you used for your spells."

Cassie's face slowly drained of color. Her breath became a death rattle. This would kill her.

I'd gotten everything I needed from Bob, and we still had the other members of Cassie's little play group to interrogate. Steve hadn't yet been able to crack Cassie's laptop, and I was guessing she was much too smart to keep anything that would connect them.

The witch was the biggest threat right now. I forced myself to lean against the wall.

"L-l-l-lydia Miller."

Cassie's eyes rolled back in her head and she slumped in the chair.

Gloria sucked up the death magic, her eyes glowing for a single second. "Mmm," she said. "Delicious."

I attempted to ignore Gloria, but my face must've told her what I thought of that, because she didn't stick around. I peered up at Samael. "Lydia Miller is one of the McCormick descendants."

"Yes."

I closed my eyes. I'd known Samael hadn't killed them all after they'd attempted to harness his power. I'd watched some of them flee, and Samael's people had been tracking them down one by one so far.

"We will find her," Samael said. He took my hand in his and brought my knuckles to his lips. We stood there, staring at each other in the cell for a long moment. Then I sighed.

"We need to talk to the kids."

"I know."

"Let's go."

We were both silent as Samael flew me back to the tower. He'd arranged for everyone else involved to be interrogated, and then custody of them would be handed over to Albert.

Cil and Zip were still awake when we got up to their floor. The nanny made herself scarce.

I eyed the kids. Both of them sat on the sofa, their faces the picture of innocence. I wasn't buying it. It all made sense now— the attack on Samael's tower had been too risky to shut up a couple of kids.

"I know you guys have the amulet," I said. "I need you to hand it over.".

Zip's eyes widened. Cil just looked resigned.

I waited them out. Within a few moments, Zip's lower lip trembled. "We were just meant to keep it safe for Merrill.

We were going to bring it back. And then dad was hurt."

"Tell me what he said when he gave it to you."

Cil sniffed. "He said *take this and keep it safe, boys. I'll need it in a few days. And if anything happens to me, you give it to your dad.*"

He clapped his hand over his mouth. That had been Merrill's voice. Gloria's spell hadn't entirely worn off yet.

"Okay. Then what happened?"

"I said we would keep it safe, and he said *good, I knew I could trust you. Remember, don't tell anyone that you have it. Promise me.*"

I ground my teeth. Something had tipped Merrill off. Likely, one of the humans had been following him, or maybe he got spooked when James offered to buy the amulet. Either way, his decision to use the kids had gotten him killed, Gary hurt, and put the Cil and Zip in danger.

I forced myself to keep my rage from my voice. As pissed as I was at Merrill, the kids hadn't done anything wrong.

"So you promised him."

"You're not supposed to break promises." A tear rolled down Cil's gray cheek and I reached out my hand and wiped it away.

"In this case, it's a good thing that you told me. Now, I need you to tell me where it is."

He shook his head in instant denial and I gave him a stern look. "Cil. This is important. Merrill died for the amulet, and your dad almost did too."

"I thought you got the bad guys."

"We did. But we know there were other people who

didn't attend the meeting tonight. Besides, where there is one group, there are usually more. When your dad wakes up, he'll take you home, and we need to make sure you guys are safe."

"Because they could try and hurt us again?"

"Anyone who wants that amulet will do whatever it takes to steal it. You know I'll keep it safe, right?"

It would be going straight back to the light fae, who had hopefully learned a lesson about complacency.

Cil glanced at Samael. He nodded. The kids gazed silently at each other, deep in some wordless conversation.

Then Cil buried his hand in their bag of treasures and pulled out the amulet. I scowled.

I'd stared at this bloody amulet when I peeked in their bag of treasures, but I'd ignored it. The light fae enjoyed things that were bright and shiny, and the amulet was old and tarnished. It looked like it would be sold at a flea market somewhere.

My assumptions had cost me.

I reached out my hand. "Thank you, Cil."

"Wait," Samael said. I glanced at him and frowned. The demon looked shaken— something I'd never seen before. His eyes were on the amulet as he shot to his feet. "Don't touch–"

Cil dropped the amulet into my palm and the room disappeared.

White fog. All I could see was fog.

"Cil? Zip? Samael?"

Nothing. There was nothing but fog. Until there wasn't. My surroundings slowly came into view and I froze.

I was in some kind of… library?

Shelves stretched out before me as far as my eyes could see, and each was bursting with leather-bound books. Flame as tall as me bordered the library, caging me in. I swallowed and scanned my surroundings. How the hell was I getting out of here?

The books themselves looked ancient, and I took a few steps forward, scanning the titles.

They were in a language I couldn't read, and disappointment pricked at me. But as I watched, the letters on the spines blurred, rearranging themselves until the titles were in English.

"Whoa."

The books seemed to all be about… demons. I scanned the titles. *Wings in flight: A Study of the Demon Form, Volume One, Two, and Three.*

Demons: A History, Volumes one through nine, Powers and Limitations.

History, family trees, even detailed explanations of their wingspans… it was all here.

I surveyed the books. I was completely, utterly alone, in a library filled with all the information that I'd ever need to understand Samael and his people. I grabbed *Demons: A History, Volume One* and hefted it into my arms. Jeez, it was huge, and there were nine other books just like it.

I hauled it with me toward a blank spot on the floor, planning to sit cross-legged on the ground. A sofa appeared out of nowhere and I jolted.

It was *my* sofa. Complete with my coffee table. Wow, a cup of coffee and I'd be set.

My favorite cup appeared on a coaster, the coffee still steaming. I gaped at it. All I needed was my cat and I could curl up for hours.

I froze. "I didn't mean that. Please leave Lia alone."

Silence, but she didn't appear. I swallowed and sat on my sofa, which seemed much, much more comfortable than it usually was. I cracked open the book. It started with names I couldn't recognize, and I skimmed the first few pages, then flicked to the index and ran my finger down the page.

"There."

Samael. Jeez, he was mentioned a lot. I flipped to the first mention of his name and began to read.

Samael, son of Nisroch and Labassu, both deceased.

I frowned and flicked to his father's name in the index, reading forward.

Nisroch was a high level general who bonded with Labassu, daughter of the underking.

I'd known Samael was a prince from the memory he'd shared with me. But reading about it solidified it in my head. According to the book, the royal family had been slaughtered by… Lucifer.

I kept reading. Lucifer was the current underking, but he hadn't always been. He'd been one of Samael's grandfather's top advisors, and he'd planned his coup over several centuries.

This was who Samael's *enemy* was. Lucifer himself.

I forced myself to put the book away. I needed to find a way out of here, and when I did, I needed to talk to Samael. Lucifer had been centuries old when Samael was just a child. How could he hope to go up against him?

I placed the book back where I found it and wandered. I'd managed to get turned around, and whenever I drifted too close to the flames, the heat pouring off them warned me away. Something was glowing to the right. I followed the tiny white sparks and frowned.

A single leather-bound book sat on a stand. The book blazed with white light, illuminated as if from within. I stared at it.

The Nephilim Prophecy.

Everything around me disappeared, and I lifted my hand, reaching for the book.

No. Opening a magic book in a strange realm definitely wasn't a good way to stay alive.

The compulsion pulled at me, and I gritted my teeth, frozen in place. I couldn't back away, couldn't seem to move, except to take another step forward. It was as if I was caught in thick, unyielding glue.

I palmed one of my knives. I broke wards with my blood. I'd break this too. I sliced my hand and the world turned purple. The book left its stand, floating into the air, and my magic streamed from me, mixing with the white sparks dancing above me.

The book fell, and I watched as my hands opened.

I caught it.

Every instinct I had, every part of me urged my hands to put it down. I couldn't explain the clenching of my gut, the pounding of my heart, but I knew that if I opened that book I was in deep, deep shit.

My hand moved to the cover.

"No, goddamn it."

I focused every ounce of my willpower on my hand. I dropped my shields and pushed my magic against the compulsion.

It made no difference. My hand moved, and I opened the book.

CHAPTER TWENTY-SIX

SAMAEL

I paced back and forth. "Get that seelie woman here. Now."

Sitri turned and pulled up his phone. Across the room, Lilith shook her head at me. "You can't dodge fate, Samael."

"Fuck fate."

"If she's in the library, it's too late. Humans are such curious creatures."

I whirled and focused all of my attention on her. Lilith paled and went silent. I turned and went back to pacing.

"Mariam is on the way," Sitri announced. "She said that if she'd known about the prophecy, she never would've sent her after the amulet."

I closed my eyes. *"So far, they've lost a sword, an amulet, and a belt,"* she'd said. And I, who'd been so focused on controlling the situation, the prophecy, and Danica herself, hadn't bothered to clarify which amulet it was. Instead, I'd been distracted by the vision she presented in her dress the night of the ball.

And now we'd all pay for it.

A rumbling BOOM shook the room. I glanced around, ready to order an evacuation of the tower, but the room itself wasn't shaking.

That sound had just warned every demon alive.

Bael's face was expressionless. "She opened the book."

Lilith shook her head. "And so it begins."

DANICA

I frowned. My head ached like I'd been hit, and my stomach clenched uneasily. I blinked my eyes opened and the light burned my eyes, making nausea roll through my body.

All I wanted was to close my eyes again, but I forced myself to sit up. The library was a mess, shelves fallen, books sprawled on top of each other. None of them seemed destroyed, but I felt bad anyway. I loved books.

Except for the book next to me.

The book had seemed thick at first, but it actually only had one page, which it was opened to. I scowled at it. Whatever had happened, to both me and the library, was because of that stupid book. I leaned over to close it, once and for all, and my hand stilled.

One sentence. The first page only contained one sentence.

When the Morning Star goes to war with the Nephilim of his bloodline, only one shall survive.

A Nephilim. I was a Nephilim. I snorted. I was pretty sure my mom hadn't been getting it on with Lucifer on the downlow. I flicked the page, and as I watched, the following pages turned to ash, crumbling into nothing.

A deep sense of unease was crawling up my spine.

I stared around the library. I didn't want to be here anymore. I clicked my heels together. "There's no place like home."

My voice sounded hoarse. I was oddly numb. I didn't

exactly know what I was doing here, but it didn't bode well for me. All I wanted was to be back in my apartment.

"Uh, hello? I want to leave now." I brushed myself off and wandered back the way I'd come. Now I was dodging piles of books and shelves that had fallen like dominos.

There. In the distance, something was glowing. I scowled. I'd been lured in by glowing in the distance last time, and all I had for my troubles was a roaring headache and a sense that I'd fucked up on a grand scale.

I turned and let my gaze wander over the mess behind me. The path I'd just walked down was no longer there. I couldn't get back unless I wanted to climb over bookcases and books. And the flames still bordered the library at every turn. Guess I was moving toward the shining light.

I hadn't realized how far I'd walked. But this time, the light wasn't a book. It was a portal. I pulled the amulet from my pocket. It glowed in the same silvery white color.

With a deep breath, I walked through the portal.

Strong arms grabbed me, pulling me to a hard chest. I panicked, pushing away, and they immediately released me. I was back in Samael's tower, the kids nowhere to be seen.

"Holy shit, what did you *do?*"

The kids' room was a mess. Someone had rampaged through it, and I was pretty sure it was the demon in front of me.

"You better fix this," I said absently, focusing on Samael. He turned and strode away.

"What's wrong, Samael?"

"What's wrong? You opened the fucking prophecy, that's what's wrong."

I went very still. "How do you know that?"

Samael was the picture of frustration as he whirled, baring his teeth. "Because I felt it. Every demon alive would have."

I studied the man in front of me. I'd never seen him worked up like this before. Samael typically got cold, icy, and silent when he was pissed. This wasn't anger… this was fear.

"Tell me," I ordered.

He let out a low growl and my pulse increased. "Tell me."

"You already know. You're Nephilim. And you're of Lucifer's line. According to the most famous seer in all the worlds, you are the key to his undoing."

"I don't believe in prophecies."

He laughed at that, but it was bitter. "Well, darling, they believe in you."

I stared at him. "Who is my father?"

"Lucifer's son."

I swayed on my feet. Lucifer was my grandfather. *The* Lucifer. Samael held out a hand to steady me and I stumbled away from him.

Harriette had lied to me. No, she hadn't lied exactly. She'd skirted the truth the way the fae always did.

"He was a high demon who was in the underking's inner circle," she'd told me.

"Where is he?"

"He disappeared before you were born."

"I know that. Is he back in the underworld?"

"No. My spies say he hasn't returned and is believed to

be dead."

I swallowed. "If I'm so dangerous to Lucifer, why hasn't he killed me?"

His eyes were very hard and very cold. "Because the bastard can't leave the underworld, and the people in this world are loyal to *me*. The only way for him to wield enough power to take my grandfather's throne was to bind his lifeforce to the underworld. Until you opened that book, he had no idea you existed. Now, every demon alive knows the Nephilim is alive."

I didn't like the way he said 'Nephilim,' as if I was nothing more than a tool.

I stared at him. *I don't like when my tools are broken before I'm finished using them.* He'd said that to me soon after we first met.

My heart twisted. "Tell me you didn't know who I was. Tell me you didn't know I have the power to take down your oldest enemy. The man who slaughtered your family."

He gazed at me steadily and I lunged toward him. He made no move to stop me as I held Misty to his throat.

"Tell me."

A muscle twitched in his cheek, but his expression stayed blank. Inscrutable bastard. I let out a bitter laugh.

"You knew who I was this entire time, and you let me stay ignorant. Worse, you were probably planning to use me to take down your enemies. Deny it."

Betrayal had sharp teeth and vicious talons. It ripped through me until I was one big, gaping wound. All this time I'd been asking Samael about my mother, when I really should've been asking about my father.

Did all of Samael's people know who I was? Did Vas? I'd begun to make… friends.

"Tell me you weren't planning to keep this from me forever. Tell me you weren't planning to use me against Lucifer."

I'd let him in, I realized. Somewhere along the way, I'd let him crawl beneath my rib cage, and he was buried there, where my fucking heart should be.

I was going to be sick.

My breath caught in my throat as Samael's hand blurred toward me, and Misty went flying. His hand slid to the nape of my neck, his hold warning, possessive. He'd moved faster than I could blink, and I reached for my Nim Cub. His other hand plucked it from my sheath.

"I don't think so. You *will* listen to me."

Fine. I gazed somewhere over his left shoulder. I didn't believe he'd kill me. After all, he needed me for his revenge plans.

There was a gaping hole inside my chest. A wound that would never heal. Despite knowing who and what he was, I'd started trusting him at some point. And he'd taken that trust and strangled it.

He cursed as my face told him everything I was thinking. Either that, or he felt it down our fucking bond. "Don't look at me like that. I was planning to tell you."

"Let me go."

"You will allow me to explain."

"I don't want to hear your explanations. I don't ever want to see you again."

The hand holding my wrist stroked the gold mark that

represented our bond, silently reminding me that I'd be seeing him until he decided otherwise. Fury burned like a fireball inside my chest and I yanked my hand. He let it go.

Trust was like a rope. Every betrayal frayed that rope until it was frail, barely holding together. But there were some betrayals that were so shocking, so all-encompassing, that they were a sharp blade, slashing through the rope and instantly severing it forever.

I'd considered letting Samael feed from me. I'd imagined a world in which I could convince him to free me from the bond, and we could *date*.

I let out a bitter laugh. His face tightened, and something that looked a lot like panic shifted through his eyes.

"Danica–"

"Stop."

If this was the last time I ever saw him, he'd do what he had promised.

"Show me my mom."

He jolted in surprise. Then his expression hardened. "Why would you want this while you are already upset?"

"There's no good time to see my mother's body, Samael." And I had no intention of spending any time around him ever again. "You said you would show me. So do it."

He stared at me for a long moment. I narrowed my eyes, waiting. That muscle twitched in his jaw, the one that let me know every time I was driving him insane. "Close your eyes."

I did.

And then I was inhabiting Samael's memory. Once

again, I was inside his body, as he stood on the sidewalk in South Durham.

My mom had been so young. I'd forgotten that somehow. I'd been born when she was just nineteen, and as I stared down at her, lying alone and cold, I let my gaze drift over her face. There were no wrinkles by her eyes, no laugh lines around her mouth. She was frozen, ageless.

The pictures had shown me her body. But they hadn't shown me the chill in the air. They couldn't communicate how quiet it was, on that street where she had died, alone and in pain. Her nails were ragged and caught, and a sharp fury stabbed through my chest. The investigators could've searched for DNA. Even if the murderer had been a paranormal, it would've told them what kind of creature had killed her.

I studied those hands. The hands that had held me when I was sad, checked my forehead for fever when I was sick. Those hands would never grow wrinkled and old. Instead, they were cut with defensive wounds, one of her nails torn completely off.

My mom had fought for her life. It hadn't made a difference, but I was proud of her for that. She'd had two kids, and despite everything that had happened between us all, she'd fought to stay alive for us.

Oh god, it hurt so much.

"Boss?"

Samael turned. *I* turned. Bael was approaching, and he glanced down at my mom's body, something like relief in his eyes.

Relief.

Samael's voice echoed inside my head. *He thought it was my lover. We both did. Bael was concerned that I would rip this realm apart in my vengeance.*

I attempted to push Samael's voice away. Either I succeeded, or he fell silent, and the body I inhabited turned back, glancing down at my mother.

"A shame," Samael said. "Have the High Coven notified."

Bael nodded. "It's already done."

Samael turned and walked away. He walked away and left my mother lying on the ground.

The memory faded and my stomach clenched as I stared up at him. "How could you leave her there?"

"I had imagined the coven would arrange for her murder to be investigated. I didn't want to destroy the evidence."

I doubted that. She'd just been another dead witch. Why would he give a shit? Samael went very still at whatever he saw on my face.

He let me go and turned away. "But why would you believe that? Every member of your coven taught you not to trust. Including your own mother."

"Don't you dare psychoanalyze me."

He shook his head. "You expect betrayal. It's your default. So congratulations, bounty hunter. You found what you were looking for."

He let me go, taking a careful step back. His face turned blank as he gazed at me. For the first time in weeks, he reminded me of the high demon I'd met while sneaking into his club. The demon who'd casually considered my death.

My phone vibrated and I slid it out of my pocket. My

throat was so tight I had to clear it a few times before I could talk.

Samael watched me out of dark, fathomless eyes while I talked to the nurse.

"Gary is awake," he said when I hung up.

"Yes. I need to take the kids to the hospital."

"Fine. But we're not done here."

I shook my head. "We were done before we got started."

"If you believe that, Danica, then you don't know me at all."

"Everything I learned today proves I never had a chance of knowing you, Samael."

I turned and walked away. He was smart enough that he didn't try to stop me.

Cil and Zip were too excited to catch onto my mood, chattering eagerly about all the things they were going to tell their dad.

I put on a happy face for them as I drove to the hospital. The fae healer gave me a nod as I arrived, her expression softening as she took in the kids.

"He's waiting for you," she smiled at them.

"Is he still sleeping?" Zip stage-whispered as we walked into Gary's room.

Gary opened his eyes and gave us a weak smile. "Just resting. Get over here."

They climbed up on his bed. I took a seat in the chair next to him and gave him a long look. "You scared the crap out of me."

"Yeah, well, you did the same to me."

It took me a moment to understand what he was referring

to, and then I snorted. One of Gary's last memories would be the way I'd lost control of my power and threatened him in his own store. So much had happened since then that I'd almost forgotten.

"I'm sorry about that."

Gary cleared his throat. "Your demon friends told me what happened. Told me you've been hunting for the people who did this to me ever since. You kept my boys safe." His eyes glistened as he clutched them close. Zip burrowed into his side. "I was so scared for them, but I knew you'd make sure they were okay."

"Don't mention it. Well, maybe mention it when I come in asking for a discount." I winked at him and he rolled his eyes, but a chuckle escaped his throat. He winced at the movement and I narrowed my eyes at him.

"You look tired," he said. "And sad."

I shrugged. "Just personal stuff. We arrested everyone involved and we've spread the word that you don't have the amulet anymore, so you guys should be okay now. But call me if you need anything." I jerked my head toward the kids. "My sister would be more than happy to look after them at the coven while you recover."

He shook his head and gestured toward two small beds that had been set up in the corner of the room. "Your demon friends thought of that too."

The lump in my throat was so big I could barely speak. "Okay, great. I uh, need to get going. I'm glad you're okay."

His eyes were already sliding closed again. "Get some sleep. You look like shit."

"Dad! That's a bad word."

"Sorry."

CHAPTER TWENTY-SEVEN
DANICA

I slept for twelve hours, and then I went to Evie's. She was waiting outside for me when I pulled up, and her eyes narrowed on my face. "What's wrong?"

"Bad dreams. I'm fine."

"Uh-huh."

I scowled at her disbelieving tone. "I need a favor from you."

She eyed me warily and I couldn't help but laugh. "You can say no."

"Let me hear it."

I reached into Samael's car and pulled the cat carrier out. The car would be going back, but I'd needed to come here. Needed to see Evie and simply breathe.

Lia let out a tiny squeak of a meow and my sister *melted*. Her mouth dropped open, her eyes went wide, and then her gaze darted between me and the cat. "Are you serious?"

"I'm never home." My eyes were hot, and several razorblades had somehow gotten stuck in my throat. "It's not fair to her."

The razorblades cut me to pieces as I said the words, and Evie's face softened. She threw her arm around my shoulders.

"Of course I'll take her. I've been thinking about getting a pet for a while now. You can visit her any time you want," she vowed. "And if you have some time off work, you can take her for a few days. We'll share cat custody."

"You're a great sister, you know that?"

"Hey, you're the one giving me a pet."

We strode into the house and sat at the kitchen table, where Evie put a plate of cookies in front of me. "I bake when I'm stressed," she said. She crouched down and opened the cat carrier. "Hello gorgeous."

Lia purred and batted at my sister with her paw, her claws tucked away.

"She likes to bite," I warned her. "They're not hard… I call them love bites."

Lia narrowed her eyes at me. I stroked her soft little head. "I'll miss you, cat."

She let out a low meow and rubbed her head against my hand.

Evie looked up at me. "I've missed *you*." I frowned at her and she laughed. "I mean over the past few years. I'm sorry for everything."

"I'm sorry too." I heaved a sigh. "Look. What happened to us sucked. We were kids. We loved each other, and no one told us why we couldn't be together. They ripped us apart and left us lost and confused. We trusted the adults in our lives and they stole our chance to grow up together." I reached for her hand and squeezed it. "We deserved better."

Evie's huge aquamarine eyes were wet. "We *did* deserve better. I'm glad you're here. I know it's hard dealing with the coven, but I'm glad you're here."

Lia bit her gently on one finger and she laughed, stroking her some more. "Do you want to... hang out next week? Gemma and a few of the other coven leaders are going to meet with a coven in New York and she's put me in charge while she's gone. I'll be hanging around here most of the week, but you could come stay. We could watch movies in the attic like we used to."

I smiled. While I had been desperate to get out and see the world, my sister loved this house. Loved it so much that I'd once teasingly told her she'd spend the rest of her life in it.

"That sounds good. Oh, before I forget, these are for you." I reached into my utility belt and pulled out the diamond studs. Evie's eyes darted to my ears, and I filled her in about Harriette and mom's jewelry box.

Evie carefully placed the earrings on the table, obviously with no intention of ever wearing them.

"Mom built protection spells into them, Evie."

She could feel them, I knew she could. Could feel the love mom had for us. She shook her head. "I don't want to talk about her."

"Samael saw her soon after she was killed. He'd gone to the area because he was worried it was a witch he was seeing. I made him show me his memories."

"Why would you do that?" Evie was fighting to sound disinterested, but her hand tightened around her mug.

"I'd seen pictures, but I'd never seen what really happened. She... fought for her life. She was brutally slaughtered. Anything she'd wanted to achieve throughout the rest of her life, any secrets she finally wanted to tell us, any bridges she wanted to rebuild… all that was ended. I don't know why she came back here— maybe she'd decided that we could move back. Maybe she wanted to see you. Maybe someone lured her here to kill her— I dunno. But she didn't deserve to die that way. No one did."

Evie sniffed, glancing away. "Why are you telling me this?"

I needed to be careful here. Evie and I were finally repairing our relationship. "I think you've been so busy being mad at mom, that you've never truly grieved her. And I get it, believe me I do. I was so, so mad at her for such a long time that when she died, we were barely speaking. The last thing I said to her–"

I cut myself off and took a deep breath. "She may not have been perfect, and she may have done a lot of things that hurt us both, but she was our mom. Burying it all down only means that it'll come up when it's the least convenient." My panic attack the other day had proven that.

I pulled out the other set of earrings from my pocket. Grief flashed across Evie's face as she took in the blue beads, and then she ripped her gaze away and stared into her coffee. "I'll think about what you've said. That's all I can say."

I placed the beaded earrings on the table next to the diamond studs. "That's all I ask."

A witch named Brooke waltzed in. Her hair was a similar shade to Evie's, and almost as long, and she had the same curvy build. She raised her hand as she walked to the fridge. "Sup."

"Hi," I replied.

She took out a can of coke and pointed it at Evie. "Don't forget about tonight."

Evie grinned and I raised one eyebrow. "What's happening tonight?"

"Dress up party at Meredith's."

I frowned at that. "Mere doesn't usually do private events."

Brooke nodded. "Yeah, but Jessica is one of her besties. She convinced Mere to let her have her thirtieth at the bar, as long as we opened it up to the public at midnight. You should come!"

The underworld would freeze over before I voluntarily put on a fancy-dress outfit and dealt with drunk witches.

Evie grinned at whatever expression I'd made. "Danica's busy. Maybe next time."

I cleared my throat. "Yeah. Maybe next time." Misty glowed red and I covered the dagger with my shirt. Traitor.

Brooke wandered out and Evie cleared her throat awkwardly. "Are you… seeing Samael?"

"No."

"Dani–"

I took a deep breath and filled her in. By the time I was finished, her eyes were wet with sympathy. Maybe eating my feelings would help. I reached for a cookie and took a bite.

"Wow, this is good. Don't look at me like that. Samael lied to me. This whole time. He says it was because he was 'protecting me' and he didn't want me to find the prophecy. But I know him. He was planning to use me to take down

Lucifer."

"He loves you, Dani."

I gaped at her and burst out laughing. "You're a romantic."

She narrowed her eyes at me. Lia swiped at my hand and I shook my head. "He doesn't know what love is."

"He's a demon. You know more than anyone that he has no experience dealing with humans. He's not used to having to compromise. You need to teach him."

"You know what I was thinking when I arrived in that library? Wow, this is so cool. I can't wait to tell Samael about this." I pressed the heels of my hands against my eyes.

"You love him too."

I let out a startled laugh. "I feel… something for him," I admitted. "But sometimes that isn't enough."

"I'm rooting for you guys."

I laughed. "Okay." My shirt had ridden up and Evie reached out and brushed her finger along the hilt of Misty. The dagger glowed blue. We both froze. I'd never seen that happen.

"Whoa. It just talked in my head." Evie's wide, panicked eyes met mine. I was pretty sure mine were just as wide.

"What did it say?"

"It said '*finally, there you are.*'" She shuddered. "It has a creepy voice." She jumped. "It did it again. It said '*that wasn't nice.*'"

"It does that sometimes. But it hasn't talked to anyone but me so far. If… if Samael knew"– god, even saying his name hurt– "he'd probably take it back. Keep this to yourself, okay?"

She nodded. "Of course."

I got to my feet. "Be good, cat." I scratched her under the chin and she purred.

I was doing the right thing. I was never home. But it still hurt like a bitch.

"You can visit her every single day if you want," Evie vowed. "Even if you don't feel like hanging out with me, you can just let yourself in and chill with her."

"I'll always want to hang with you, Evie."

She stared at me. And then her lips curled into a wide smile. "I'll always want to hang with you too."

"We need to talk about the way you fell asleep in fae territory."

She winces. "Oh. That."

"Yes, that. Vas found you curled up in the drivers' seat. You can't do that again, Evie. It's too risky."

"I won't. I'm not an idiot. My power has been… fluctuating recently. Besides, I knew Vas was above me. He's not exactly subtle."

I laughed. "No he's not. Okay, I've got to get going. Things to do, vengeance to plan."

Evie laughed, and then winced as she realized I was serious. "Don't be too hard on your demon, Dani."

"Uh-huh. Says the woman who sent a box of bespelled dicks after the last man who got on her bad side."

I left Evie playing with Lia and headed for the Mage Council. I'd attempted to tell Keigan that it wasn't a good idea for me to be anywhere near the facility, but he'd told me firmly that he was a Discipulus Mage and the last time he'd checked, he was still allowed guests.

Albert had really pissed him off when he'd had me brought in.

Keigan met me downstairs, sending fierce frowns in the direction of anyone who whispered or gaped at me.

"You know, I wouldn't put up with this shit for anyone else," I told him, and he laughed.

"I've added you to my guest list. That means your ban is revoked."

"I won't need to come back here," I told him gently. "I no longer work for the Mage Council."

He shook his head at me as we signed in. The bowl of water turned green and I marveled at it as we got into the elevator.

Keigan cleared his throat. "Did you or did you not tell me that you planned to start your own business one day?"

"I mean yeah, once I found out who killed my mom and moved to California. But I was thinking I'd buy some shack on the beach somewhere and just do enough work to pay for rent and food."

Keigan looked at me for a solid three seconds. And then he threw his head back and laughed. "Ah, the ignorance of youth. I forget how little I knew myself when I was your age."

"And just what is that supposed to mean?" I asked pissily.

He shook his head as the elevator doors opened and led me into his office. Up here, it was easier to ignore the shocked looks as I walked down the fifth floor. If Albert found out I was here, heads would roll. It wasn't like Keigan to have a pissing contest with his boss.

"That means what you think you want would be the worst thing you could give yourself. The boredom would drive you crazy within three days."

I wasn't a sulker, but my lower lip was coming perilously close to sticking out in a pout. Because I had a pretty good feeling that Keigan was right.

"Take a seat," he said as he broke the ward on his office door and gestured me inside.

I picked up a stack of files off his guest chair and held them above his desk, searching for a clear space.

"Oh, just put them on the floor," Keigan waved his hand.

This wasn't like him. The Keigan I knew kept his office spotless. "Uh, are you okay?"

He smiled absently at me. "Never better." He opened a closet and unlocked a beat-up file cabinet, pulling out a manilla folder which he handed to me.

I opened it, frowning down at the photos. It looked like some kind of... store?

I glanced up at Keigan and for the first time he seemed flustered. "When I became a Discipulus Mage I knew I wanted to make some smart financial decisions. With the state of this world, putting my money in the bank didn't make much sense. So, I turned to commercial real estate."

I had no idea where he was going with this. He smiled at whatever he saw on my face.

"This is one of my properties. The tenants have given their notice as they're moving to South Carolina. It will be empty in a few weeks."

Was he... offering it to me? I gaped at him. His smile widened.

"It's not much, but there's room for an office and a small cell. I don't have a mortgage on the property, so you won't need to pay me rent–"

"Hold it right there. If I'm doing this, I'm paying you a fair market rent."

Tears pricked at my eyes. With the money I'd made from Mariam, I could more than afford to rent it and still pay my other bills. And Mariam had promised to give me a reference. I'd also bargained for access to the library. She'd said she would talk to the fae king about allowing me to visit occasionally.

Screw the Mage Council, I'd do just fine without them.

My mind was racing. Despite all the details I had to consider, I still had to resist the urge to call Samael and tell him my news. I pushed the urge away.

I'd relied on Samael and his people far too much in this investigation. I didn't regret it— the kids were safe, and so was my sister. But I was done using his resources. Including Steve.

As much as I liked him, I needed to find my own hacker. I'd hire some mercs for when I had more than one suspect to take down. Once I was making some decent money and I'd built up a reputation, I could probably even hire a receptionist.

Keigan cleared his throat. He was still waiting for me to say something, but from the amusement in his eyes, he knew what I was going to say.

"I'll take it. Thank you Keigan." I wasn't a hugger by nature, but I got up, rounded his desk, and wrapped my arms around him.

He flushed. "You're welcome, Dani. I know you're going to be successful at anything you put your mind to."

CHAPTER TWENTY-EIGHT
DANICA

The sun heated my skin as I walked across the field toward Gary and the kids. Twenty or so black chairs had been set up on the grass, and I took a seat next to Zip. The chairs had been chosen with respect for goblin stature, and I stretched my legs out in front of me.

Gary let the kids fill me in on everything that had been happening over the past week. When they'd finally run out of things to tell me, he smiled at me. "Thank you." His voice was hoarse.

"You've already thanked me. Should you be out of bed?"

He gave me a dark look, and we both turned our attention toward the pyre that was being built twenty feet away.

Goblins didn't believe in burial, so Merrill's body would be burned on a pyre. His daughter was helping to light it.

"Dad, can we go watch them light the fire?"

Gary craned his neck. Merrill's body was nowhere to be seen. "Don't get too close."

The kids jumped off their seats and

made their way over to the pyre. Gary was silent for a few minutes. Then he cleared his throat.

"I had to come. Merrill and I, we were competitors. But we were also friends."

"He put your kids in danger."

"I didn't say he was perfect. He never would've wanted anything bad to happen to my boys. Or to me. Sometimes, bad things just happen."

We were both silent. And then he let out a long sigh. "You're probably wondering what happened to their mother."

I turned in my seat. Gary's face was blank, but his eyes... I'd never seen sadder eyes.

"You don't have to talk about it."

He ignored that. "Frez came through the portal with me. We'd been together for so long, through the Decade of Despair, through all of it. We had the boys and she stayed home for a while, but then she wanted to get back to work.

"She got a job in the unseelie king's court. She did low-level tasks— mostly running errands— she never met him directly, but I guess they found out who she was, and that she had a connection to the king.

"She was walking home one night, probably distracted. Zip had been having some problems and she felt guilty for leaving the boys to go to work. But we needed the money."

He wiped away a tear and forced a smile as Cil turned and waved at us. "Frez was killed by a human hate group. She was trying to get home to our boys and never saw it coming. They hit her with a car and drove back and forth over her body until she died."

The blood drained from my face. "Did the authorities find them?"

"No. She was just a lesser unseelie, and we couldn't afford to retaliate against the humans. Now, they tried to take everything from me again. They almost left my boys orphans."

Uh-oh. "Gary–"

"It's beginning," he said, and his tone told me he wouldn't be listening to reason anytime soon. Shit.

Yexa found me after the service.

"Thank you for what you did."

"You're welcome. I'm sorry it can't bring your dad back."

"So am I." She surveyed the crowd. "I think he'd like this, you know? He always loved it when his friends gathered in a big group. He used to talk of the old days, before he came through the portal— and realized he didn't have enough power to get back."

"I didn't know that— that some lesser fae can't get back through the portal."

"We keep it quiet. I could go through if I wanted, but there's nothing for me there. Although, there's not much left for me here either. Anyway…" her voice trailed off.

"Wait," I said as she turned to walk away. "I have some people to introduce you to."

I led her over to where Cil and Zip were sitting by their dad.

"Yexa," Gary got to his feet with a smile. "I met you when you were a little girl. You probably don't remember me."

I turned my head, and my gaze slammed into Samael's. He stood alone at the edge of the field, his feet planted as he watched me.

We stared at each other. Samael took a step closer, wearing his inscrutable expression once again. If he came any closer, people would notice him. I was surprised they hadn't already.

I murmured a goodbye and left Yexa talking to Gary and the kids. Then I made my way over to Samael.

"What are you doing here?"

"We need to talk, Danica. Now that you know about the prophecy–"

"I don't believe in fate. And I don't have to attempt to kill Lucifer if I don't want to. The prophecy says only one of us will live. Which– let's be real– means that *I'll* be the one to die. I'm not going anywhere near the guy."

"You can't bury your pretty head in the sand over this. The moment you opened that book, Lucifer learned all he needed to know. He'll send his people after you. You're a threat to his power. To his *life*. He'll never let that stand."

Bitterness flooded my mouth. "Oh, *now* you care what happens to me? Maybe you shouldn't have left me ignorant then. Maybe if I'd known about what would happen if I read the prophecy, I would've been on the lookout for glowing books."

Samael's voice was a blade coated in sweet poison. "Be very careful, bounty hunter. I have given you freedom I have never given anyone else. If I wanted to, I could make you do anything I wished. Everything I've done was to prevent you from reading that prophecy. You may thank me whenever you please."

He turned and walked away. My eyes burned and I blinked furiously. I wouldn't cry over him. Not again.

Thank him my ass.

I ordered a Lyft and waited on the corner of the street.

Samael had gotten through my wards while I was sleeping and left the keys to the car I'd borrowed on the counter. I'd dropped the car back at his tower and left the keys at the front desk.

He'd simply walked back through my wards and left them on my counter again, the overbearing jackass. Later today, I'd be replacing my Toyota.

But first, I had a meeting. I was done being Samael's toy. By now, it was evident that he wasn't removing the bond and getting the hell out of my life unless I made him.

The Lyft pulled up and I got in. The human driver realized I didn't want to chat and hummed quietly along to a song on the radio. I stared out the window. Samael's tower shot into the sky in the distance and I forced my gaze away. No matter what happened, that tower would always stand as a reminder of the demon who lied to me at every turn.

I closed my eyes. Samael had already enjoyed centuries of life. I'd had less than thirty years. The writing had been on the wall since the moment we met. One day soon it would come down to me or him. And I was choosing me.

Meredith nodded at me from behind the bar as I walked in. I waved at her, turning toward the corner where I'd met the bladesmith last time. He was waiting, his eyes sharp.

I sat. "Thank you for meeting with me."

"You're welcome. I was intrigued by your message."

The bladesmith tilted his head. "What is it that you need?"

I took a deep breath and handed him the arrowhead Cara had given me. The pointy end was still wrapped in soft cloth. I didn't know how much it would affect me, but I definitely needed to find a way to protect myself from the arrow. The last thing I needed was to fall and impale myself on something that could kill demons.

But I finally had a weapon that would protect me from ending up as Samael's toy.

"I need you to make this appear invisible to demons. Even the most powerful high demons. And if possible, I'd like to be able to clip it under my lanyard."

He let out a low whistle. "You don't ask for much, do you? I love a challenge, but that has Rowan in it."

"I'm aware. That's why I need it hidden."

David shook his head. "Hiding rowan wood from a demon would require demon blood for the spell."

I gave him a slow smile. "Would half-demon blood work?"

"Well, now that's an intriguing prospect. I'd need to ask the witch I work with." He narrowed his eyes at me. "It will be expensive. Are you sure you want to do this?"

"I'm sure." Thanks to the money Mariam had wired into my account, I could afford to work with the bladesmith. Besides, at this point in my life, I couldn't afford *not* to work with him.

David reached for his phone and murmured into it while I signaled for a drink. He hung up and looked at me. "The witch happened to be just around the corner. She agreed to come meet us."

Mere brought me my drink, gave the bladesmith a wary look and hurried away to a group of unseelie near the door.

"Where is your friend who likes to watch the pretty barmaid?"

I gaped at David. "Who are you talking about?"

"The demon who's always here sitting at that table and flirting with everyone who moves while keeping his gaze fixed to the woman who just brought you that drink."

I choked on my own spit. "Do you mean Vas?"

The bladesmith shrugged and I pulled up a photo of the demon. He nodded.

Vas had a thing for Meredith? Enough of a thing that he was coming in here and watching her work?

How did I miss that?

"Ah, here she is now."

I turned toward the door as it opened. Hannah walked in and shot me a wide smile.

"Halfling," she smiled in greeting. "Now this is interesting."

"It sure is."

Trust Hannah to be involved with this.

The bladesmith explained what I needed and Hannah gazed steadily at me. "Are you sure about this? If the spell fails and the demon finds you carrying rowan wood…" her face paled at the thought.

I swallowed "I'm sure. How can we guarantee the spell won't fail?"

Hannah's face turned somber and she frowned, the deep lines of her face making it clear I'd disappointed her. "There are no guarantees when dancing with demons, child. If you haven't yet learned that, it's about time you did."

Well.

"Okay. What can we do to give it the highest chance possible?"

She shrugged. "Between the bladesmith's craft, my knowledge, and your power, if we can't do it, it can't be done."

"Okay. I'm ready if you are."

Hannah leaned back and laughed. "Oh, this will be interesting." Her gaze dropped to my wrist. "You're still wearing the bracelet I gave you." Her eyes turned distant in a way that told me she was attempting to read my future, and then she shook her head. "All I know is that it will be important one day. Don't take it off."

"I won't."

"Okay then. We will go to my house and get to work. I hope you're ready to bleed for your vengeance, Danica."

I stared at the arrow on the table, my mind conjuring images of the threat in Samael's eyes as he told me he could make me do anything he wished.

"I am."

* * *

Thank you for reading Dance with the Demon.
The wild ride continues in the next book in the series: Inner Demons.
If you'd like to hang out with a fun group of like-minded fans, come check out my reader group on Facebook- Stark Society.
Want to go along for the ride as Danica hunts for the Mistilteinn Dagger?
Click here for your free copy of Fool the Demon and see what happens when Danica goes up against Samael for the first time.
Featuring a dragon, a look-away spell, and a masquerade ball. You won't want to miss it.